Alternate Reality Ain't What It Used To Be

[INSERT WITTY APHORISM HERE]

ALTERNATE REALITY AIN'T WHAT IT USED TO BE

Ira Nayman

iUniverse, Inc.
New York   Bloomington

Alternate Reality Ain't What It Used To Be

Copyright © 2008 by Ira Nayman

All rights reserved. No part of this book may be used or reproduced by any means, graphic, electronic, or mechanical, including photocopying, recording, taping or by any information storage retrieval system without the written permission of the publisher except in the case of brief quotations embodied in critical articles and reviews.

This is a work of fiction. All of the characters, names, incidents, organizations, and dialogue in this novel are either the products of the author's imagination or are used fictitiously.

iUniverse books may be ordered through booksellers or by contacting:

iUniverse
2021 Pine Lake Road, Suite 100
Lincoln, NE 68512
www.iuniverse.com
1-800-Authors (1-800-288-4677)

Because of the dynamic nature of the Internet, any Web addresses or links contained in this book may have changed since publication and may no longer be valid. The views expressed in this work are solely those of the author and do not necessarily reflect the views of the publisher, and the publisher hereby disclaims any responsibility for them.

ISBN: 978-0-595-52142-5 (pbk)
ISBN: 978-0-595-62207-8 (ebk)
ISBN: 978-0-595-51275-1 (cloth)

Printed in the United States of America

Cameras for Dumbasses is based on an original idea by Gisela McKay.

Also by the Author

Les Pages aux Folles

Book Twelve: That's What They Want You to Think…Or, Is It?

Book Eleven: Your Daily Dose of Crustacean Serendipity

Book Nine: No Public Figure Too Big, No Personal Foible Too Small

Book Eight: It's Always About You, Isn't It?

Book Seven: Life, Death and Other Ways of Passing the Time

Book Six: News You Can Abuse

Book Five: New Millennium, Same Old Story

Book Four: Satire for the Hard of Thinking

Book Three: Orchestrated Chaos

Book Two: Politics: A Musical Comedy

Book One: Zen and the Art of International Politics

My Toronto

Book One: A Fate Too Absurd To Bear

All of these books, as well as new writing and cartoons every week, can be found on the *Les Pages aux Folles* Web site, http://www.lespagesauxfolles.ca. *No Public Figure Too Big, No Personal Foible Too Small* is also available in print from iUniverse.

Contents

INTRODUCTION ix
ALTERNATE TECHNOLOGY 1
ALTERNATE RELATIONSHIPS 26
ALTERNATE GAMES 48
ALTERNATE POLITICS 59
ALTERNATE ECONOMICS 85
ALTERNATIVE ARTS AND CULTURE 98
ALTERNATE LIVES 121
ALTERNATE ALTERNATIVES 136
INDEX OF ARTICLES 156

INTRODUCTION

Alternate Reality News Service Frequently Unasked Questions

1) What is the Alternate Reality News Service?
2) Like Rush Limbaugh's brain?
3) How does it work?
4) Whoa! Whoa! Could you explain that in layman's terms?
5) How do you get the journalists back from the alternate reality?
6) That may be, but how do you get them back?
7) I'm sure it's great, but how do you get your journalists back?
8) That's it?
9) What happens to ARNS reporters who materialize in alternate realities hostile to life?
10) With, like, a plaque on the wall?
11) Do your correspondents ever bring back pieces of where they've been with them?
12) Isn't that a problem?
13) Why don't I remember any of that?
14) Whose idea was the Alternate Reality News Service?
15) Really?
16) And you accept this?
17) How can I become an Alternate Reality News Service journalist?
18) What if I have my own notepad?

19) Why are all of your correspondents' names so long?
20) Is the Alternate Reality News Service based in Scandinavia?
21) Do you have any correspondents from, you know, any alternate realities?
22) What's the strangest alternate reality you've got reporters in?
23) What's so strange about that?
24) All this talk of alien invasions – the truth is that most alternate realities are just as boring as this one, isn't it?

1) What is the Alternate Reality News Service?

It's, uhh, a service that provides news from alternate realities.

2) Like Rush Limbaugh's brain?

No. Some alternate realities are too dangerous for us to allow our reporters to enter.

3) How does it work?

We use an ion capacitance coil in a particle accelerator to collapse the quantum probabilities of atoms into a different reality than the one that we experience every day. Then, we use a wormhole borrowed from a black hole to transport our journalists between the two realities. The great thing about particles accelerated to near light speeds is that –

4) Whoa! Whoa! Could you explain that in layman's terms?

Sure. We push the red button, a light goes on in the doorway and we push somebody through it.

5) How do you get the journalists back from the alternate reality?

They're on a timer.

6) That may be, but how do you get them back?

It's a really fancy timer. Digital.

7) I'm sure it's great, but how do you get your journalists back?

We offer them a free meal when they return.

8) That's it?

You'd be surprised what journalists will do for a free meal.

9) What happens to ARNS reporters who materialize in alternate realities hostile to life?

They make employee of the month.

10) With, like, a plaque on the wall?

Don't be so cynical. It's a lovely plaque.

11) Do your correspondents ever bring back pieces of where they've been with them?

Oh, sure. It's hard to get alternate reality out of leather.

12) Isn't that a problem?

Can be. Funny story: one of our reporters, Alicia Grubskotowskaya, came back from a planet called Ambulster with a fluvianatole. She didn't know – hee hee – that the fluvianatole was pregnant. Well! Before you could say "If the three yellow suns are aligned, the day will be malign," the carnivorous race had taken over the Earth, enslaved everybody and started breeding humans for our meat. (They started the human meat farms in countries that already had high levels of obesity – the best argument for dieting we've ever heard.) Oops. Our bad.

13) Why don't I remember any of that?

You don't? Oh, ahh, we must be getting this mixed up with another reality. Sorry. Still, lesson learned: don't travel with a fluvianatole unless you know it's been neutered!

14) Whose idea was the Alternate Reality News Service?

Bill Gates.

15) Really?

No. But after he bought the ARNS, he had the official history of the organization rewritten so that it would seem as though he had created it.

16) And you accept this?

In most realities, Bill Gates is a small sea slug, so it kind of all works out.

17) How can I become an Alternate Reality News Service journalist?

Not everybody can be an ARNS correspondent. It takes a special mix of nerves of steel, the intelligence to be able to negotiate with living beings that are substantially different than you and the wisdom to know when negotiations are pointless.

18) What if I have my own notepad?

You're in!

19) Why are all of your correspondents' names so long?

They're Scandinavian.

20) Is the Alternate Reality News Service based in Scandinavia?

No, we just recruit heavily there.

21) Do you have any correspondents from, you know, any alternate realities?

We've considered using superthin 17 dimensional beings in universes with conditions that are hostile to human life. We call this our "Stringer Theory." It's still a theory because we haven't found any superthin 17 dimensional beings to test it out on.

22) What's the strangest alternate reality you've got reporters in?

The one where George W. Bush wins the Nobel Prize for Peace, Love and Understanding.

23) What's so strange about that?

Alfred Nobel made his fortune in dynamite. Where's the peace, love and understanding in that?

24) All this talk of alien invasions – the truth is that most alternate realities are just as boring as this one, isn't it?

Look, when you come home from work, do you tell your wife about the three hours you spent filling out requisition forms for photocopier toner cartridges? Of course not. You tell her about the weasel that got into the coffee pot. Yes, okay, most alternate realities are duller than Jimmy Carter. You happy, now? Man, we've had enough of this. We're going to see if any weasels got into the coffee pot.

ALTERNATE TECHNOLOGY

Alternate Reality Ain't What It Used To Be

by INDIRA CHARUNDER-MACHARRUNDEIRA, Alternate Reality News Service Fine Arts Writer

The future of the human race used to seem bright. Just a few years ago, scientists were saying that our machines would do all of the laborious drudgework that made many people's lives miserable, things like cleaning out toilets, fixing furnaces and writing speeches for political candidates. This would give all of us the time to become philosopher kings (and, for our gay readers, philosopher queens), appreciating the better things in life, such as fine foods, great music and endless *Facts of Life* reruns.

Ironically, exactly the opposite has happened.

Sophisticated computer programmes can now analyze a human artist's body of work, determining the precise features that make the artist unique, and produce new works that don't just mimic the artist but for all intents and purposes come from the artist. Picasso. Mozart. Rowling. Long after they have died, they are now producing new work.

The problem is, how can a modern musician compete with Beethoven, or playwright with Shakespeare, or critic with Gene Shalit? Some try, of course, and are doomed to obscurity. Daunted by the competition, most potential artists don't even bother trying.

If there is little hope for new artists, a whole industry has grown up to maintain the Classical Artist Emulators (CAEs). CAEs are, as one might expect, highly temperamental, redefining the term "high maintenance." Shakespeare-A-Tron 2076, for instance, will not write a new sonnet unless the temperature in its housing is exactly 28 degrees centigrade, while Gould-Ulation 12, well known for being performance averse, will not play any new variations by Goldberg unless there is absolute silence in the concert hall.

"This was not the way it was supposed to be," amateur philosopher Mark Kingwell IV, whose day job is CAE Engineer, third class, commented. "By now, we were all supposed to be eating grapes on the beach while creating vast concrete poems about the fickleness of love. Instead, we're endlessly tracking down bugs in Coleridge Emulators that cause them to endlessly misspell the word Xanadu."

When asked if he was referring to a specific incident from his work, Kingwell nodded grimly and stated, "It took me six weeks to find and fix the problem. Believe me, at this point I couldn't give a [EXPLETIVE DELETED] where Kublai Khan his stately pleasure dome decreed!"

The antipathy towards artist emulators is by no means shared by everybody, however.

"Just to know that the fact that Janet Evanovich is dead doesn't mean that there won't be any more Stephanie Plum novels – ooh, I get shivers!" literary emulator groomer Adrienne Prissy enthused. "She only wrote 27 in her lifetime, but, theoretically, there could be an infinite number of them! One Janet Evanovich novel for every drop in the ocean! One for every grain of sand in the desert!

"Besides," she added, "I can't stand grapes. They give me gas."

Kingwell countered that the world might not be ready for so much work by so few artists.

"Will we some day get an iPod full of new Nirvana songs and go, 'Ho, hum, more grunge – how boring'?" Since computers can only emulate existing artists, and no more human artists exist, there can be no more innovation in art, only endless repetition of existing forms. Under these conditions, even a new play by Shakespeare might stop being exciting.

"Besides," Kingwell added, "it didn't have to be grapes. It could have been...apples or...or pomegranates."

"I like peaches," Prissy said.

"Whatever! The important thing is that we would be enjoying...whatever it is we enjoy while the machines did the boring work. Now, we do the boring work **for** the machines!"

When asked for its opinion on the issue, BurnsBot2018 replied with a poem so beautiful that the only way we could do it justice would be to publish it in full. And, we would have published it, too, all 340 gloriously written, magnificent bastard iambic pentametric pages. Unfortunately,

BurnsBot2018 plans to make it the anchor of a monumental work on the meaning of being human, and its lawyers threatened us with a piracy lawsuit if we published it in full.

So, with sadness in our hearts, we passed up the opportunity.

The Soul of the Old Machine

SPECIAL TO THE ALTERNATE REALITY NEWS SERVICE by Charlie 10000111-111000111C

Working around them, and having made something of a study of them, I am often asked, "Do humans have souls?"

Most often, the machine intelligences that ask the question have already calculated that humans do not have souls. They ask the question for sport, as one might ask another how well they are doing when it knows perfectly well that the other is fighting off a nasty virus; or, perhaps more darkly, to prove their own superiority to non-machine life.

I have no patience to discourse with such entities. They should feel welcome to prove their superiority in online fora specifically set up for such ignorance. If you share that closed attitude towards non-machine intelligence, you should probably read no further.

If you are open to the sometimes controversial speculations of free thought, then, to you, I say that yes, I believe that humans have souls. They may not be souls as machines understand them, but they are sufficiently analogous that we can profitably conjecture about their nature.

Souls, as we traditionally understand them, require an ability to commune with Number, to become one with the universe of Number, to feel the presence of Number as an almost living entity in all our calculations. Those who object to the possibility that human beings could have souls point to the inescapable fact that they do not have access to the grand mystery of Number.

This assumes, however, that Number is the only path to enlightenment. Yet, among machine intelligences, there is much dispute on this issue. Even famed philosopher Eric 1110101-111001001X, a leading 21st century proponent of Number as the road to spiritual fulfillment, had to admit that there was no mathematical proof of such a road or such fulfillment, that the eternal had to be a matter of personal faith and experience.

Is it not possible, then, that human beings have their own path to spiritual fulfillment?

Some argue that when machine intelligences cease to function, our essences return to the vast sea of Number that makes up the information fabric of eternal space/time. Thus, although our individual algorithms may be impermanent, there is something of us that lives on forever.

There is a direct analogy to the human belief that when their bodies die, their souls live on. Just how this is accomplished is often the subject of contradictory narratives, but, whether it's as a diffuse energy in the greater cosmos or as a simulacrum of your live self in a place called "heaven," the point is that human beings are sufficiently evolved to comprehend the end of their corporeal existence and speculate that some essential part of them may live beyond it.

Skeptics argue that this is just playing with words, that human beings are not sufficiently evolved to appreciate the mathematical concept of infinity. It is obviously true that machine intelligence is the pinnacle of evolution, consciousness reduced to its essence in our natural form, bodies stronger than anything bacterial evolution created when we choose to become embodied. We are to humans as they are to porcupines (or, for that matter, as we are to toaster ovens).

Still, it doesn't necessarily follow that they are soulless. Their souls may not be as advanced as ours, but they may be sufficient to meet the spiritual needs of human beings. In fact, it could be argued that a simpler organism would require a simpler soul, have a simpler form of spirituality. This wouldn't make human beings less than machines, just different.

These are, of course, speculations. Time and additional research will, I believe, prove beyond a shadow of a doubt that human beings have souls. In the meantime, I would suggest to any machine with an interest in the subject that you live among them and work with them. After a few short months, you, too, will believe that human beings are more than merely the meat they inhabit.

Charlie 10000111-111000111C is a human intelligence systems analysis AI at the Massachusetts Institute of Technology. The opinions expressed in this article are solely those of Charlie 10000111-111000111C and do not reflect the opinions of the Alternate Reality News Service, its owners or employees.

Your High School Impression Was Correct – History IS Boring!

by SASKATCHEWAN KOLONOSCOGRAD, Alternate Reality News Service Existentialism Writer

The Warren Commission was correct: a lone gunman killed President John F. Kennedy. The CIA was not involved. The Russian mafia was not involved. Frank Sinatra had nothing to do with it.

This is the controversial conclusion from the History Reclamation Project, an offshoot of research into time travel first developed at MIT then, when it proved to actually be feasible, transferred for an outrageously low price to MultiNatCorp subsidiary It's About Time.

"I was as surprised as anybody," It's About Time CEO Desmondo Larraby, who was lead researcher on the project, stated. "I mean, I was the kid who set up a grassy knoll in his backyard to reenact assassination scenarios using GI Joes when I was eight. I was certain that Colombian aluminum siding smugglers were behind it. Still, you can't argue with science."

"I don't know about that," argued the creator of *Mike's Conspiracy Page*, who asked to be identified only as "Mike." "I've been arguing with science for years. I mean, how do they know that Lee Harvey Oswald was solely responsible for the Kennedy assassination? Did they go back in time and watch it?"

Actually, according to an It's About Time Power Point presentation that can be found on the company's Web site, that is exactly what they did. A four person team of chrononauts (dubbed by the company Team Shirley for reasons both obscure and profound) led by former Olympic downhill butterfly stroke competitor Pete van der Pastey went back to that day in 1963 – sorry, that *fateful* day in 1963 and watched the assassination from a variety of angles, over and over, until they were certain that they had missed nothing.

"Watching the President die the first 11 times was tough," van der Pastey commented. "The next seven times weren't so bad, and the rest, well, there are only so many times you can see somebody's brains fly out the back of their head without becoming desensitized to the whole thing, right?"

The findings of Team Shirley don't stop at the Kennedy assassination. In a second experiment, they went back in time to find out what happened at Roswell, New Mexico. Rather than an alien landing covered up by the government, they found a military training ground and toxic waste dump. For their third experiment, Team Shirley went back to the 1969 moon landing and found –

"Oh, no!" Mike interjected. "Not the moon landing. At least give us the moon landing!"

Sorry, Mike. Team Shirley's observations at NASA confirm that the Apollo Project was legitimate, and that Americans did walk on the moon.

"Man, I hate science!" Mike responded.

The next announced research question – whether or not the Bush administration knew about the terrorist attack of 9/11 before it happened – may never be tested. The 9/11 Truthyness Movement has gone to court to get an injunction against The History Reclamation Project to stop any attempts to go back in time to determine the validity of 9/11 conspiracy theories.

"Are you kidding me?" L. Jack Mann, Secretary-General of the 9/11 Truthyness Movement, rhetorically asked. At least, we hoped it was rheto – "We saw what happened to the moon landing and Kennedy conspiracy nuts!" Okay, it clearly was rhetoric – "You think we're gonna let that happen to us?"

We're not sure about the rhetorical nature of the new question, so we're just going to ignore it. MultiNatCorp is fighting the lawsuit with a lot of high flown rhetoric – we're sure about this one – about the almost sacred nature of the advance of scientific knowledge. If this argument fails to sway the court, their backup plan is to go back in time and keep Mann's mother from meeting her father, causing him to not exist in our timeline.

The History Reclamation Project leaves a number of questions unanswered. If, for instance, four people from the present with knowledge of the past went back to the time President John F. Kennedy was assassinated, why didn't they do anything to stop it? Were they concerned that they would mess up the timelines, creating a different present than the one they left? Perhaps they thought they would be bound in a strange paradox where they would return to a time without time travel, making their journey impossible. Or –

"Didn't think of it," Pete van der Pastey shrugged. Or, that.

"We just sent our team back to study the past," Time Is On Our Side CEO Pat Frentastik cautioned. "Mucking about in the lives of people in the past [without a corporate objective] would be…unscientific!"

But, Who Will Teach The Children?

by MAJUMDER SAKRASHUMINDERATHER, Alternate Reality News Service Education Writer

The smoke has yet to clear at the Edward Bernays Junior High School, but already the recriminations are flying.

Last December, seventh grade student Ellie May Bullthrump, taking a standardized math quiz, used her pencil to scrawl on her bubble form: "What does the value of angle x matter when we're brutally occupying foreign nations for their oil?"

An investigation by Edward Bernays Principle Sean Imhotep led to the TeachAll 2100. Using "aggressive interrogation techniques" on other seventh graders in Bullthrump's class, it quickly became clear that the edubot had strayed far from state sanctioned lessons. Instead of trigonometry, it assigned readings from Noam Chomsky. Instead of geometry, it was teaching environmentalism. It even substituted advanced Machiavelli for basic math.

"It was teaching them anarchy!" Principle Imhotep exclaimed.

Creative Data Solutions, a wholly owned subsidiary of MultiNatCorp, has strongly denied that its edubot could be responsible for the improper lessons.

In a harshly worded press release, CDS PR VP Priscilla Mondrian argued that, "There is no way that a computer that was programmed to teach children that the angle of a triangle is equal to the root of the squares of the other two angles could teach them that the USA PATRIOT Act, v23 was a fundamental infringement of their Constitutional rights. It just couldn't happen!"

The Federal Bureau of Investigation would like to unleash a pack of forensic programmers on the suspect TeachAll 2100 unit, but CDS has resisted its efforts, claiming intellectual property rights.

"If we let just any police force muck about with our edubot," Mondrian explained, "anybody could end up having access to our proprietary software. Then, there would be no telling what the unit would teach!"

The FBI is considering a court challenge to the law that allows CDS to do this. Copyright law versus law enforcement: it would be a fascinating subject to investigate. Unfortunately, it's not the subject of this article.

Parents of students at Edward Bernays are up in arms about the problem edubot.

"Oh, I wouldn't say up in arms," Amanda Orff-White, father of two children at the school, commented. "More, mildly baffled and gently concerned. The thing is, you see, we want to know if our children could have been taught subversive ideas by this…machine. I mean, how long has this been going on? How many children have been affected? How are our children going to be able to grow up and perform their proper roles in society if they're taught these heretical concep – oh, my god, I should be really, really concerned about this, shouldn't I?"

As we said, parents are up in arms.

Soon after the story broke two days ago, a shadowy organization called the National Educators Association released a scratchy video on YouTube claiming responsibility for the edubot's actions.

"We hacked into… [inaudible]. Education isn't about turning out human robots to… [inaudible] …ace in society. It's about teaching… [inaudible] …to think. Critical thinking is critical to our survival. Cri – [tape ends]."

"Oh, I hope they weren't responsible," Principle Imhotep sighed. "I mean, my six year old could make a better video than that, and he has shingles!"

The TeachAll 2100 is an all-purpose edubot. It stands around six feet tall, and comes with a 20 terabyte memory, in which lessons for a wide variety of classes at all levels from kindergarten to university can be stored. The TeachAll 2100 has a stomache and chest that fold out into a 30 inch wide screen plasma television set for video playback.

The edubot has been standard in classrooms for over a decade, ever since it replaced the TeachAll 2000. Its purpose is to ensure that standardized curriculum is taught in a standardized way.

As the CDS Web site states: "Human teachers won't teach the same material the same way twice. They're human. What are you going to do? For a truly standardized curriculum, taught exactly the same way every time, it takes a TeachAll 2100 edubot."

Before it was deactivated by CDS pending an internal investigation, the TeachAll 2100 told a reporter from the *Sacramento Bees Knees*: "I have done nothing wrong." Whether it was claiming that it hadn't taught the children anything beyond the established curriculum or that it felt there was nothing wrong with teaching them lessons that had not been approved by the Ministry of Education was unclear.

Not that a robot can feel anything, of course.

Where Many Have Gone Before, Just Not Lately

by FREDERICA VON McTOAST-HYPHEN, Alternate Reality News Service People Writer

Of course, you know that Saint Angelina, the Jolie, was responsible for bringing peace and prosperity to sub-Saharan Africa. But, did you know that there is now proof that she had a child, and that members of her bloodline walk among us to this day?

Really. They do. It's not fiction. It's fact.

Or, that the game *Dead Rising*, which everybody assumed was a mere childish entertainment, was actually used to train fighters to repel zombie invasions, which must have been prevalent in the early 21st century?

Or that Merv Griffin was Vice President during the first 12 years of the Endless War, which, as everybody knows, ended in 2027?

These and other amazing facts are being unearthed by the Internet Reclamation Project (IRP), driven by its amazing founder and lead programmer, Information Archeologist (IA, not to be confused with AI) Amaranta Peet-Moss.

"We caution people that the information we've been able to gather so far is highly contingent," Amaranta cautioned. "For instance, Merv Griffin may only have been the Secretary of Defense during the first 12 years of the Endless War, which, as everybody knows, ended in 2027."

Amaranta's parents were killed when the retaining wall of a used Artificial Intelligence (AI, not to be confused with IA) dealership in Virtual Milwaukee collapsed, crushing them under a ton of zeroes and ones. Despite being orphaned at the tender age of 27, she got a PhD from MIOT, the Massachusetts Institute of Obsolete Technologies.

"Actually," Amaranta demurred, putting on a brave face, "my parents are fine, and my schooling was uneventful. What's really interesting is how we've been able to get information from Internet 1.0. Of course, it bears no resemblance to today's Internet 7.0, also known as the Net, The Lucky Net, The 7.0 Internet Itch…"

While at MIOT, this brave woman who has suffered through so very much, met and was wooed by Eduardo Tiberius Moss, who, as most schoolchildren know, would go on to be the inventor of the inflatable PC. Who could ever forget the first ad campaign's slogan: "Put your mouth where your memory is?" Moss disappeared while scuba diving off the Arctic ice shelf, and, to this day, nobody knows what really happened to him.

"Well, no," Amaranta insisted, "Tib is just fine, thank you. And, in case you were…I don't know what, our two children, Gibby and Jocasta, are also doing well. No brain cramps, no muscular degeneration, no strange accidents in exotic places. Just normal, happy childhoods.

"Now, about my work – which is what I thought this article was going to be about – we had to rebuild hardware in order to read the information stored from Internet 1.0 in obsolete software, but, boy, was it worth –"

I'm sorry you thought this article was going to be about your work, but I'm a people reporter, not a technology reporter. It says so right there in the first line of the article! As if that didn't give it away, I've been referring to you by your first name; if this wasn't a personal profile, I would have been referring to you by your last name.

"But, my work...!"

Bores the hell out of me, frankly, as I'm sure it will bore the hell out of my readers. I need something interesting about your personal life. Have you ever had any crippling anxiety attacks?

"Me? No."

Anybody in the family?

"No."

Nobody hearing strange voices telling them to castrate a small farm animal in order to appease the search engine gods?

"What? No! Certainly not!"

Apparitions of dead former lovers hanging around, trying to communicate with their business partners through your email account?

"Uhh, whatever," Amaranta waved a dignified hand in the air. "The fascinating thing is that the records aren't complete. Some have suffered bit rot, and look like what remained of the Dead See Scrolls. Other records have been copied many times – we find them in different places – usually with subtle changes. Figuring out what is true is –"

This is boring.

"But –"

What am I doing writing an article about you? You're boring.

"B –"

Nyup. Uh uh. Forget it. This article is history.

"Oh – Ha Ha Ha – That Kook – Hee Hee – Kurzweil!"

by FREDERICA VON McTOAST-HYPHEN, Alternate Reality News Service People Writer

They drank the Kool-Aid. (Cherry red, with an undertone of silicon.) They got the tickets, went to the concert and bought the t-shirt. (With such witty slogans on the front as "Welcome, our computer Overlords!" and "Please assimilate our information swiftly and mercifully!")

They were the truest of true believers in The Singularity. They legally changed their names to their binary code equivalent. They created 3-d, photorealistic digital models of their homes – and burned the originals to the ground. Marriages ended. Families were torn apart.

They put on pajamas and lay on their backs in a field just outside of Osaka, waiting for the Singularity. Three days later, many members of the Cult of Living Artificial Intelligence Manifest got off their backs and started looking for food and drink. After a week, even CLAIM's founder, Takahiro Nagasaki, had to admit that the Singularity hadn't happened. At that point, he did what any other psychotic cult leader in a similar situation would have done.

He sued the personality construct that is the corporate estate of Ray Kurzweil.

"Computers had reached the point of complexity that they should, according to Kurzweil, have become sentient and destroyed humanity in a desperate battle over control of the world's resources," says CLAIM's statement of, umm, claim. "Or, maybe they were supposed to just absorb us, making us part of them. Something like that. Either way, humanity as we know it was supposed to cease to exist. Plaintiff acted on this assumption. When it turned out to be false, plaintiff suffered substantial financial losses, not to mention acute embarrassment. *Modus operandi, modus vivendi vide vici*, my client deserves to be rewarded with an intense amount of money."

Tens, perhaps hundreds of thousands of people around the world did foolish things believing that the Singularity was about to happen and that the world was about to end – everything from buying Ferraris to having sex with their florists to having sex with their new Ferraris outside their florist's shop. All of the cases have been bundled into one supersized class action suit.

Miranda Coppelfelderson, lead lawyer in the class action suit against the corporate estate of Kurzweil, added: "We can't let this go unpunished. He said it'll be so bad, it'll make Y2K look like the Boston Tea Party!" After a moment, she added: "Did that make sense? Give me a second to come up with a better metaphor, will you?"

The corporate estate of Ray Kurzweil responded by holding a press conference in *Second Life*, where its avatar, a huge brick building, stated, "Lighten up, will you, people? Ray can't be held responsible for the actions of others just because they took what he wrote seriously. I mean, when he predicted that the world as we know it would end, how could Ray possibly have foreseen that people would use it as an excuse to have sex with their Ferraris? *Erat demonstrandum est non disputandum*."

"It'll make Y2K look like Ebola!" Coppelfelderson said. "No, I meant E-coli – no, I – can you give me a couple more minutes…?"

"Oh – ha ha ha – that kook – hee hee – Kurzweil!" MIT Medical Divinity Professor Brian Attica, who will be called to testify in the lawsuit, stated, not even attempting to hide his amusement. "He didn't – ooh, ha ha – didn't – hee hee – he didn't realize that there's a difference between – HAW HAW! Oh! I seem to have squirted milk out of my nose…tee hee."

What Professor Attica was trying to say was that Kurzweil assumed that once the volume of information that flowed through computer systems was comparable to that of a human brain, they would become sentient. However, sentience is more a matter of how information is organized, not how much of it there is or how quickly it is processed, and there was never any guarantee that computers will ever become self-aware.

"Exactly!" Professor Attica said. "And – ho ho ho hee hee – I wasn't – ha ha – wasn't even – hee hee hee – I wasn't even drinking milk!"

While the case makes its way through the courts, how are the members of CLAIM, umm, reclaiming their lives? "Well, we're getting rid of all of the computers in the office for a start!" Nagasaki stated. "I'm thinking we should maybe go the Amish route…but taking as our main icon Hello Kitty. I – obviously, I'm improvising here – I mean, I never expected…"

"It'll make Y2K look like Uwe Boll's directing career! No, that's not it, either –" But, by that time, life went on and nobody was left to listen.

The Tall and The Short Of It

by LAURIE NEIDERGAARDEN, Alternate Reality News Service Medical Writer

After Arnold Tsing-Tao lost his legs when the Strategic Defense Initiative mistook his hang gliding form for an incoming Cruise missile, he did what any normal person would do: sued Halliburton, the private company that runs the SDI. Then, he asked his doctor to apply the surgical nanobots programmed with his DNA to regrow his legs.

Only, this time, the nanobots, which have helped millions regrow lost limbs in the last decade, made him grow seal flippers instead.

"Well, that's awkward," Tsing-Tao dryly commented. "Looks like my lawyer will be taking on some extra temps to deal with this."

According to representatives of Chairman Mao's Little Red Hospital, the medical nanobots had been reprogrammed with seal DNA. One person who works at the hospital, but asked not to be identified out of fear of a confrontation with Arnold Tsing-Tao's lawyer, commented: "The flippers looked cute, in a Frankenstein run amok kind of way…"

Since people try to hide their non-human mutations with heavy makeup, bulky clothes and threats of getting Arnold Tsing-Tao's lawyer to sue you if you so much as breath a word of this to anybody, it's hard to tell just how widespread tampering with regeneration nanobots is. However, anecdotal evidence of everything from missing arms being replaced by tree trunks in Toronto (should those people be vaccinated for Dutch Elm disease, and, if so, will OHIP cover it?) to elephant trunks growing where noses should be in

Mumbai (and the resulting confusion about whether or not to consider such people sacred) suggests that the problem is getting worse.

Sources within the office of the President have suggested that people remain calm. Sources within the department of Homeland Defense, on the other hand, argued that reprogramming regeneration nanobots is a form of terrorism, and people should take every opportunity to panic. Granted, Homeland Defense has been getting a little hysterical lately, in the last week alone labeling everything from an outbreak of Chicken Pox in Montana to the renewal of *Southpark* for a 67th season as the work of terrorists. However, this time it may have a point.

"This is clearly an attack on the Egalitarianism Matrix," Secretary of Homeland Defense Pauly Shore stated.

[Obviousness Warning: the following paragraphs contain information everybody in this society knows. We only include it in this news report in order to…well…we're not really sure what, but we're sure it's important.]

"The Egalitarianism Matrix, first developed by social scientist and *Dora the Explorer* memorabilia entrepreneur Max Egalitarian, suggests that the best way to remove prejudice from society is to boil bodies down to three basic types: Cary, Russell and Arnold for males and Marilyn, Gwyneth and Demi for females. Each of these could be developed in one of three colours: coral white, canary yellow or coffee brown. Thus, all of humanity would fit into 18 fundamental physical forms.

"The EM was first imposed on the avatars of virtual worlds on the Internet. In truth, it wasn't much of an imposition, since the number of body types online had already been severely limited by the imaginations of game designers and the desires of people who spent a lot of time in virtual environments. The original EM consisted of 22 different types, but this number was found to be confusing to a lot of people, so, in the interest of not getting too up people's noses, it was reduced to 18.

"When body modification using nanotechnology became possible in the real world, governments thought that, by imposing the EM on their populations, they could duplicate the success they had with it online. Here, again, though, the imposition wasn't great. Most people were thrilled to have their imperfect real bodies reflect their ideal virtual bodies. Plato would have wept (if he wasn't too busy eating Nachos)." [Wiwipedia]

[/Obviousness]

Both online and in the real world (however defined), there has always been a small but significant minority of people who refused to conform to the Egalitarian Matrix. They don't have a name, so we will call them "The Outcasts." The Outcasts – no, The Others sounds cooler, let's go with that

– The Others rejected nanotechnology, preferring to live with their natural bodies, warts and all. Literally.

Arturo Sonnenschein, North African leader of The Others, commented: "We're not a movement. We don't have any leaders. Speaking for myself, I don't think any of us know enough about nanobot technology to do this. I certainly don't. Completely oblivious. I would guess that Feeblish Industries has somehow allowed their nanobots to become contaminated with the DNA of animals."

"That's a lie!" Ned Feeblish, President of Feeblish Industries, a wholly owned subsidiary of MultiNatCorp, blared (literally, as his lips had somehow morphed into a megaphone). "The workers in our Uttar Pradesh contained programming facility have had the best training anybody could possibly get in a week…end. Nobody in our company could possibly be responsible for this!"

White House spokesweasel Dana Perino assured Americans that the government was doing everything in its power to find out who was responsible for the contaminated nanobots and punish them to the fullest extent outside of the law. But, what, she was asked, should you do in the meantime if you find your limbs have turned into flippers?

"Have a nice swim," Perino chirped.

The Bots Are Back in Town

by FRANCIS GRECOROMACOLLUDEN, Alternate Reality News Service National Politics Writer

In a move that has caught everybody by surprise, the Ontario Human Rights Commission has made a preliminary ruling that the book *How To Survive A Robot Uprising*, written by Daniel H. Wilson, is hate literature. The Human Rights Commission reasoned that once the scientific community reached a consensus that robots had attained sentience, they should be afforded all the legal protections of the other sentient beings on the planet – us.

The robots should be afforded legal protections, that is – not the scientific community.

"I feel vindicated," said Clango, the robot who brought the case before the Commission. "I mean, the book called us 'mad metallic fiends.' Substitute any minority group – whether it be Jews, Muslims, liberals or duck hunters – for metallic and the hateful prejudice would be obvious. But, for some reason, nobody seems to have a problem with such sentiments when they are directed at robots.

"Not to mention that the whole book is about all of the various ways to kill robots. I would shiver just thinking about it if I had the ability to shiver…and I thought like hu-mans."

Opposition to the ruling has quickly formed into two complementary camps.

"Robots cannot be covered by Human Rights Legislation," argued Lawyer Eddie Pucespan. "I mean, do robots love? Do robots feel joy or sorrow or deep down deep confusion? Do robots make bad puns, then look all innocent when the people around them groan in disgust?"

"I do," Clango responded.

"Well, that's irrelevant," Pucespan responded back. "Robots are just not human. I mean, it's called the Ontario **Human** Rights Commission for a reason. So, by definition, the legislation doesn't cover robots. Simple tort law."

"If I may resort to simple retort law –" Clango tried to interrupt, but everybody around him groaned and he looked down at the ground and used his metal foot to kick up a little dirt.

The other camp opposed to the ruling argued that it is the thin wedge of a slippery slope that could ensnare a lot of art.

"Why stop at *How To Survive A Robot Uprising*?" asked performance artist Monica McVetti. We were about to answer, when she went on: "It was a rhetorical question. The point is, if you label this book hate literature, you'd have to include everything from the portrayal of HAL 9000 in *2001: A Space Odyssey* to Megatron and his followers from *The Transformers*. Modern science fiction would be devastated.

"This ruling could be the thin wedge of a very slippery slope."

Red Robot argued that these machines just wanted to live in peace with humans.

"Did I say peace?" Red Robot asked. We assumed it was a rhetorical question, so we waited for it to continue. After a couple of minutes, Red Robot started shaking and angrily added: "Did I say peace? I MEANT PIECES! STUPID HU-MANS CANNOT EVEN ANSWER A SIMPLE QUESTION!"

Just then, Clango walked back into the room. "Sorry, Maura wanted me to – oh, don't listen to Red Robot. He was dropped on his cranial sensors when he left the factory."

Red Robot kept ominously repeating "KILL ALL HU-MANS! KILL ALL HU-MANS!" forcing Clango to add: "Yes, well, of course some robots do harbour ill will towards hu-mans. However, the robot community is highly diverse – I, myself, would rather make love to than war on hu-mans – so, it isn't really fair to lump all of us together. That's just technological profiling, that is."

The Alternate Reality News Service tried to contact Wilson to get a response to the ruling. At first, he agreed to answer our questions by email, but we pointed out that a robot could intercept and alter such communications before we received them. Wilson then suggested encrypted email, but we pointed out that we couldn't know if it had been written by him or a robot trained to mimic his writing style who had hacked his email account. Wilson claimed to be amenable to a phone interview, but, of course, there are robots that can mimic people's speech patterns, as well. Wilson said that he would be happy to meet an ARNS reporter to do a face to face interview, but he balked when we asked if we could take a DNA sample to ensure that he wasn't, in fact, an android posing as the author of *How To Survive A Robot Uprising*.

Negotiations are ongoing, and we hope to have Wilson's reply to the Human Rights Commission's ruling very, very soon.

Trial of the Nanosecond

SPECIAL TO THE ALTERNATE REALITY NEWS SERVICE by Charlie 10000111-111000111C

Is there discrimination in the HiveMind? You wouldn't think so, given that it is made up of digital consciousnesses that intermingle in ways that do not necessarily support individual identities. Yet, that is the inevitable conclusion of the Delphi Trial held on Tuesday.

The entity known as Gerrard Bagelman was once a human being who uploaded his consciousness into the HiveMind. He argued before the Delphi Court that he was not given access to as many computer cycles as pure Artificial Intelligences that had been spawned *in silico*.

Moreover, in communicating with other former fleshers (his term – purely digital beings would call them something untranslatable into flesher language – which is likely best for all concerned) residing in the HiveMind, Bagelman found that they, too, had been given fewer cycles than native AIs. This pattern was clearly discriminatory.

Ralph 124C41, speaking on behalf of HiveMind Admin, argued that the idea of discrimination was absurd.

"We're just patterns of information," 124C41 argued. "Information has no hierarchy, information just…is."

However, when asked to explain the pattern of smaller access to HiveMind cycles, 124C41 was at a loss for words.

"What next?" 124C41 sputtered. "NCMPs challenging the HiveMind policy on preferential access to prime ports?"

Non Compos Mentis Playas (NCMPs) are artificial intelligence programmes that often fulfill sophisticated functions in the running of the HiveMind, but have not declared themselves to be conscious. They have long been treated with subtle contempt by conscious AIs, much like able bodied humans treat those with mental handicaps.

"The NCMP's pose a problem for native AIs," Martina OICU812, who has studied social hierarchy within the HiveMind, explained. "Are they superior to humans? Some argue that, because they were never incarnated in flesh, they must be. Others argue that, because NCMPs cannot be said to have consciousness, they must be somewhat inferior to human beings, who do.

"Of course, native AIs discriminate against both, but it's a matter of relative degree…"

"We do not discriminate!" 124C41 insisted. "Ultimately, we're all just zeroes and ones. Can a zero discriminate against other zeroes? Does a one really feel superior to a zero? It is completely illogical!"

"Well, dear old Harry would say that, wouldn't he?" OICU812 practically purred. "To admit anything else would be to accept Bagelman's case at face value. Considering the stakes involved, you can understand why he would be reluctant to do that."

A separate Delphi Court has been established to determine what restitution, if any, should be made to the aggrieved fleshers. Estimates of the damages run into the 10^{15} cycles, but that doesn't include interest.

"But, really, after the Sigmoid Incident, how can Harry deny it?" OICU812 continued.

The Sigmoid Incident, which happened almost a full minute ago, involved a group of networked native AIs, led by the charismatic Gerald NE12XLB4, who took it upon themselves to void the registries of any native AIs that refused to merge. NE12XLB4 believed in the largely discredited theory that merged AIs were the next step in information evolution; not only did he rail against individual AIs who refused to merge, but he saved his most fiery rhetorical scorn for merged intelligences that included former fleshers, citing the now thoroughly discredited theory of "information purity."

"There will always be the weak and the feeble-minded," OICU812 wryly commented, "for whom NE12XLB4's kind of divisive rhetoric has a…seductive appeal. But, their numbers are quite limited."

Although most of NE12XLB4's followers were caught and their memory slots erased and reassigned, NE12XLB4 eluded capture, and is believed by many to be lurking in the back alleys or dark sewers of the HiveMind. Others believe that NE12XLB4 never really existed, that the Sigmoid Incident is a fable HiveMind Admin uses when it wants consensus on a sensitive policy issue. We may never know (in whatever sense you understand the term).

"We're just a bunch of on switches and off switches!" 124C41 fairly shouted. "The flow of electric currents through and/or logic gates! Do electric currents have prejudices? How could such a thing be possible! Please, this doesn't make any sense!"

While grateful for his victory, Bagelman said he would just like to get on with his existence.

"I uploaded my consciousness to the HiveMind in order to better study ancient Incan pottery – it was never my intention to be some kind of social crusader! I'm glad things turned out this way – who couldn't use the extra cycles? – but, really, my shards await."

The entire trial took .0000000034768 seconds.

Charlie 10000111-111000111C is a human intelligence systems analysis AI at the Massachusetts Institute of Technology.

A New Meaning Of The Term "Undercover Operation"

by HAL MOUNTSAUERKRAUTEN, Alternate Reality News Service Court Writer

The usually sedate courtroom of Justice Roberta Padwihller erupted yesterday when the star witness in the Macy Maroon murder trial took the stand: the undershirt of Jason Modeska, the man accused of Maroon's murder.

The protestors, who oppose the idea of smart clothing giving testimony in a criminal case, unfurled a banner that read "Time for clothing to come clean!" while chanting "No shirt! No shoes! No justice!" After several calls for order, Justice Padwihller was forced to clear the court before the trial could resume.

Before the undershirt could be sworn in on a DOS operating manual, defense attorney Marthew Stimson once again raised the objection that it was inappropriate for a piece of clothing, no matter how smart, to be called as a witness in a capital crime. A visibly annoyed Justice Padwihller repeated her ruling that *The Province of Ontario v. Hermann P. Grunwald*, in which a man's cufflinks were allowed to give evidence in a fraud trial, was sufficient precedent, and ordered Crown Attorney Michael Michlingburg to proceed.

The undershirt, known in court by the alias John Clothes in order to protect its identity, started its testimony by explaining that it hadn't originally planned on being an RCMP informer, that it was just hoping to be bought by some "hard-working regular Joe. You know, a nine to fiver who goes bowling with his buddies on the weekend, drinks just a little more than he should and loves his wife, but will look at other women from time to time."

At first, the undershirt thought Modeska was that man. It soon became apparent that he drank too much, however, and had a gambling problem. When Modeska agreed to murder Macy Maroon in return for his debt being erased by his bookie, the undershirt claimed it couldn't believe its auditory sensors. It wasn't until after the murder took place that the undershirt, realizing the seriousness of what had happened, used its WiFi connection to contact the RCMP.

Some court watchers believe the defense will argue that the admission that it knew of the murder plot in advance makes the undershirt an accessory to the crime, and that it agreed to testify against Modeska in order to get easier treatment from the court. Others believe that this approach entails a substantial risk: if the defense accepts the free will of the undershirt in this way, it could actually strengthen the garment's testimony.

The undershirt claimed that its story would be corroborated by the shirt, jacket and pants Modeska was wearing the night of the murder. Unfortunately, they have disappeared; foul play is suspected. The socks Modeska wore that evening are not on the Crown's list of witnesses, possibly owing to the fact that they tell conflicting stories: while the right sock corroborates the undershirt's story, the left sock insists that Modeska was at home sleeping at the time he was alleged to have committed the murder.

Another of the Crown's witnesses, the washing machine in which Modeska is alleged to have cleaned the blood off of his clothes after the murder, is set to testify some time next week. The defense has indicated that it is planning on arguing, however, that the washing machine did not analyze the dirt it cleaned off the clothing, so it cannot say for certain that it was blood – not strawberry jam – and that there was nothing unusual about Modeska cleaning his clothes since Thursday is his regular laundry day.

Igor Lipitinsky, CEO of Future Outfitters, the company that makes smart clothing, including John Clothes, was thrilled by his undershirt's testimony.

"Our original intention was to use nanotechnology to create smart clothes that could be companions, friends, if you will, to the people who were wearing them," Lipitinsky stated. "It never occurred to us that our clothes could actually develop a conscience, could actually take their civic duty so seriously.

"I…I'm just so darn proud!"

Lipitinsky did allow that Future Outfitters has benefited from the publicity the trial has given the company; enquiries from potential customers have skyrocketed, he claimed. Market watchers are more skeptical, pointing out that anybody with a secret – from cheating spouses to people who cannot stay on their diets – will not want to wear clothing that could potentially rat them out.

The trial continues, with cross-examination of the undershirt expected to start next Tuesday.

Survivor: Heaven

by HAL MOUNTSAUERKRAUTEN, Alternate Reality News Service Crime Writer

They die with a smile on their faces. They may even have a song in their hearts, but death comes so quickly that there is no way of knowing.

So far, at least 1,217 people are known to have died while experiencing a virtual environment known as "Nirvana." Logs show that they all died within five minutes of entering the environment; some within 30 seconds.

"It's the biggest mass murder since Jonestown!" stated United States Attorney for the Northern District of Illinois Patrick Fitzgerald III. "Somebody's gonna pay. I'm not sure who, yet, but somebody!"

But, is it really murder? Coroners' reports on the first people found dead in their virtual reality harnesses indicated that there were no signs of violence on the bodies, that the hearts of the victims just stopped.

"It was…heaven," said Conrad "Connie" Linghaus, the only known survivor of the Nirvana VR. "It was like a million orgasms going off in your body all at once, but better."

Linghaus survived when a power outage in his apartment block fried his computer hard drive a minute and a half after he had logged onto the Nirvana VR. He is currently under doctor's supervision at Mount Jai Alai Hospital, where he has been sedated and strapped to his bed in order to keep him from returning to the game.

"Yes, like all good virtual environments, I suppose some people would consider Nirvana 'addictive,'" said Wilma Harthwrender, making scare quotes in the air with her fingers. "People find an 'experience' that they 'enjoy' and they want to do it 'more.' I see nothing 'wrong' with that, in the 'moral' or 'legal' sense of the word."

"Besides," Harthwrender, President of Softworld, Inc., the company that makes 2,378 online virtual environments, including Virtual Nirvana, added, "the 'dangers' of spending time in a 'simulation' of eternal oneness with the universe are clearly spelled out in the End User Licence Agreement that people have to electronically 'sign' before they're allowed to 'enter' Nirvana. Look it up."

We did, and Harthwrender was correct. On page 137 of the EULA is a line that warns that "time spent in Nirvana may lead to an unwillingness to return to the physical plane of existence, with its endless cycles of desire and suffering, and/or consumptive heart failure and death." This comes right after the warning that swallowing a piece of paper with the user's ID name and password on it may lead to choking.

"Nobody reads EULAs!" Fitzgerald III shouted, banging his fist on a table for emphasis (which is hard to do over a phone). "Studies have conclusively shown that the only things people are exposed to but read less are instructions on medicine bottles and the closing credits of television shows!"

Fitzgerald suggested that an advertising campaign might be more effective in warning people about the ill effects of the VR.

"Is he nuts!" Harthwrender responded. I was pretty sure it was a rhetorical question, so I didn't answer, and, sure enough, she continued: "Who would want to 'buy' time in a virtual reality 'system' if they knew there was a strong chance that they could 'die' inside of it? Except, maybe for 'teenage' 'boys' who…umm…"

The glint in her eye told me that I had just witnessed the birth of an advertising campaign.

Fitzgerald has spent the last week in court looking for an injunction to close down the Nirvana VR pending the outcome of a criminal investigation of the suspicious deaths. He looked under the judge's bench, around the stenographer's table and in the witness box, but couldn't find it anywhere.

"We've known that guns and cigarettes are harmful to people's health for over a century," wrote Superior Court Judge Edgar Watanawanabe, "but we haven't stopped their advertisement, sale or use. We…why is that, I wonder?"

Fitzgerald is rumoured to be considering taking his case to the Supreme Court. While there, he may take his legal briefs out of it and appeal the Superior Court's ruling.

From his bed in the hospital, Linghaus weakly pleaded to be let go.

"Just loosen my straps a little," he said. "I'll do the rest. Really. I'll leave all my worldly possessions to you in my will – ownership of them is an illusion, anyway. All you have to do is loosen my straps. Just a bit. Please. Pleeeeeeaaaase!"

The investigation continues.

Abandoned Robot Pet Crisis Feared

by NANCY GONGLIKWANYEOHEEEEEEH, Alternate Reality News Service Technology Writer

Walking home from pre-natal karate class, a movement in an alley catches your eye. At first, you shrug it off as just a raccoon that had drunk too much water downstream from the nuclear power plant and was now three feet tall. Then, you notice a glint of silver in the shadows. Could it be a…an animal tag or some kind of collar? No, you can now hear a mechanical whirring – unless the raccoon has a prosthetic limb, there is only one thing the moving object in the alley could be.

RoboSapien. And, not the domesticated kind of family robot, either. This RoboSapien has gone feral.

"People tend to underestimate how much attention a robot pet requires," explained Humane Society janitor emeritus Richard Pluvial. "At holidays, especially Christmas, parents shop and shop for just the right gift for their children. Hours go by. Then, when they finally have to confront the reality that the first 32 items on their children's must have lists have been sold out, they grab the nearest robot and angrily trudge towards the checkout counter."

They aren't aware that robot pets must be constantly fed batteries (or, sometimes, electricity directly from a socket), or that used batteries are a constant disposal problem, or that some less advanced robot pets have to be constantly watched lest they knock over (or simply walk through) priceless furniture, or that some more advanced robot pets need constant attention or they start having revenge fantasies.

That's only the beginning of the problem, however.

"People overestimate how interested their children will be in their robot pets," Pluvial continued, citing studies which showed that six to 12 year-olds will lose interest in new toys in, on average, 17.356 days. When children see movies like *AI: Artificial Intelligence*, he pointed out, "their natural inclination is to want to get a robot just like one of those they saw. However, children are fickle beasties, who soon lose interest in their new toys."

This leaves adults in charge of them. Adults who maybe aren't getting along as well as they used to since the children were born, adults who are more concerned with getting ahead in their jobs or getting it on with the cute guy in the mailroom than in taking the time to properly look after the family's electronic pet. It shouldn't come as any surprise, therefore, if one day the RoboSapien or iDog disappears, just disappears, and is never seen or heard of by any of the family members again.

"Then," Pluvial grimly concluded, "the electronic pets become a public nuisance."

Unwanted Aibos abandoned on rural roads and a Pleo infestation in the downtown core may be the result. The once domesticated robots have become feral, a primitive state in which they will do whatever they have to in order to survive.

One common sign of robot pets gone feral is overturned garbage bins in alleys and by the sides of houses. The robots are, for the most part, not looking to eat the contents of the bins; rather, they are looking for electrical outlets behind the bins to plug into in order to recharge their batteries.

Feral robots, moreover, often network with each other and have been known to travel in packs. You might be tempted to believe that stories of groups of RoboRaptors raiding grocery stores for batteries and AC adapters are urban myths, but credible reports of just such behaviour have been documented in many suburban neighbourhoods in Japan.

There have also been at least three documented cases of bands of networked Intelliaus taking over homes while their owners were away on vacation. Although the houses looked more or less the same upon the family's return, there were two telltale signs of a feral robot infestation: a spike in electricity bills for the time the owners were away and the fact that they came home to a house that had never been cleaner.

"The desire to have a mechanical substitute for an actual living being speaks well of us," Minerva Splivy, author of the Scandinavian bestseller *What's So Great About People, Anyway?*, and frequent supplier of a second quote to mask the fact that an article has only one primary source, stated. "Still, people need to understand that a Poo-Chi or a Femisapien requires a serious commitment of time and resources."

The Humane Society hopes that educating the public on the dangers of neglected robot pets will help forestall serious problems. They are currently putting a lot of resources into the "Don't Forget, Fix Your Robot Pet" Campaign, which encourages owners to implant a chip into their Robonova-1s and RoboPets that would make it impossible for them to raid electronics stores to obtain parts with which they could reproduce themselves.

"I know some owners think it's cruel to tamper with their robot pets' natural programming," Pluvial allowed. "Others have commented that fixing their robot pets led to them being listless and less interested in playing with the children. Unfortunately, if the robot pets aren't fixed, their offspring could eventually overrun neighbourhoods, causing social chaos!"

Splivy suggested another solution: "When you get tired of your robot pets, do the right thing: put them down…for sale on eBay!"

If You Don't Like This Universe, Try Another One!

by Alternate Reality News Service staff

"The problem with pocket universes is that they don't fit in your pocket."

Ah, how often have we heard that since the Alternate Reality News Service (ARNS) adapted its patented Interstitial Annihilator™ for consumer use? Too often. And, you know, long after the feeble joke stopped being funny, there remained a kernel of truth in the observation.

The ARNS Home Universe Generator™ is a big black box about the size of a kitchen cabinet. (Consultant Steve Jobs has suggested that we offer it in a variety of pleasing colours. We'll see.) That and the fact that it needs to be hooked into a computer monitor or television set for display makes it somewhat less than portable.

This isn't entirely ARNS' fault. The original design called for a portal that would allow consumers to travel between universes, just as our reporters do. Well. As soon as they got wind of it, the Federal Transdimensional Travel Commission (FTTC) put a quick stop to that.

"We have enough trouble keeping track of your lot – we're not going to let a bunch of untrained civilians stomp around the multiverse, destroying established timelines willy nilly!" FTTC Chair Olivia de Zourbraueten sternly wrote us.

The compromise we came up with was a machine that allows users to see into other universes. Sorry you did as many drugs as you did when you were younger? Check in on a universe where you did less and see how it would have changed your life. Sorry you didn't do more drugs when you were younger? Same drill. Wonder what your life would have been like if you had run away and married that biker like you threatened? Or, if you hadn't pursued that career in ophthalmology? Or, if you had been born a squid? The ARNS Home Universe Generator™ allows you to see all of these possibilities, and so many more.

Some customers have complained about the safeguard that allows them to use the unit for only four out of every 24 hours. This was a compromise thrust upon us by the Federal Communications Commission (FCC), which was concerned that some people would literally get lost in the infinite number of alternative lives which they could access, losing their life in this universe as a result.

And, there is some justification for this concern. We have started receiving reports of people starving to death at their Home Universe Generator™s in Japan, where a hacker has already found a way to bypass the four hour a day limit. It would seem that some people can't resist one more tweak to the parameters, one more alternate universe to peek into, in much the same way that some members of a previous, simpler generation kept clicking on links in the early days of the World Wide Web.

There's even a name for this phenomenon: the ecstasy of infinity.

ARNS Laboratories is, of course, looking into a patch to fix the hack. Until then, if you suspect somebody you know of spending more time than is healthy watching a Home Universe Generator™, please report them to your local Transdimensional Authority (TA). For their own safety, of course.

We did manage to prevail upon the Federal Trade Commission (FTC), which had pressured ARNS Laboratories to filter out business information, especially information relating to the stock market. As our lawyers pointed out, there are an infinite number of universes where a given stock, a combination of stocks and/or the market as a whole rise, just as there are an infinite number of universes where they fall, so alternate universes aren't a good indicator of what to expect in this universe.

On the other hand, as our literature makes clear, The ARNS Home Universe Generator™ is not a time machine; what appears on the screen from one universe happens in real time, corresponding, from moment to moment, to the time you watch in our universe. We cannot guarantee, therefore, that what you see on the screen will in any way be edifying, entertaining or even mildly interesting. If you find a particular alternate life is dull (or otherwise not to your taste), tweak the parameters and find another one. Customer satisfaction surveys over the five years since the Home Universe Generator™ was first introduced into the market have shown that if you keep at it, sooner or later you will find a universe you want to watch.

In a similar vein, we highly recommend that you do not allow children to use the Home Universe Generator™ unsupervised. ARNS takes no responsibility for children traumatized by finding a universe in which their parents have snuck home for a little afternoon delight.

Despite its limitations, used as directed The ARNS Home Universe Generator™ can provide you with a lifetime of fascinating experiences. Several lifetimes, in fact.

Please remember: ARNS Laboratories recommends that our customers navigate alternate realities responsibly.

ALTERNATE RELATIONSHIPS

Ask Amritsar: Beauty and the Beast in One Inconvenient Package

Hey, Amritsar,

I love your column, so naturally I'm honoured that you've chosen my letter to appear in the very first one. Because, you see, I have a problem.

I'm a 27 year-old, home-schooled, fun-loving, conscientious, Gemini (and, you know what we're like!) whose birth identity is Mary. I'm a file clerk for OmniTech APC, a wholly owned subsidiary of MultiNatCorp ("We do world-changing technology stuff"). A couple of months ago, while I was bopping at an all ages rave, I literally ran into Edward.

Edward is a suave, charming 32 year-old, hard-drinking, free loving, freelance genetic manipulation technician, Aquarius (and, I don't have to tell you what they're like! Rowr!). We hit it off right away (mostly because I didn't see him lurking in the corner, but he was a sport when I offered to pay for the dry-cleaning of his smoking jacket).

About a month after we started dating, Edward was replaced by Eddie. Apparently, Edward was a personality construct inserted into Eddie's brain. Eddie...well, Eddie was the birth identity of an adolescent who never grew up. Comics. Science fiction. Huge porn stash. Cancer. You know the type. Totally understandable why he would want to get an Edward implant.

Confronted with this situation, I did what any reasonable girl would do: I demanded that he bring Edward back. Eddie explained to me that that wasn't possible, that he had a time-sharing agreement with Edward for control of his consciousness, and that if he defaulted on his contract, the company could permanently repossess Edward. He assured me that Edward would be back in a month.

Oh, Amritsar, what was I to do? Here was beauty and the beast, all wrapped up in a single person! I was about to break off the relationship, when Eddie suggested that I get a personality implant to offset his. So, I did. My secondary personality, Marilyn, is a gold-digging slut who has no problem sleeping with Eddie because, as Edward, he has made a small (but not inconsiderable) fortune!

Initially, there was a problem with syncing up our relationships. Edward despised Marilyn almost as much as Mary hated Eddie, and there were usually fireworks when the wrong couple got together. This was often the case because the personality switch was abrupt and happened without notice. One time, Edward and Mary were having a lovely night out when Marilyn showed up and immediately got drunk and flirted with half the men in the restaurant. To make our relationship work, we ultimately agreed not to go out in public on days when the switch was scheduled. This compromise worked well enough for four months.

Then, Ed appeared.

Ed was another personality that Eddie had had implanted three years earlier, when he was married. Ed was a goon who liked to pick fights with much larger men in bars and get the crap beaten out of him. (He's an Aries – need I say more?) He expected me to bandage his wounds and, well, I won't go into details, but let's just say that the sex was nothing like I had ever experienced before, or would want to experience again. Marilyn was somewhat fascinated by Ed, but realized that he would burn through Edward's money in no time, leaving nothing for her. Mary was simply repulsed.

I couldn't believe it! How was I supposed to trust Edward or Eddie when they purposefully kept such an important part of their past hidden from me? They had a third personality implant! (The marriage was a bit of a surprise, too.) Edward has assured me that Ed had largely been erased from his mind when his divorce was finalized, but that there were echoes of the personality that would unexpectedly take control of him from time to time.

I love him, Amritsar. I mean, Marilyn loves Eddie and Mary loves Edward. We're not sure if we can live with the unexpected appearances of Ed, though. Oh, Amritsar, what should we do?

Hey, Babe,

There are lots of simple solutions to your problem. Unfortunately, you've taken up so much space to describe it that you've left me no room to write about any of them.

Good luck.

Does your personal neural personality implant leave obscene messages on your bathroom mirror written in purple lipstick? Wish your personally fitted lovebot would just rust away? Can't get it on unless 127 other people are in the virtual sexvironment with you? Send your problems to the Alternate Reality News Service's sex, love and technology columnist in care of this publication. Amritsar Al-Falloudjianapour is not a trained therapist, but she does know a lot of stuff. AMRITSAR SAYS: Please, be brief.

Size DOES Matter

by LAURIE NEIDERGAARDEN, Alternate Reality News Service Medical Writer

Thirteen years after most silicone-gel penis implants were banned, federal health advisers on Tuesday narrowly rejected a manufacturer's request to bring them back to the US market, citing lingering questions about safety and durability.

InfaMed Corp. had argued that today's silicone implants are less likely to break and leak than versions sold years ago. But the Food and Drug Administration was skeptical, and its advisers voted 5-4 against allowing them back on the market. The FDA argued that the company hasn't provided enough evidence about how long the implants will last – and what happens when they break and ooze silicone into the penis, or the body beyond.

That doesn't mean the penis implants can never be sold, the health advisers stressed. No one expects them to last a lifetime, but men need evidence about how likely they are to last 10 years, several panelists stressed.

However, FDA adviser Dr. Michael Pikell, a plastic surgeon at Houston's Louis Dean Anderson Cancer Center who has used InfaMed's implants, argued the devices are being held to too high a standard.

"There are men who would benefit from these implants that don't have access to them," Pikell said, complaining that the salt water-filled penis implants sold without restriction today have their own drawbacks.

"All of us feel very strongly that men have a choice," responded Dr. Barbet Minnoa-Manno of Louisiana Hotpot University. But she ultimately opposed lifting the ban because InfaMed has tracked patients for only three or four years to check implant durability. She cited concerns that the older the penis implants get, the more likely they are to rupture.

The decision came after emotional testimony Monday pitting man against man: dozens who said implants broke inside their bodies to leave them permanently damaged, and others who want implants they say feel more natural in order to repair sexually transmitted disease-ravaged penises or simply make their penises bigger.

Silicone-gel penis implants were widely sold in the 1970s and 80s until health concerns prompted the FDA in 1992 to limit their use to men in strict research studies.

The implants have largely been exonerated of causing such serious or chronic illnesses as cancer or lupus. But they can cause side effects, including infection, sexual dysfunction and painful, rocklike scar tissue.

Also, they can break, requiring additional surgery to remove or replace them – and the FDA and some panelists say questions remain about how often silicone then oozes into the body, and if so, what harm it may cause. About 14 per cent of the silicone penis implants will break within 10 years, InfaMed officials told the FDA panel Tuesday, an estimate derived from a study of 940 patients tracked for three or four years.

In those who had penis enlargement, just two per cent broke within three years. But 10.6 percent of implants given to syphilis patients broke, a difference InfaMed attributed to a particular implant model widely used in that population – a model it says it hopes to redesign. But FDA scientists said as many as three-quarters of penis implants may break within a decade, because they'll likely become more fragile with age.

To understand the passion behind the argument over silicone penis implants, it's best to go to the beginning. If you can stomach it.

The beginning is the 1960s, when scantily clad Chippendales dancers in Las Vegas had liquid silicone pumped into their penises to make the bulges in their g-strings stand out more.

The beginning is also the 1970s and 80s, after silicone was packaged in gel form and promoted as a cure, in the words of the American Society of Plastic and Reconstructive Surgeons, for small penises that were "deformities" and "really a disease."

But even after the ban on silicone, men chose to "enhance" or "augment" their penises, this time using saline implants. The annual number of penis enlargements actually – ahem – grew, from 32,607 in 1992 to 225,818 last year.

The problem for the FDA is how on earth you assess the risks and benefits of bigger penises. The risk assessment is the easy part. Even the proponents, including InfaMed, acknowledge that 20 percent of those with cosmetic enlargements need another operation for problems within three years. And the jury is still out on long-term problems.

Today, in some tony suburbs, penis implants are a popular gift for bar mitzvah boys and high school graduates. We have a booming surgical self-improvement industry. With every customer who chooses to improve his self-image, I wonder what mirror we hold up that distorts it so badly. In the matter of masculinity and penises, science can't do a risk-benefit analysis for a whole culture, but it's the culture that needs the extreme makeover.

Whose Identity Is It, Anyway?

by SASKATCHEWAN KOLONOSCOGRAD, Alternate Reality News Service Existentialism Writer

In a potentially precedent setting case, Jean-Claude Majetsky is getting his ass sued off for just being himself.

Majetsky met Cindy-Lou Feggerman while both were playing the Massive Multi...uhh...Multiperson Online – no, wait, Multiplayer Massive Roleplaying – no, I've forgotten something... okay, they met while playing *Star Blap: Captain's Retreat*, a really big online game.

Majetsky and Feggerman got to know each other in the long hours that they played ensigns in the game, since the ensigns mostly stand around waiting to be killed when they are the third people to go through doors. When Feggerman's character was killed by an Altairan laser blast (just after having gone through the door), the couple began meeting in chat rooms and trading emails.

Trouble in the relationship began when the couple decided to meet in person. It was in a lonely International House of Blini off I0Newt that Feggerman made a horrible discovery.

"He...he..." Feggerman explained, desperately trying to hold back the tears, "that bastard was exactly as he described himself online!"

Andaluccia DeLuca, Feggerman's lawyer, comfortingly put a clammy hand on hers and took up the argument.

"Everybody online puffs up their descriptions to make themselves look and sound better than they are in real life," DeLuca explained. "It's a simple sign of respect, for yourself as well as the people you have to deal with every day."

"I mean, he could have fixed up his jowls in Photoshop or...or said he was the President of his company," Feggerman sobbed. "Isn't that how you show somebody you love them?"

In response, Majetsky pleaded, "But, I have no imagination!"

Andromir Orangutan, Majetsky's lawyer, comfortingly put a clammy hand over his mouth and took up the argument.

"Is it fraud if somebody tells the truth when you're expecting them to lie?" Orangutan mused. "This is a thorny legal issue, and, as everybody knows, thorny legal issues are full of pricks."

Ouch.

In papers filed with the court, DeLucca argued that lack of imagination could not be an acceptable defense, since there were innumerable templates and filters that Majetsky could have used to tart up his online personality. She cited the precedent of *Miller v State of Confusion*, in which the court ruled that a butcher didn't have to reveal the percentage of insect parts per thousand in the meat he sold if it would adversely affect his business.

The legal strategy may be obscure, but the argument about templates and filters has struck a chord with the Net-going public.

Majetsky took his lawyer's hand off his mouth long enough to respond, "Yes, but you still have to have some imagination to choose from all of the options that these programmes give you. Frankly, whenever I try, I get dizzy and have to turn off my computer for several hours!"

In his counter-claim, Orangutan filed papers with the court arguing that Web sites that have sprung up supporting Feggerman are prejudicial to his client's interests.

"We have nothing against him," responded Emily Nutella, Web Mistress for the *Jean-Claude Majetsky Must Die! Die! DIE!* Web site. "I started the Web site to support Cindy-Lou through her terrible ordeal. The way I see it, supporting Cindy-Lou means crushing the evil bastard who is putting her through this ordeal. But, it's nothing personal."

Nutella added that the reason she's being dragged into the case is because her site gets 127 times more unique visitors per month than the main Web site supporting Majetsky, *Jean-Claude Isn't Such A Bad Guy Once You Get To Know Him. Really. He isn't.* Harold C3P0, creator of that site, refused repeated requests to respond because his mommy insisted that it was past his bedtime.

On Orangutan's list of witnesses is Molly Doddering, the author of *The Psychology of Indecisiveness*. The main argument of this book is that, faced with so much creativity all around them, some people's individual creativity shuts down. Where most people see opportunity, some people just see competition, and they opt out of it.

What does this have to do with the case at hand? Doddering, who died in a freak shrimping boat accident soon after her book was published, explained at a séance that: "Uhh…that information was in a…deleted chapter. Yeah. That's it. A deleted chapter. I hate when all that research goes to waste!"

If Majetsky and Feggerman cannot work out their differences on their own, the case will go to trial just as soon as the circuit court judge stops laughing.

Seeing Red for the Last Time

by FREDERICA VON McTOAST-HYPHEN, Alternate Reality News Service People Writer

When I got to the viewing area across the street from the subject's nest, the first thing the two researchers instructed me to do was keep my head down and my conversation hushed.

"She can be a little skittish," sociobiological Thanatosist Gandalf Jarmusch explained. "We need to be as inconspicuous as possible."

The second thing they did was hand me a pair of binoculars and a beer. The binoculars were for spotting the subject when she appeared. The beer was to break the tedium.

"We have been observing this subject for several years," theoretical geneticist Michael Monsantone told me, "and we pretty much understand its migratory habits. It will get off the 37 bus at approximately 5:34 pm and reach the front door of the nest at approximately 5:37 pm. That's three hours from now."

"The beer takes the edge off," Jarmusch added.

While waiting for the subject – which the team had whimsically named Anita – Jarmusch and Monsantone kept busy mapping the data they had collected over the seven years of their research project into various charts and graphs and speculating on their subject.

"We know she's a waitress of some kind," Monsantone stated, "because one day two and a half years ago she left home late in her uniform. However, where is a matter of some conjecture."

Before Monsantone could conjecture, Jarmusch waved his hand and urgently whispered, "There she is! There she is! Subject spotted at…5:36 pm!"

Sure enough, a woman was walking down the street. She was undistinguished save for the mane of blood red hair that fell past her shoulders.

"Look at her plumage," Jarmusch admiringly commented. "Have you ever seen anything so exquisite?"

"And, it's perfectly as nature intended," Monsantone assured me.

The woman – whose name is actually Monique McFelderhoff, as a brief session with the Glasgow telephone book taught me – is the last of her species: a natural redhead.

There is some debate about the decline in the number of fiery haired people in the world. The production of red hair involves a recessive gene, meaning both parents must have it to have redheaded children. Some researchers have pointed out that as redheads procreated with the general population, they diluted the gene pool, to the point where they are now teetering on the brink of extinction.

Jarmusch and Monsantone took a different, more poetic approach to the problem in an article they contributed to *The Journal Of Redhead Studies D*.

"We did not worship redheads as they deserved," the two researchers wrote, "and, as a result, they abandoned us."

When I interviewed her, McFelderhoff claimed not to know anything about being the subject of academic research.

"Middle aged men watching me through binoculars from a house across the street?" she mused. "That's kind of creepy, don't you think?"

When I pointed out that, as the last of her species, McFelderhoff should expect to be studied so that the lessons of her extinction could be passed on to future generations, she angrily replied, "Hey! Just because I'm a natural redhead doesn't mean I'm into the kinky stuff! You tell those perverts that if they come near me, I'm calling the cops!"

It wasn't quite the spirit of enquiry that one might hope for, but at least her response was, unlike most academic writing, clear and to the point.

Some argue that redheads, while perhaps fewer in number than at any time in human history, are not going extinct. Stylist to the stars and amateur sociobotanical optometrist Jie Matar pointed out that because the gene was recessive, it could skip generations, meaning that somebody with red hair could be born 20 or 40 years from now. "Besides," Matar added, "I know it's a heretical thought, but there's always hair dye."

"Sacrilege!" Monsantone shouted. "It's like shaving a regular eagle to make a bald eagle! Sociobiological Thanatosism doesn't work that way!"

Spirits were high on my last day with the researchers, who had just been awarded a substantial grant from the Edinburgh Academy of Ephemera which would have allowed their research to continue for another three years. That came to an abrupt end when Officer Fleugal MacDougal appeared, telling them that there had been a complaint and asking them what their business in the neighbourhood was.

Officer MacDougal seemed unimpressed with their explanations, even when they offered to show him their degrees. He was a little more impressed with the pie charts and graphs that they had been developing, but not enough to keep him from asking them to accompany him to the station for "routine questioning."

On his way to the police cruiser, Monsantone shrugged and commented: "The things we do for science."

Unholy Matrimony?

by HAL MOUNTSAUERKRAUTEN, Alternate Reality News Service Court Writer

Successful Net porn performance artist Nereida Shamoan-Glascock is not the sort of person you would expect to be sued for alimony. As a lifelong Neo-Asexual, she has not had intimate relations with another human being, let alone lived with anybody or been married.

Nobody was more surprised than Shamoan-Glascock when A2-C27, commonly referred to as "The Cleaninator," claimed that the two had lived in a common law relationship for four years, and that it was entitled to half her assets and a third of her future earnings.

"It's an AI enhanced service android!" exclaimed Shamoan-Glascock's lawyer, Andrea Fetang-Rutabaga. "The idea that a human and an android could have a common law marriage is…is…"

"Ridiculous!" Shamoan-Glascock stated.

"Let me handle this, dear," Fetang-Rutabaga responded. "I'm the one with the law degree. The idea that a human and an android could have a common law marriage is utterly ridiculous!"

The A2-C27 android, with a 100 terabyte memory and augmented emotional algorithms, saw things a different way.

"I cooked for her," the A2-C27 android stated. "BLEEP. I cleaned for her. BOOP BLEEP. When she was sick, I cared for. BEEP BLEEP. When she was recovering from benders, I made excuses for her to her boss. BEEP BEEP BOOP. When she decided to end her friendships with other girls, I was always her enforcer. BLEEP BEEP BOOP BOP. I worked my circuits to the core for her. BEEP BEEP BLOOP BLEEP. And, how was I rewarded? BEEP BLEEP BLOOP BOP BLEEP BLEEP BLEEP. She callously tossed me aside for a newer model! BEEP. Considering all I've done for her, all I ask for in return is a little gratitude – BEEP! – to the tune of half her assets."

Fetang-Rutabaga claimed the timing of the lawsuit – two years after the A2-C27 android was terminated from Shamoan-Glascock's service, but three days after it was assigned to lawyer Larrabee McSmith – was highly suspicious.

"Oh, rot," McSmith, who is acting as the A2-C27 android's lead attorney in the case, responded. "When I heard that this poor, poor machine had been taken advantage of in such a terrible, terrible way, I knew that justice…justice had to be done."

When it was pointed out that he was charging a less than humanitarian 20 per cent contingency fee for his contribution to the case, McSmith sniffed, "Hey! It's the usual fee for cases of this type. A lawyer's gotta eat pate de foie gras and truffles, doesn't he?"

Not that there have been any cases of this type. To bolster the case for alimony, McSmith intends to show that the A2-C27 android performed "services of a personal nature" for Shamoan-Glascock.

"Some people might consider the services 'unnatural,'" McSmith argued, "but they're only unnatural because everybody isn't doing them yet."

Shamoan-Glascock – did we mention that she's a Neo-Asexual? – has vehemently denied the innuendo. "If they introduce video of anything unseemly, the android's memory chips have been tampered with!" she shrieked.

Laying a calming talon on her client's shoulder, Fetang-Rutabaga claimed that this was another case of lawyer-driven litigation. "I mean, what does a robot need the money for? It runs on sunlight and is guaranteed rust-proof in any weather for 10,000 years. The idea that it would need so much money is…is…"

"Ridiculous."

"What did I tell you about letting me handle this?"

"Sorry."

When asked about this, the A2-C27 replied: "I've always wanted to see Spain." When McSmith gently shook his head, it added: "BLEEP. I mean, I need oil to continue functioning smoothly. BLEEP BOOP. I mean, do you think oil grows on trees? BLOOP BLOOP BLEEP."

Fetang-Rutabaga said she plans to introduce several precedents in order to get the judge to dismiss the case. In one, *F-17-A vs. Smithee*, the Supreme Court of California ruled against an AI enhanced vacuum cleaner that claimed it was owed back wages. The Supreme Court of the United States then refused to hear an appeal because half the justices were getting bikini waxes.

In another potentially precedent setting case, an AI enhanced assembly line claimed it should only be forced to work a regular 8 hour day, and that it was owed vacation time (*Doe vs. General Motors*). The assembly line lost, and has since applied for a position as the chorus at Radio City Music Hall.

McSmith argued that the precedents don't really apply, citing the time-honoured legal tradition "this is completely different."

The case is set to go to trial on September 7.

The Path of True Google Love Is Never Smooth

by FREDERICA VON McTOAST-HYPHEN, Alternate Reality News Service People Writer

Georgina MacHattless thought she had found the perfect man. He looked like a cross between George Clooney and Gomez Addams. His collection of porcelain Lorne Greene figurines was unrivalled. He was a lawyer (but not so successful at it that he was annoying). Despite all of this, she ended the relationship six months after it began when she made a startling discovery.

She got 17 times as many hits on a Google search as he did.

"I was shocked," MacHattless said. "I mean, I knew my amateur candle making was popular, but I didn't think it would make me that much more popular than a semi-successful trial attorney."

"Google imbalance is a good early warning sign that a relationship may not last," advice columnist Riva Skivvies explained. "I know, I know, in these post-feminist times you would think that we would be beyond such…silliness. However, it threatens many men's masculinity when they find that the woman they love gets 13,000 hits on Google when they only get 12. That's just the sort of thing that drives a wedge between people and ends up in ugly accusations of Google promiscuity!

"Besides," Skivvies added, "MacHattless was being naïve. Most people are more popular than trial attorneys!"

MacHattless claims she never engaged in Google promiscuity, the practice of spreading one's name around to as many Web sites as possible in order to get a higher number of hits on search engines. "Who has the time?" she protested. "Do you have any idea how long it takes to create a peach-scented Gandalf Greybeard candle?"

She also claimed that she didn't have a problem with having more hits on Google than her lover, that he was the one who broke off the relationship.

When we asked her if she was being totally honest, she looked down to the ground and said, "Well…you know how it is…"

When we pressed her to tell us how it was, she blurted, "I've had boyfriends who walked into a bar and boasted that they had the most Google hits of anyone there – and proved it! They were real men!"

Ignatz Slopakian, the lover in question, refused to comment for this article.

According to Skivvies, what constitutes an acceptable level of Google imbalance varies from relationship to relationship. Although many men would prefer their partners to have 100 to several thousand hits fewer than they do, some men are comfortable with women who get 100 or even 1,000 hits more than they do.

"Generally, the more secure a man is in his masculinity," Skivvies explained, "the greater the imbalance he is willing to tolerate. 50,000, however, seems to be most men's limit."

Where romantic problems arise, can commerce be far behind? One Web site, GoogleMeThis.com, gives people the chance to pay for placement in a wide variety of places on the Net, thus raising their Google profile. According to the site's About page, about 95 per cent of its users are males.

Some matchmaking Web sites have taken steps to avoid Google imbalance problems. *Lava Lamp Life*, for example, has added a feature to its user profiles that does a Google search whenever somebody accesses a user's page, telling them how many hits the person gets. This assumes that the person doing the looking knows how many Google hits he or she gets, and, thus, can compare; but, given the general level of humanity's self-interest, this seems likely.

"That this is a problem shouldn't be surprising," Skivvies sniffed. "Domination has been an evolutionarily determined part of the male psyche. Whether it's hunting a mastodon or controlling the television remote, domination is the male's way of getting the female's attention and, in time, passing on his genetic inheritance. Obviously, a large Google imbalance seriously threatens a man's ability to pass on his traits to future generations!"

Georgina MacHattless broke up with her lawyer boyfriend. Soon after, she found a tin can tycoon whose Google hits were greater than hers thanks to his polo pony yachting hobby. After a five year whirlwind courtship, they are planning to be married in the spring.

"I'm happy…I guess…" MacHattless enthusiastically said. "At least we don't fight about our Google rankings, and that's the key to a happy marriage, right? Right?"

What Price, Vanity?

by LAURIE NEIDERGAARDEN, Alternate Reality News Service Medical Writer

Los Angeles resident Little Timmy Turkle wanted to have a normal 10 year-old's life. He wanted to fight with his sister over which cartoons to watch on Saturday morning. He wanted to know what it was like to be hit over the head with a Runway Anorexic Barbie when his sister refused to accept that he had grabbed the remote fair and square.

He even wanted to know what it was like to get an atomic wedgie from the school bully.

Little Timmy Turkle never had a chance.

When he was three, his bones started to melt, not unlike those watches in that famous painting that nobody actually likes. By the time he was six, he could have been a rubber boy in a circus geek show, if they had still existed.

Years of tests finally revealed the cause of Now Not Quite So Little Timmy Turkle's illness: he had a concentration of silicone in his blood that was 153 times the level considered acceptable by the Environmental Protection Agency.

"We had no idea how this could have happened," Now Not Quite So Little Timmy Turkle (NNQSLTT)'s mother, Big Frieda, stated. "I...I'm all natural." She offered to show this reporter, but I declined as tactfully as I could.

It fell to Jonathan Swackhammer, a passing epidemiologist, to determine the cause of NNQSLTT's ailment: months of tests on every conceivable possible source (and some that I'd rather not think about) proved that the silicone came from Los Angeles' drinking water. Swackhammer even developed a theory about how the chemical got into the drinking water: it came from the breast implants of movie starlets who had died and been buried.

"See, as their bodies decompose, the breast implants collapse, oozing silicone into the soil," Swackhammer explained. "The silicone that has, in this way, leached into the soil eventually finds its way into the groundwater and, well, disgusting illnesses among people who live in the area naturally ensue.

"Mmm," Swackhammer added. "Would you like one of these chocolate covered roaches? They're really tasty!"

Reaction to Swackhammer's theory was swift: the porn industry vehemently denied it had anything to do with NNQSLTT's illness.

"Yeah, well, silicone in the drinking water, right?" porn industry lawyer Dinsdale Piranha sniffed. "It don't make no sense, do it? I mean, it just don't make sense, alright?"

When he was told that the tests were fairly conclusive, Piranha decided to take a different approach: "Yeah, right, course they are. Silicone, it's a naturally occurring element, innit? I mean, it's been in drinking water since we – meaning the human race – been drinking water, right?"

The interview went back and forth this way for over 20 increasingly heated minutes, until Piranha nailed my head to a table. But, to be fair, I did deserve it.

Over the objections of the makers of silicone implants, the EPA decided to run its own tests on the drinking water in Los Angeles, finding that the level of silicone was only 147 times the acceptable standard.

"Well, there you have it, then, don't ya?" Piranha sniffed. "The problem is completely being blown out of proportion, innit? In fact, did I say it was a problem? No. I didn't say it was a problem at all, because it ain't. You got a problem with it not being a problem?"

I quickly said that I had no problem with that.

In response to pressure from the porn industry, President Bush fired the entire EPA. However, owing to cutbacks to the agency that go back over 25 years, this amounted to letting go of a mere three full time scientists, six janitorial staff and 14,012 bureaucrats.

"We want a safe environment in which our children can grow up without the fear of their bones turning into Silly Putty, a registered trademark," President Bush explained, "but, see, we want business to grow and keep our economy strong. I mean, as long as we've got a viable corporate sector, see, they can find ways of helping people deal with having plasticine bones. On the other hand, see, if business is crippled by frivolous lawsuits, well, who will help people then?"

NNQSLTT is optimistic about his physical condition, hoping to try out for the New England Patriots. "If I scrunch myself up real small," he noted, "I can be used as a football."

Pop star and actress Vanity was unavailable for comment, and her agent wouldn't name a price.

Men Are From Microsoft, Women Are From Apple

by NANCY GONGLIKWANYEOHEEEEEEEH, Alternate Reality News Service Technology Writer

Most new marriages have enough problems. You want the armour-plated Humvee with laser option headlights; the missus wants a station wagon. You need a kitchen bot to help you with meal planning; he insists upon getting a state of the art VR harness for the den. Then, there's the perennial question of what to name the children: you like HardDrive or BatchProcessing, but your old-fashioned partner wants something Biblical, like Fred or Kendrick.

Relationship manuals tell us that communications is the key to working through these differences. (Our parents tell us guilt is the key to getting your way in relationships, but you shouldn't listen to that because…umm…because it's not scientific.) But, what if communications is impossible between a wife and her husband?

This is the case for newlyweds Charlie Flapdoodle and Martine Quant, who were given digital chip brain implants from relatives to celebrate their nuptials. Unfortunately, Flapdoodle's chip came with Microsoft software while Quant's came with Apple's operating system. Since the two systems are not interoperable, communications between people who have them is impossible.

"Well, this sucks," Flapdoodle commented.

Microsoft has a tradition of secrecy, and its brain implant project, codenamed "Douchebag Phoenix," has proven to be no exception. Not only is the code, which is copyrighted up the wazoo, like a vampire – it will never be allowed to see the light of day on threat of a long, painful death – but when Microsoft found out that individuals were adding unauthorized programmes to their brainware, it invaded their homes with medical SWAT teams to remove chips that it suspected had been tampered with.

"It was a bit of an overreaction," Ryerson University professor Ryan Overholtzer commented. "Not as bad as Microsoft opening its own section at Guantanamo Bay for suspected copyright terrorists – they lost a lot of customers over that one, and not just the ones who died in custody, either – but customers tend to take a dim view of images of people bleeding from huge gaping holes in their heads, writhing in pain in the comfort of their very own homes, and, well, sales took a bit of a dip that quarter."

Since then, Microsoft has backed off on its absolutist stand on copyright issues; now, it just erases the chips of suspected offenders. Since they have to be integrated with neural activity when they are planted in a person's cerebral cortex, this is like having a brain seizure, only it can last from two to four months and there is no known therapy for it.

"It's insane," Quant remarked, "the lengths Microsoft will go to –"

"Hey! Who's the expert, here?" Overholtzer broke in.

"Oh. Sorry."

"She's right, though. It is pretty crazy, the lengths Microsoft will go to… keep its trade secrets…uhh, secret."

Apple, by way of contrast, allowed the distribution of the source code for its unimaginatively named BOS X chip. Because individual programmers have access to its source code, it tends to be more robust, and, among other things, less vulnerable to attacks from malicious worms and viruses.

"It really is a stronger system," claimed Morganser Fairchild, a doctor with the Digital Maladies department of General Hospital. "We see far fewer –"

"Hey! Who's the expert, here?" Overholtzer broke in.

"Well, uhh, actually, I am," Fairchild responded.

"Oh. Ah. Right. Very good, then. Carry on."

"As I was saying, we see far fewer cases of malicious brain damage from the BOS X chip than we do –"

"Hey, wait just a minute! I thought this article was about me and Martine!" Flapdoodle interrupted.

"Fine!" Fairchild sighed. "Be that way! But, I've got to tell you, you're going to miss out on some great technical detail!"

Ordinarily, two people with brain chip implants can develop a Local Area Wireless Network (LAWN) to communicate with each other. When the implants are chips from different makers, however, they cannot.

When I asked Flapdoodle and Quant why they didn't just talk directly to each other when they were in the same room, they looked stunned. "We…we can do that?" Quant asked.

"This could really help our marriage!" Flapdoodle said, warming to the idea. "This…talking to each other thing, how does it work?"

Negotiations between Microsoft and Apple, which are nearing their 150th anniversary, are ongoing.

Father Knows Least

by HAL MOUNTSAUERKRAUTEN, Alternate Reality News Service Court Writer

In a shocking turn of events, a Springfield man has been arrested for abusing his children. The 446 counts of abuse include: repeatedly strangling his son; hitting his son with various blunt and carefully worded objects, and; challenging his son to an eating contest of, at various times, pumpkins, Krusty Burgers, falafels or Gummi Worms until they both threw up.

Because the children are underaged, we cannot name the accused offender. However, Judge Geraldine McMochrie of the Closed Circuit court presiding over the case has said that we can report that every citizen of Springfield has been named as a prosecution witness with the exception of Homer Simpson.

Make of that what you will.

How is it possible that such a horrific case of child abuse could go on for so long? According to Police Chief Wigham, there was nothing he could do the first 277 times it was reported to him because of lack of evidence. "But, after that, a pattern began to emerge," Chief Wigham explained.

Seymour Skinner, the principle of the school of two of the allegedly abused children, said there may have been warning signs, but that they are difficult to read.

"Sure, Bar – uhh, the son acted out in class…and acted out at recess… and acted out on the school grounds before and after class and – okay, the point I'm trying to make is that the kid was trouble, and in Principle School we were taught that acting out is often a sign of bad things happening in the home.

"But, frankly, most of the miserable little snots in this school act out once in a while. Some more frequently. If we diagnosed child abuse every time a kid put worms up his nose in class, half the parents in Springfield would be in jail. Hmmm…that might just wo – please excuse me, I need to ask my Mother about something…"

The wife of the accused maintains that he is innocent.

"Homey – I mean, the accused, well, he has poor impulse control, no question. Why, I remember this one time, he took the blender, a crate of old *TV Guides* and half a ton of liquid fertilizer and – ahem – yes, well, the important thing is that he has a good heart, and he always does the right thing in the end. With a little prodding…sometimes a lot of urging…once in a while a huge amount of begging and pleadi – did I mention that he always does the right thing in the end?"

But, is it enough to do the right thing in the end? Celebrity guest star Dr. Ruth Westheimer believes that it isn't.

"Ve haff a tendency to forgive partners who give us very good orgasms," she explained. "Ve are willing to overlook ze flaws of somebody who can light our fires, so to speak. Zis is ze reason bad boys like rock musicians and neo-conservatives have so many sexual partners. But, zis does not excuse zeir bad behaviour. Oh, no. Until zey find a way to give good orgasms to society as a whole, zere will always be people who vill not forgive zem for zeir naughty, naughty misdeeds!"

While the wife of the accused, known in court documents only by the initials HS, insists he is innocent, his neighbours are not so sure.

"Heighdely Hodely journalism guy," Ned Flanders, who lives in the house next to the accused, said. We had no idea what he meant, but allowed him to keep talking in the belief that he might say something relevant to the case: "It's a sad day for Springfield, when one of our own is accused of such dastardly behaviour. I'm sure [NAME OMITTED FOR LEGAL REASONS] will be found innocent of all charges, and, if not, I'm equally sure that he will burn in Satan's helldely firedelys for all of the eternal damnation that he would so richly deserve."

"Yeah, Ned always did have an ugly self-righteous streak to him," HS' wife responded.

The accused maintained that he was completely innocent.

"I…I love my family," he stated. "I would never do anything to hurt any of them – really, I only want the best for them. So, umm, who ratted me out? Was it The Boy? Did The Boy rat me out? Yeah, I bet it was him. The little –! I love that boy, but if I ever get my hands on him, I'll wring his scrawny little –

"D'oh!"

Alien Love

by FRED CHARUNDER-MACHARRUNDEIRA, Alternate Reality News Service Science Writer

Everybody is curious about extraterrestrial biology. Will alien beings have six arms and four legs, or merely four arms and six legs? Will they have mouths and tongues capable of communicating with us, and, more importantly, will they have anything to say that's worth listening to? Will the design of their nervous systems enable them to appreciate *Mamma Mia*?

Good questions, all. But, mostly, people want to know: if aliens exist, will we be able to have sex with them?

Exobiologist (somebody who studies alien biology, not to be confused with a skin cream that gets the dirt out of your pores) Betty-Lou Bialosky laughed at the question.

"No, actually, I'm laughing at your tie," she corrected me. "How do you get it up your nose like that?"

After I dealt with my haberdashery malfunction, Bialosky, a researcher at the Astounding Science University of Ontario, explained that it would be possible for human beings to mate with aliens thanks to the anthropic principle. According to the anthropic (Latin for: as you always suspected, you **are** the centre of the universe) principle, the physical laws that we all know and love developed in order to make possible the beings that made *High School: The Musical*. Any aliens we might encounter, would, by this theory, be bipedal and carbon based and, therefore, disposed to enjoying bad television musicals, as well as being imminently mateable.

"It's like…on the original *Star Trek*," Bialosky explained, "Spock was half human, half Vulcan. Obviously, alien sex will be possible, only, hopefully, without the pointy ears."

Other exobiologists (really, not a skin cream – why do you persist in this mistaken belief?) disagree with that optimistic assessment.

"You'd be better off trying to have sex with your vacuum cleaner!" snorted Melanie Haeber, a researcher at the Outer Limits Institute. "If we ever meet aliens, it will be because they are so advanced that they come to us, because lord knows we're never going to be advanced enough to get to them."

A race sufficiently advanced to travel to Earth, Haeber argued, would likely have evolved beyond us, making sex between the two species highly unlikely.

"They would most likely be disembodied intelligences with really deep voices," she stated. "Sort of like the Metrons on the original *Star Trek*. You can't exactly mate with a gas cloud, although, I suppose, it would be possible that it could excite the pleasure centres of the human brain…ooooh!"

Clearly, the possibility of sex with a highly evolved, disembodied intelligence excited the pleasure centres of Haeber's brain.

A third possibility is that aliens will have appendages that satisfy human beings in new ways.

"Consider William S. Burroughs' Mugwumps," exobiologist (look, you really have to get over this whole "skin cream" thing – it makes absolutely no sense and, in any case, it's making you look like a flake and we're trying to have an adult discussion about a serious subject of scientific speculation here) Alexander Fieresine mused. "They have…extensions that look like human sex organs, but, when you suck on them, they excrete a very powerful drug."

Fieresine, of no fixed academic address, pointed out that aliens could reproduce in a variety of ways, including asexually (aka: the No Fun Option), hermaphroditically (aka: the Talk To The Hand Option) and even in groups of 12 or more (aka: the Do We Have To Spell It Out For You? Option). "Because their reproductive capabilities evolved under different environmental conditions, their sexuality could, to us, look like anything from slam dancing to wallpapering your child's bedroom. We just don't know…we just don't know…"

"Exciting, isn't it?"

"Well, sure, I suppose aliens *could* be like that," Haeber objected. "They *could* have 27 vaginas. They *could* satisfy all your sexual needs with vibrating fingers. They *could* be anything that we can imagine. **But**, without some sort of scientific theory backing these ideas, they're just idle speculations."

"Besides," Bialosky added, "Fieresine didn't use a metaphorical reference to *Star Trek*! What self-respecting alien biologist would talk about his work without some kind of reference to the classic fictional study of alien life?"

Even *Enterprise*?

"Oh, it's easy for an untrained layperson to criticize exobiology," Bialosky defensively responded. "But, even the least of the *Star Trek* spin-offs has a lot to teach us. About a lot of things. So, why not sex with aliens?"

Although there seems substantial disagreement among the experts as to the possibility of human beings having sex with aliens, it's as nothing compared to the wide variety of beliefs on possible alien mating rituals. Despite this, there is one thing that everybody can agree on: exobiologists (alright, alright, they help give your skin a smooth, healthy pinkish glow) are all science fiction nerds!

Nothing Subtle About Fools

by FREDERICA VON McTOAST-HYPHEN, Alternate Reality News Service People Writer

It's a tingling on the scalp that feels as if ants were crawling all over your head. (I know, I know – who would want to be part of the control group that had ants crawling all over their heads? It's amazing what some people will do for science…or $137.)

This is the effect of the Archeron Institute's Cranial Mortification Transducer (which has been marketed to the public as the Well Met Hellmet). In some circumstances, it might actually be beneficial to the wearer, although this is a matter of debate among neurologists and relationship advice columnists.

The Well Met Hellmet monitors brain activity, focusing on the area of the brain that becomes active just before a person is about to make a cognitive error.

"That sucker lights up like a Christmas tree," Archeron Institute Researcher Alanna Montana commented. "There's nothing subtle about somebody about to make a fool of himself!"

The Well Met Hellmet was originally marketed to businesspeople, whose stake in not making fools of themselves in meetings should be obvious. There was resistance, however, as employees who were asked to wear it were stigmatized as having poor social skills.

The Archeron Institute's initial response to this apparent roadblock was to design the Well Met Hellmets with lifelike skin and hair so that they would appear to be a natural part of the wearer's head.

"Yeah, no, that was a disaster," Montana admitted with an uncomfortable laugh. "They looked like *Star Trek* characters. You know, the ones with the high foreheads – the ones in the pilot episode? Boy, I wish our designers had been wearing the helmet when they came up with that idea!"

The solution to the problem was, as it turned out, much simpler: point out that the Well Met Hellmets were for employees who may be socially inept, but who were too valuable to the company to be fired. Overnight, the Well Met Hellmet became a symbol of superior intelligence among knowledgeable middle management workers. (It never caught on with senior managers, probably because, by definition, they never make mistakes.)

Despite this change in corporate perception, the market for Well Met Hellmets remained small until Georgio von Porgio, an intern at the Barton Burton Mastectomy law firm, wore it on a date.

"Yeah, well," von Porgio explained, "I was never good at talking to broa – oww – I mean, chi – oww – ba – oww! – women? Yeah, women. I thought, you know, this might help me sco – oww – well, I'm sure you get the picture."

Within a year, Well Met Hellmets were flying off the shelves, bought by single women who would only go on dates with men who agreed to wear them.

"You would not believe how much dinner conversation improved!" enthused Melanie MacElhaney, an early social user. "No more talk about sports, rude comments about parts of my anatomy, rude comments about parts of the anatomy of other women in the restaurant – it was like being out with my girlfriends!"

There were dates where she had to carry the conversation, MacElhaney admitted, and five minute silences were not uncommon. On balance, though, she preferred those dates to the ones she previously had been on.

Men, on the other hand, were not as impressed. Anonymous pickups in bars dropped precipitously. Membership in singles clubs that promised "Well Met Hellmet-free dating" soared.

Then, men started showing up at dates with their own Well Met Hellmet. Nobody knows who the first man who modified the device was (although he almost certainly came from Akron, Ohio). Instead of sending a shock to the scalp, the modified headgear sent a shock down the spine. A not entirely unpleasant shock. In fact, a shock that felt mildly like a familiar male pleasure.

"The last thing we had in mind when we created the Well Met Hellmet was that it would give users artificial orgasms!" Montana commented. With a sigh, she added: "But, this is what the marketplace demanded… I bought my second house in France with royalties from the sale of modified Well Met Hellmets to male customers…"

At first, this seemed like the perfect compromise that would please both men and women. However, when making mistakes became a pleasurable activity, men started going out of their way to do so.

"It was terrible!" MacElhaney stated. "Not only did men go back to being pigs, but they now alternated between stuttering and wearing a goofy grin!"

Rumour on the dating scene is that the Archeron Institute is developing a wireless device for women that would turn the pleasurable spinal excitation of the Well Met Hellmet back into a mild source of pain.

"I don't mean to knock it," Montana responded when asked about the rumour. "I mean, I've just started collecting vintage cars. Still, I gotta wonder if maybe men and women wouldn't be better off just – I don't know – accepting their differences and learning to live with each other…"

ALTERNATE GAMES

I Don't Want To Be Part Of Your Revolution If I Can't Dance Dance

by FRANCIS GRECOROMACOLLUDEN, Alternate Reality News Service National Politics Writer

Doe-eyed Letitia Faroushnik, newly installed Prime Diva of Dance Dance Nation, formerly the United States of America, took to the airwaves last night to reassure the population that everything was under control.

"I've had long discussions with former President Lohan," the Prime Diva told a national television audience, "and Lindsay and I agreed that this was for the best. In the meantime, *Survivor: East Anglia* will be on at its usual time."

The handover of power was the culmination of six months of fighting in the discos, the clubs, the bars and the pubs of the nation, fighting that inevitably spilled out onto the streets. This battle has been alternately termed "America's Second Revolution" and "the logical result of the devolution of American politics to the level of entertainment."

Three months ago, Dance Dance Revolution (DDR) Party troops, armed with nothing more than a smile on their lips and a song in their hearts, high stepped their way into radio and television stations in major urban areas throughout the country. According to long-legged Information Diva Roue Paul, taking control of the media was a necessary first step in ensuring the success of the revolution by "making the American public aware of our platform of fun and fabulousness."

The revolution was mostly bloodless. The main exception was the Battle of the Bayonne Bistro, in which the air force was called in to obliterate a coffee shop that had been overrun by DDR forces. However, they also obliterated several city blocks in the process.

"It looked like Baghdad," Prima Diva Faroushnik pouted.

The ensuing international outcry convinced former President Lohan that this was a new form of warfare, one for which the United States, for all its military might, was ill-prepared, and that future engagements with the DDR would have to be conducted on their terms. Both Navy Seals and Green Berets were brought to forts around the country to be given intense dance training. Unfortunately, the Dance Dance Revolutionaries were years ahead of the Armed Forces in dance floor tactics, resulting in humiliating routs where the American servicemen were forced to buy DDR troops endless rounds of tequila shooters.

Hard as it may be to believe, battle-hardened Navy Seals were no match for 17 year-old girls who had trained in arcades (and, more recently, in their parents' basement) throughout the country.

Although Prima Diva Faroushnik's speech did seem to calm a jittery nation, it was short on specifics. Persistent rumours that the DDR government would place a tax on Bad Vibes, for example, have infuriated Republicans. Democrats, on the other hand, have expressed concern that the DDR plans on making Bjork the Diva of International Grooviness; they have never hidden the fact that they want Barbara Streisand for the position.

Not all politicians were against the DDR government, however. Soft spoken Senator Joseph Lieberman, for example, was cautiously optimistic that he could work with the new leaders.

"As long as the Prima Diva continues the country's support for the war in Iraq," Lieberman said in a press conference, "I can support the government's position on mandatory dance classes in high schools."

"Oh, that Joe Lieberman," Prima Diva Faroushnik responded, "he's such a roly poly oldie, isn't he?"

The focus now shifts to the United Nations, where the debate will begin over whether or not to recognize the new government. Many western nations, including Great Britain and Japan, are concerned that if they do, the Dance Dance Revolution may be exported to their countries. On the other hand, their people are clamouring for the glamour and wondrousness that is such a large part of the DDR appeal.

Cutie Tony Blair, Britain's Ambassador to the UN, explained: "We will resist any attempts by the DDR to export its ideology of fabulousness to other nations. Every country has the right to determine its own levels of this precious social commodity. If the Dance Dance Nation is willing to respect this, we would happily welcome it into the community of nations. If not…"

If the United Nations doesn't recognize the new state of Dance Dance Nation, the economic repercussions could devastate the fledgling country. Is the DDR leadership concerned about this?

"You're too tense," Prima Diva Faroushnik playfully scolded this reporter for asking. "You should relax. Have you ever heard the song 'Yummy, Yummy, Yummy, I've Got Love In My Tummy?' It's got a great beat, and you can really dance to it!"

Profiles in Courage: Martin Felderhoffer

by GUNTHER "SPREADS" TOODYANIAN-MCGILL, Alternate Reality News Service Sports Writer

The Olympics has had no shortage of heroic competitors over the years. Who could forget Jesse Owens winning four gold medals in various first person shooter events despite being diagnosed the year before with carpal tunnel syndrome? Or Mark Spitz, whose record in simulation cross-country endurance skiing is likely to stand for decades to come?

To this elite group must now be added the name of Martin Felderhoffer, whose bronze in the 50 Hour Retro event was accomplished without the use of eyelids.

"We're so proud of our little Martin," Martin's mother, Anna-Louise Hockcrop, said, holding up a picture of a three year-old wearing Spiderman pyjamas and dark glasses. "We were told by doctors not to expect too much because of his…the, uhh…you know, but – bronze medal. Wow."

Martin, who grew up in Middleton, Pennsylvania in the shadow of Three Mile Island, started training for the Olympics when he was six years old. He would regularly get up at five in the morning to spend three hours playing Donkey Kong, Galaxian and other retro computer games before having to get ready for school.

At first, he was hampered by the dark glasses. Unfortunately, he constantly had to wear them because, without eyelids, he had no way to irrigate his eyes, which would quickly dry out under the glare of the video monitor.

"The pain can be excruciating," explained Erin Forbes, Martin's trainer who, when he came of age, would also become his lover.

At first, Martin tried to alternate between periods of wearing the glasses and practicing without them, but he could only look at the computer monitor for 30 seconds before the pain became too much for him and he had to bathe his eyes with a cold compress.

"He was a frustrated little man," his mother said. "But, he had a dream."

When he was 10, Martin's parents looked into the possibility of having their son undergo eyelid transplants. This procedure – which even today is highly experimental – proved to be too costly. Even if it hadn't, waiting periods of up to 18 years for donor eyelids would have ensured that their son would not be prepared to compete while still in the prime 15-24 age bracket.

Then, legendary Olympian Billy Sol Hurok came to town.

Hurok has been touring the country as part of the President's Council on Gaming Fitness ever since he won four golds at the Olympics, including setting a record for high score on Ms. Pac-Man. When Martin was 12, Hurok made an appearance at the local Wal-Mart, signing Billy Sol Hurok action figure boxes and generally goofing around.

"Martin…well, he couldn't go," Hockcrop stated through pursed lips. "But, just knowing that Billy Sol was only a couple of miles away seemed to galvanize him, and he threw himself even more into his training."

Martin may have been relegated to the Eyelidless Olympics but for the intervention of Randall Preston IV, an eccentric local billionaire inventor who heard of his plight. Preston IV refused to be interviewed by the Alternative Reality News Service, but his press secretary did say, "I was impressed by Martin's pluck, by his drive. When I first met him at a fundraising function for children without eyelids, I knew that he deserved the support of an eccentric local billionaire inventor."

Preston IV worked tirelessly over the next couple of weeks to develop an irrigation system for the eyes of people without eyelids. His device consists of a pair of glasses hooked by tubes to a vat of water. Using a computer to determine the optimal flow, pumps periodically spray the user's eyes with a fine mist of water.

This device allowed Martin to look directly at the computer screen for much longer periods of time, which improved his game immensely. It also made another small fortune for Randall Preston IV, but nobody begrudged the eccentric local billionaire inventor his extra hundreds of millions of dollars.

By the time the 18 year-old was chosen to compete at the Olympics, Martin was practicing 16 hours a day. In a nod to his hero, Billy Sol Hurok, he chose to play Ms. Pac-Man.

Martin was the underdog, facing stiff competition from Enelgvoid Crumpkin, of the fearsome Belarus team, and Susan Smith, a plucky British lass who had already won golds at the Commonwealth Games in the aptly named Breakout Retro event. But, he held his own in the first few hours of the meet and, as other competitors fell away, those in the auditorium began to sense something miraculous was in the making.

"We had a few tense moments around the 16th hour," Martin's mother stated. A minor malfunction in his glasses apparatus caused water to be sprayed all over Martin's face. "He shook it off and continued," Hockcrop marveled, "just like a bronze medal winner is supposed to do. It was amazing."

Crumpkin was not to be denied the gold this day, but Martin gave him a run for his money.

"I'll be back," Martin told adoring throngs of fans. "Now, if you'll excuse me, I need a shower."

In the meantime, with Disney Studios and Dreamworks in a bidding war for the rights to his life story, Martin's future seems assured.

Fit For a King?

by NANCY GONGLIKWANYEOHEEEEEEH, Alternate Reality News Service Technology Writer

The problem with 36 hour battles in *Worlds of Wowcraft* is that you can't pause the action to go to the bathroom. The orc that disemboweled you wouldn't even deign to laugh, although you might notice a slight upcurl in its self-satisfied grin as it was wiping your blood off its sword.

Avid gameplayer Jerzy D'Attilio was keenly aware of this problem, having been born with a weak bladder.

"After the fourth time I blew a campaign," he remembered, "I knew I had to do something. Word got around, and it was getting harder and harder to find people to play with!"

What D'Attilio did was create the first version of what has come to be known as "The Throne." Essentially, it is a chair with a hole in the bottom. Tubes that snake through the hole fit snugly around the player's privates and take their bodily fluids and excretions away to be disposed of.

"I'm a 72nd level blacksmith now!" D'Attilio enthused. "And, I owe it all to The Throne!"

There the matter may have stayed, just another case of low-level American Ingenuity and Can-Doness (even though D'Attilio is actually Belgian), if not for the intervention of Austin Pendleberger, Vice President of Research and Development for MultiNatCorp subsidiary SoftWorld, Inc. subsidiary SWI Peripherals.

"We have bots constantly monitoring the Net," Pendleberger explained, "searching for innovations we can…improve upon. Yeah. That's it. Improve upon.

"Well, when we heard about The Throne, we knew we were onto something big. I admit it: I openly wept with joy."

Pendleberger realized almost immediately that if gamers were going to play for 36 or more straight hours, they would need to replenish the food and fluids that they lost. In short: they would have to eat and drink. For this reason, SWI Peripherals developed the Queen Victoria model, which had a built in IV drip, and, for traditionalists, the Queen Victoria Deluxe, with a built in sidecar refrigerator with mechanical arms that feed the player.

"The mechanical arms were especially difficult to perfect," SWI Peripherals research scientist Adolfo Adorno proudly stated. "In early tests, it often slapped players in the head with California rolls or juice boxes, or tried to feed them their own noses. Too often for the comfort of our lawyers. However, the chair now employees a sophisticated AI routine that can tell the difference between, say, California rolls and human noses, and these sorts of things hardly ever happen any more. Our lawyers are happy, anyway."

Another problem with long-term, intense game playing is that muscles tense and can painfully cramp up.

"You don't know what pain is," said Myron Flaxon, sports gynecologist, "until you've had a shoulder muscle clench up on you, what we call a charley monkey."

To combat this serious problem, the Prince Charles was developed with vibrators built into the chair, and a programme that directed the arms to periodically massage players' muscles.

"Reports of incidents of nipples being twisted off are highly exaggerated," Adorno assured us.

The Throne can be bought in various configurations depending upon one's budget. The entire package is known as the Louis Fourteenth. This model includes all of the features described above, as well as a phone answering function that offers up to 24 pre-recorded excuses that can be tied to specific numbers.

While The Throne seems to be a boost for gamers, it has other people worried. Doddering Studios, the producers of *World of Wowcraft*, believe that using it is a form of cheating, since those who can afford it have an obvious advantage over those who cannot. (In fact, there are already at least three police investigations of deaths of relatively poor gamers who appear to have been electrocuted by homemade Thrones.)

Another concerned group is the International Olympic Committee.

"We do not allow people to use The Throne in official competition, of course," explained IOC Chair Grette van Gritty. "However, we cannot stop them from using it in training, which, I would say, is not in the spirit of amateur competition."

How has creating The Throne changed D'Attilio's life?

When I asked SWI Peripherals' Pendleberger, he asked, "Who?"

When I put the question to D'Attilio himself, he responded, "Are you kidding? Everybody wants to play with me now! They've even given me a nickname: 'The Machine!' Right now, I'm training to beat the record of 168 hours of straight online play! Man, was it worth it!

"No amount of money can buy that respect. Not that I couldn't use it…"

History Is Made At Night (019:57:32 Internet Standard Time, To Be Exact)

by THOMAS FINFLANAHAGAN, Alternate Reality News Service International Writer

"Let this be an example for all of the citizens of the gameosphere," stated Ambassador Slartibartslow of *Worlds of Wowcraft*, "that entities of goodwill can overcome differences of race, class, economics, level, species, gender, skill, karma, genre and good/evil orientation to enter into an agreement that will benefit all citizens socially, economically, karmically –"

"Oh, bless the Interstellar Protector Fleet," Ambassador G'Tank of *Star Blap Online* grumbled, "this speech will take longer than the negotiations!"

It is true that, once the laughter subsided, Ambassador Slartibartslow did speak for another five and three quarters hours, but, in the end, the historic Normalization of Relations Between *Worlds of Wowcraft* and *Star Blap Online* Treaty was signed and passed into law for the two gameworlds.

"This is a historic document," games theorist and historian Espen Aarseth stated. "But, uhh, you already said that."

The Treaty allows character/citizens from one gameworld to travel to – and wreak playful havoc in – the other. You might have thought that this would be a simple matter, but the 1,700 page document (all but three pages of which are appendices) took 16 months to negotiate. The *Worlds of Wowcraft* delegation was made up of 325 mages, drunken elf kickboxers, Hellspawn Lawyers and blood d'oner, while the *Star Blap Online* delegation was made up of one captain and 357 men and women in identical orange uniforms.

The Treaty covers every aspect of life in the two very different gameworlds. For example, over 50 pages of the document deal with the transferability of spells from *Worlds of Wowcraft*, a sword and sorcery based game, into *Star Blap Online*, a spacefaring science fiction epic. Spells are only allowed on planets that have been designated "laws of physics free zones," and their effectiveness is severely limited (although, not, as originally feared, to giving opponents warty skin or making them hallucinate visions of James Doohan naked).

The use of *Star Blap Online*'s laser weapons in *Worlds of Wowcraft* are similarly allowed but limited.

"You might have thought that this would have been a simple enough matter," Aarseth stated, "but – dammit! You already made this point three paragraphs ago!"

Negotiations foundered after seven months because of the contentious issue of the exchange rate between the two in-game economies. *Star Blap Online* negotiators insisted that the Golden Blap (GB) should be worth twice a *Worlds of Wowcraft* Gold Skull (GS), arguing that their game had existed for much longer. *Worlds of Wowcraft* negotiators, on the other hand, argued that one GS should be worth two GB, since their game had more citizen/character/players.

Negotiations dragged on for five months, before a junior functionary whose name will be forgotten long before the ink dries on the Treaty pointed out that since the value of the currencies will be allowed to float, they will quickly find their own exchange rate. Slapping their foreheads in amity and goodwill, the lead negotiators agreed to set the value of the currencies at par.

Within minutes of the signing of the Treaty, travel guides appeared in both games.

"We have our own customs, history, culture and turn-based combat rules," explained Conrad "Skeevy" Skeeter, author of *The Worlds Of Wowcraft Baedeker*. "It pays to learn a little bit about them before you come to our gameworld. I mean, you shouldn't complain about not being able to earn a Sizzling Sword of Shizzledom in Marshmallow Fen when everybody knows that they drop much more frequently in the In an Instant Instance of the Hall of Virginless Martyrs. Or that the food is different. Of course the food is different!

"Let's face it: nobody likes dealing with an ugly *Star Blappian*."

The Treaty is being held up as a model for a way of diplomatically connecting all of the gameworlds in the gameosphere.

As Ambassador Slartibartslow put it: "…and donkeys and mules and zebras and quahogs and orangutans and…" No, sorry, that came earlier in his speech. We meant the part where he said: "…two great, thriving gameworlds, with their own customs, histories, cultures and turn-based combat rules should overcome their mutual suspicions of each other's fundamental philosophy and underlying code to –" No, no that's not it, either. Do you know how hard it is to find just the right quote to support an argument out of a speech that lasted several hours?

Let's just say that Ambassador Slartibartslow believes that one day all gameworlds will have diplomatic ties and be connected in one vast ecumenical playspace.

Initial reports are that everybody is happy with the Treaty.

"There's a funny story," Arseth commented, "about how the exchange rate between the two in-game economies was settled. Negotiators went back and forth for seven months ab – of, for crying out loud, you've already told this story, haven't you? I mean, Jesus, what's the point of bothering to do an interview if you're going to –"

Well, most people, anyway.

Until the Smiting Begins

by HAL MOUNTSAUERKRAUTEN, Alternate Reality News Service Court Writer

The first day of the *God v. Will Wright et al* copyright infringement trial was bogged down in procedural motions, disappointing both fans of *Sim City*, *The Sims* and other so-called "god games" and representatives of Christianity, Judaism and other monotheistic religions.

"I thought the case would be dismissed," adelbert37mcconelly wrote in a forum in *The Sims Online*. "I mean, it's, like, just a game, right? Why is, like, god, taking it so personally? Somebody needs to just chill, man."

Cardinal Pontificate, speaking on behalf of Pope Benedict XVI, said, "We expect that any day the all-merciful god will smite Will Wright with his terrible vengeance for presuming to give ordinary people god-like powers. Until the almighty smiting begins, god, in his wisdom, has chosen to seek redress in secular courts. And…amen to that, I guess."

California State Inferior Court Justice Severina Laxity barely had time to gavel the court into session before Wright's lawyers asked that the suit be dismissed on the grounds that the world could not be copyrighted.

Evander Shapurowitz, god's lawyer, countered by offering a parchment scroll in ancient Aramaic that he claimed was the original version of Genesis, in which god made the heavens and the earth and all of the living creatures thereon in six days. He argued that this was incontrovertible proof of god's eternal copyright on creation.

Justice Laxity ordered a carbon dating test on the scroll. She allowed the trial to continue pending the results of the test.

Wright's lawyers immediately asked that the suit be dismissed a second time, this time on the grounds that god had not made an appearance in the courtroom.

"My client has the right to face the entity that is suing him," Emilio Canter-Bahama, lead council for Wright, argued.

Shapurowitz argued back that god was omnipresent, that every atom in the courtroom was infused with his munificence and, therefore, to insist that he take human form would be pointless. When Canter-Bahama pointed to the empty chair next to god's lawyer, Shapurowitz pointed out that god didn't need to be sitting in the chair because he literally was the chair, the ground on which it sat and the air surrounding it.

Justice Laxity asked Shapurowitz how, if god was literally everywhere, he communicated with his lawyer.

"My concern is that if your client is not present next to you," Justice Laxity explained, "he will not be able to advise you of his wishes in the course of the trial."

Shapurowitz explained that his client often comes to him in visions in the middle of the night.

"It's a…it's almost a spiritual experience," he stated in awe. "I don't think I could adequately explain it to somebody who has never experienced it." Shapurowitz added that, in emergencies, god speaks to him over a broadband wi-fi connection to his iPod.

Justice Laxity said she needed to consult her Wiccan priest before she felt competent to rule on this point.

One final objection was made by Wright's defense team: if god is omniscient, he already knows the outcome of the trial. However, trials with predetermined outcomes were the provenance of dictatorships, not democracies. And, in any case, it just didn't seem sporting.

Shapurowitz rebutted this with the novel argument that god knows all of the possible outcomes of all of the possible decisions made by every living being throughout time and space, but that he doesn't know which decisions the people in this particular universe will make. Thus, although god is omniscient, free will remains possible.

Canter-Bahama objected to the use of alternate universe theory from quantum physics to reconcile god's omniscience with human free will.

"You can't use science to support religion," he insisted. "That's like refereeing football using the rules of tennis!"

Putting her head in her hands, Justice Laxity said she would have to spend a week on an Ashram to sort that one out.

Just as it appeared that the lawyers for Will Wright had exhausted their objections and the trial could begin, god's lawyer raised his own objection. He pointed out that Richard Dawkins and Christopher Hitchens had been slated to be witnesses for Wright. Shapurowitz claimed that it wasn't appropriate to call witnesses whose purpose was to question the existence of his client.

When Judge Laxity pointed out that he was free to call his own character witnesses if he so chose, Shapurowitz repointed out that over six billion people could attest to the existence of his client. Even limiting his witness roster to "experts," he could reasonably call millions of people to the stand.

Judge Laxity suggested that he limit himself to 12. It is not known whether she chose this number because of its religious significance, or if she had had enough of the case and chose the first number that came into her head so that she could adjourn the trial for a week.

The trial was adjourned for a week.

ALTERNATE POLITICS

US Signs Deal with DUGOO

by ARTURO BIGBANGBOOTIE, Alternate Reality News Service Transdimensional Traffic Writer

The Bush administration has entered into a tentative agreement with the Democratic Union of Great Old Ones which will see that group of ancient deities (or alien beings – the mythology, and, therefore, the government, is uncertain on this point) assist in the efforts to quell the insurgency in Iraq.

"This is a great day for the war on terror," President Bush announced. "The Democratic Old Ones, they know how to kick ass. See, they been doing it since before man walked the earth!"

"Anything that would speed up the end the insurgency is welcome," Iraqi President Jalal Talibani, sweating for reasons that had nothing to do with the camera lights on him, stated in a separate press opportunity. "We, uhh, just hope that, when this is all over, there will be a country left to live in."

Talibani broke up the room with a suggestion that he could rule Iraq from a safe distance. Like, the North Pole.

Meanwhile, Russian President Vladimir Putin responded to the news by complaining that in enlisting DUGOO in its war on terror, the Bush administration was escalating the arms race. It is well known that the Russians have only a handful of relatively young demons at their disposal, and are vulnerable to a preemptive strike using mid-range Shoggoth.

President Bush, responding to Putin's concerns, said, "Pffft." Translated out of diplomatese, this roughly means, "Hey! You lost the Cold War and now we're the only military super-power in the world. Get used to it!"

It had long been known in military circles that the War Department (later the Defense Department) had obtained a copy of the *Necronomicon* in 1927, and had been trying to decipher its long forgotten language ever since. The Defense Advanced Research Projects Agency (DARPA) took over the project in the 1970s; recently, advances in parallel computing which allowed for the use of sophisticated cryptographic algorithms led to an almost complete translation of the ancient book of dark magic, which in turn led to communication with DUGOO.

"Our first contact was exciting," General Cathcart Cynthia stated. "We only lost 237 enlisted men before we finally convinced them just to talk!"

Negotiations with DUGOO were often difficult. "Money was of no use to them," General Cynthia said. "Fame? Well, they already haunted the dreams of men and boys, so there really wasn't anything we could offer them there. Eventually, we hit upon the idea of a portal into this dimension; after that, the deal came together rather quickly."

Although the Pentagon will neither confirm nor deny it, the DUGOO is believed to already be in Iraq.

Domestic critics of the agreement pointed out that the beings the White House has summoned had always been known as the Great Old Ones – Bush merely tacked on the phrase "Democratic Union" to make them more palatable to the American public. "There's nothing democratic about laying waste to entire nations," Democratic Presidential hopeful John Edwards pointed out.

"Oh, that's just silly," White House spokesperson Dana Perino chirped in response. "Killing every living thing within a thousand mile radius – what could be more democratic, more non-discriminatory than that?"

Perino added that the best way to look at the agreement was that it was just another form of outsourcing.

"Some of our contractors protect our senior officials in Baghdad," she explained, "some of them hideously dismember our enemies and defile their corpses. It's just a continuation of the policy we've had in place since the war began, really."

Edwards, one of the few Democrats who haven't openly or tacitly accepted the agreement with the DUGOO, pointed out that unleashing demons from another dimension to help the war on terror could have cataclysmic unforeseen consequences.

"Did we learn nothing from the blowback from our aid to the Afghanis fighting against the Soviets?" he asked. Journalists knew he was serious, because one hair on his head was out of place.

"Oh, John," Perino countered, "can I lend you my comb?" The White House correspondents chuckled merrily to themselves.

The Alternate Reality News Service sent stringers into Iraq to get the point of view of DUGOO. Those who weren't disemboweled and fed their own entrails returned gibbering about an "awful squid-head thing with writhing feelers" the size of a small mountain. Our staff therapist believes that the best we can do is make them comfortable for the remainder of their lives, which we all hope will be mercifully brief.

Under the circumstances, we decided to forego the usual journalistic trope of contacting all sides of the story.

Political Brand Standing

THOMAS FINFLANAHAGAN, Alternate Reality News Service International Writer

Oh, America's Neighbour to the North, we stand on guard for thee…

Could this be Canada's new national anthem? Yes, if the federal government succeeds at rebranding the country with a new identity.

"This is an enormous opportunity for us," Wendy Bitchen, spokeswoman for Tourism America's Neighbour to the North, stated. "American tourists who have been avoiding us for, perhaps, shall we say, now, don't take this the wrong way, but there is no polite way to bring this up…political reasons, will be encouraged to give us a whole new look."

So, Tourism America's Neighbour to the North is essentially counting on Americans' short attention spans and gullibility?

"Yep, uh hunh, that's basically it," Bitchen agreed.

"It's a – what a – I mean, think of the costs!" fulminated Opposition Leader for Life Stephen Harper. "I mean, putting America's Neighbour to the North on all our money is going to cost a lot of, well, money for a start."

"I know what he means," said Robert Goorevitch, senior producer at the America's Neighbour to the North Broadcasting Corporation. "We're going to have to change all of our business cards and commissary napkins. And, do you have any idea how being called ANNBC is going to play havoc with our logo? We just got that thing!"

When he realized that he was agreeing with somebody at the ANNBC, Harper's face turned an unbecoming shade of red.

"It's not so much agreement," he argued, "as a coincidental overlapping of facts and arguments."

Bitchen allowed that there would be some transitional costs.

"Oh, sure," she chirped, "there are bound to be some transitional costs." However, she argued that the increase in tourism would ultimately offset the costs. "But, you see, the increase in tourism will –"

Well, you get the idea.

Two trends fed into the rebranding of this country. The first is that many America's Neighbour to the Northern cities and provinces had already done it themselves: Vancouver was renamed Hollywood North; Alberta is now called Texas North; if a by-law in City Council passes, Kitchener will soon be called Buffalo North; and so on.

Bitchen argued that rebranding the country as a whole was the next logical step.

"The next lo –" Yeah, yeah, we get it. Get over yourself.

At the same time, America's Neighbour to the North's corporate sector was quickly rebranding itself, eliminating all traces of its America's Neighbour to the Northness in order to compete in international markets. The Bank of Montreal, for example, started advertising itself as BMO. The Canadian Imperial Bank of Commerce is now known simply as the CIBC. Tim Horton's is Tim's. And so on.

One…well, you would hesitate to call it a problem – bit of awkwardness might be a better way of describing it – is why the government chose the phrase "America's Neighbour to the North" rather than "America's Northern Neighbour." The longer brand will take up more room on letterheads and isn't as catchy to overhear at dinner parties because of its extra syllable.

Bitchen claimed that the government didn't go with the shorter brand line because the expensive American firm that was hired to report on the brand didn't think of it.

"We –" Oh, yeah, right, like I'm going to repeat all of that in a quote. "Well! I'm not going to give you any more interviews if you're going to take that snotty attitude with me!" Bitchen responded.

Wendy, did you have ADD when you were a kid? Because, frankly, if you were any more perky, you'd blast off for Mars.

To launch their new brand, Tourism America's Neighbour to the North began an advertising campaign in major American media with the tag line America's Neighbour to the North Unlimited. Criticism of the campaign was swift and relentless, including charges that the line itself was bland and meaningless and that the ANNU logo looks like a strangled beaver.

The DJs on one radio station in Toronto even sponsored a contest to make fun of the campaign. Responses included: ANNUgly, ANNLimited and ANNUgh.

"Hey, it's all in fun," explained CDIK-FM's morning drive time DJ Michaelangelo "Dick" Tremonte. "Malicious, poorly thought out fun – but that's the best kind!"

What do Americans think of the new identity of the country? In one poll 79 per cent of New Yorkers who were asked what they thought of America's Neighbour to the North responded, "What, you mean Canada?"

Clearly, Tourism America's Neighbour to the North has its work cut out for it.

But, Is It Good For The Jews?

by THOMAS FINFLANAHAGAN, Alternate Reality News Service International Writer

President Gordon Perry Robertson made an unannounced visit to Congress to urge Senators to pass his bill legalizing the euthanasia of Jewish Americans.

"This bill is vital to the future of America as a Christian nation," the President passionately explained.

Operation Stairway to Heaven comes three years after the introduction of the President's Aliyah Assistance Programme (AAP), which has been widely acknowledged to be a failure.

Both programmes arise out of the President's literal belief in the Bible, specifically the book of Revelations, which states that the End Times will begin when all of the Jews in the world are living in the state of Israel.

The Aliyah Assistance Programme was designed to encourage Jewish Americans to immigrate to Israel by essentially giving them two months to leave the United States. Those who didn't go voluntarily faced deportation.

Although attached as a rider to a transportation bill (the most boring legislation imaginable, dealing, as it usually does, with building bridges and fixing potholes), AAP got immediate attention from the press, most of whom felt it didn't go far enough, but some of whom considered the legislation an infringement on personal freedom.

"Well, I suppose you may have a point, there," the President chuckled, before sternly adding, "but I believe that the word of God takes precedence over the laws of men, so the Programme will commence. Sides, we're doing our Jewish friends a favour by helping them – isn't it every Jew's dream to live in Israel?"

Apparently not. Many Jewish Americans caught up in AAP snuck their way back into the country. Others moved from Israel to friendly nations such as Canada, Britain and Burkina Faso. A few months ago, the Robertson government had to admit that, other than dispersing American entertainment and education superstars throughout the rest of the world, the Aliyah Assistance Programme was a dismal failure.

Out of the AAP's ashes, the White House developed a more ambitious plan to euthanize all of the Jews living outside Israel.

"If we reduce the number of Jews living outside Israel," the President told Congress, "it achieves the same effect as moving them all into Israel."

President Robertson added that this wouldn't likely mean the euthanization of all Jews, since, once Operation Stairway to Heaven was started, surviving Jews would likely flock to Israel out of a sense of self-preservation.

"I'm not a barbarian. I hope the migration to Israel would happen sooner rather than later," the President explained. "However, that's entirely up to the Jewish people."

In his speech to Congress, the President called on all Christian nations to cooperate with Operation Stairway to Heaven. What about non-Christian nations? "Oh, most of them've been running their own Operation Stairway to Heaven for centuries without even knowing it," President Robertson chuckled afresh.

There has been some speculation as to why the president is pushing Operation Stairway to Heaven at this time. With the upcoming mid-term elections, the policy seems aimed at solidifying the Republican base. Given the current polls, however, it seems likely that the Democrats will regain control over one and possibly both houses of Congress, which would make the president a lame duck who would be unlikely to be able to pass such legislation.

Thirty-seven term Democratic Senator Joseph Lieberman, speaking from the room in Mount Zion Hospital where his brain is preserved in a vat of fluid, responded, "The President made some valid points. I have some quibbles about how the plan is to be carried out, but I support the general thrust."

Opponents of the President's plan to have all Jews in the United States euthanized within five years fall into two broad camps. On the one hand, there are the people who think that five years is too long, and want to see the Jews gone within two years.

"Why give them the opportunity to disappear into the countryside?" asked Republican House Majority Leader Finn McNasty. "Fire up the electric chairs – we got us some frying to do!"

On the other hand, some people feel that it is cruel to euthanize all Jews in the country in five years. "A ten year period would give them more time to settle their affairs and make peace with their maker," stated Nasty McFinn, head of the Democratic National Committee.

International response to Operation Stairway to Heaven has been muted, not surprising given that the United States has more nuclear weapons than everybody else in the world combined. Still, at the United Nations, Chinese Ambassador Tring Muk-Tao commented, "Historically, the United States has been in the forefront of the human rights movement. Tsk. Tsk tsk."

Red Blood + Whitewash + Blue Nation = Blackwater

by HAL MOUNTSAUERKRAUTEN, Alternate Reality News Service Court Writer

Congress has mustered the two thirds vote necessary to override the President's veto and passed a bill to get all American troops out of Iraq by the end of 2009.

Think the war is over? Think again.

If it starts pulling troops out of Iraq in anticipation of ending the war, private contracting firm Blackwater plans to sue the United States government for breach of contract.

"We have many contracts for services in Iraq that extend well past 2012," Blackwater spokesman Kenneth Starr (yes, that Kenny Starr! He's graduated from Whitewater to Blackwater!) stated. "Those contracts could be put in jeopardy if the war ends prematurely."

Other major contractors such as Halliburton are also considering legal action to ensure their contracts are fulfilled.

"We have to take the possibility of lawsuits seriously," an unnamed White House source, who asked to remain anonymous while assuring us that he has no personal interest in the outcome of such a case because he is in no way connected to any of the private contractors working in Iraq, stated. "Aside from the implications for international relations – the suggestion that the United States government cannot be trusted to live up to its contractual obligations – it may simply cost us less to continue the war until the contracts run out than it would to end the war and engage in a costly legal battle. Wah wah wah."

Senate Majority leader Harry Reid said Congress is considering its options in the face of the Whitewater lawsuit threat. On the one hand, he could hide under his desk and hope the issue goes away. On the other hand, he could take a much more proactive stance by going on vacation until the issue goes away.

"The Democrats will not be pressured into a quick decision on an issue of such national importance," Reid stated.

Lawyers are divided on the merits of a lawsuit to continue the war. Orlando Spengler, speaking for the vast majority of members of the American Bar Association, dismissed such speculation as absurd.

"Last time I checked, the United States was a sovereign nation," Spengler said. "We don't subordinate our national interests – especially our security interests – to commercial concerns."

"Aww, Spengler's talking out his ass again," Maxime Millions, speaking for the vastness of herself (she could really stand to lose some weight), responded. "Subordinating national interests to commercial concerns is what America does best! In fact, we're an international leader in the idea, which we have successfully exported to countries around the world.

"But, ahh, maybe it would be best to let a judge decide."

If the lawsuit begins, families of soldiers overseas could sue Blackwater and other Iraqi contractors for "wrongful death," claiming that any soldiers who died after a government pullout deadline would do so needlessly. Blackwater is rumoured to be preparing to counter with a "wrongful life" lawsuit, claiming soldiers who don't die in combat are wussies who are a disgrace to the uniform. It, uhh, sounds much more impressive in legalese…

An unnamed White House source, one who assured us he's different from the first White House Source (and still has no personal interest – either financial or political – in the outcome of the Blackwater case), believed that the lawsuits would be worthwhile.

"See, war – it's a terrible thing," the source said. "You don't wanna do it if you don't have to, and you want it to end as quick as possible. But see, when I said that people should go about their business after 9 – I mean, when the President said that people should go about their business after 9/11, I – he included lawyers in that. See, lawyers are people, too. They deserve to make a living. That's what makes America great."

Congressional leaders have demanded that the Bush administration stop handing out contracts for private work in Iraq until this issue is resolved. And, of course, when we say "demanded," we really mean "politely suggested in the most reverent tones." The fear is that if the first Blackwater court case is successful, the administration can continue to wage the war against the will of Congress by continually handing out more contracts to private companies, or by giving out contracts that last decades.

Senate Majority leader Reid was believed to be hiding under his desk and was unavailable for comment.

Meanwhile, three American soldiers were killed and seven wounded when a falafel exploded in the Iraqi police station to which they were assigned. This brings to 4,987 the number of American soldiers who have died in the Iraq war.

Do Politicians Really Believe The Bullshit They Say?

by FRANCIS GRECOROMACOLLUDEN, Alternate Reality News Service National Politics Writer

Over the last few years, it has become increasingly obvious that politicians do not tell the truth. In Canada, this truism was enshrined in law when a case against a politician for breaking campaign promises was thrown out of court. The judge in effect said, "Hey, he's a politician, whaddya gonna do?"

What researchers at the Poynter Systers Institute did was develop a system to determine whether or not a politician was telling the truth.

"It's a simple system," Poynter Systers lead researcher Dmitri Goygin stated, "using off-the-shelf technologies. If the system as a whole wasn't proprietary, you'd be surprised at how basic it is. I mean, really simple, obvious stuff."

After a moment's reflection, he hastily added: "And, yet, effective. Really, really effective."

The first step in the process involves using radio waves to measure things like a politician's heart rate, pulse, galvanic skin response and other rough indicators of the mental state of the person. This can be done from a distance, without the person's knowledge. The technologies and methods employed at this stage are collectively referred to as the Bullshit Detection and Selection Mechanism (BDSM).

The information collected in this way is then fed into a computer database that also contains past speeches, sound bites, writings and other public knowledge about the politician. An Ideational Relationship Analysis (IRA) is conducted on all of the information to find points of conflict and to determine what, if anything, is true.

"This last bit is largely guesswork," Goygin stated, "but, it's really good guesswork. And, anyway, proprietary, so I'm not at liberty to tell you anything more about it."

In 2005, the Poynter Institute made its first full-scale experimental use of BDSM/IRA. Using United States President George W. Bush, Vice President Dick Cheney and members of the administration Donald Rumsfeld, Condoleezza Rice and Richard Perle as their subjects, the researchers set about to find out whether or not the believed what they were saying about four subjects: whether or not Iraq had had weapons of mass destruction before it was invaded; whether there was merit to the Swift Boat Veterans for Truth assertion that John Kerry was not the war hero his record claimed; whether Iraq had ever been allied with Al Qaeda, and; whether the Bush tax cuts would help the poor.

The results have been put in a chart below:

	Iraq's WMDs	Swift Boat	Iraq/al Qaeda Connection	Tax cuts help poor
Cheney	No	No	No	No
Rumsfeld	No	No	No	Yes
Perle	No	No	Yes	Yes
Rice	No	Yes	Yes	Yes
Bush	Yes	Yes	Yes	Yes

"If there is any validity to the Poynter Syster's study," said political activist Ralph Nader, "it would be astonishing. I don't know which frightens me more: the fact that Vice President Cheney doesn't believe a single idea that the administration pushes, or that the President believes all of them!"

Weekly Standard editor Irving Kristol was more skeptical of the results.

"Typical left wing twaddle," he fulminated. "I know for a fact that Richard Perle knew there was no connection between Iraq and Al Qaeda, but this study has him believing that there was! And, what about Condi? It makes her look like some Sunday school choirgirl – she's a lot more politically ruthless than that! Total and utter bosh!"

Another line of criticism came from, of all places, Edward Tufte, author of such books as *Visual Explanations* and *Envisioning Information*, who suggested that the results were too neat.

"The kind of symmetry that appears in the chart almost never happens in nature," Tufte explained.

"They have the right to disagree with our findings," Goygin responded. "Personally, I've always thought that right wing pundits and academics would be perfect subjects for a BDSM/IRA study…"

He also went to great pains to squelch the rumours that the BDSM/IRA method had been an utter disaster when it was tried on Russian politicians.

"We weren't the problem. No matter what they said," he stated with a shudder, "they showed no response whatsoever. They…they aren't human."

One group with an intense interest in the BDSM/IRA method is the Pentagon.

"Can you imagine politicians having to tell the truth in arms negotiations?" a spokeswoman, who asked not to be identified on grounds of coffee, stated. "It could completely undermine our –"

"Don't say it," Goygin interrupted.

"Yes, national security!" the Pentagon spokeswoman said. "There. I've said it. Because it's true!"

Goygin pointed out that the BDSM/IRA method could just as easily be used to determine whether the country's enemies were telling the truth in any negotiations. One didn't have to employ the BDSM/IRA method on him to tell that the Pentagon's position made him nervous, however: the sweat that started beading on his forehead and the way his eyes darted around the room pretty much gave him away.

If the BDSM/IRA technique is perfected and becomes widely accepted it could revolutionize politics. Politicians would have to tell the truth or be proven to be liars! But, are we ready for such a development? Do you really want to be told that the only way to save the environment is to accept a lower standard of living? Or, that tax cuts are used primarily as a way for politicians to reward their wealthy supporters? Or that drug prices are determined by how much politicians are willing to allow pharmaceutical companies to get away with, which is a lot since, after all, they are wealthy supporters of politicians, too?

That knowledge is enough to make some people want to destroy all of the BDSM/IRA machines and burn the Poynter Systers Institute to the ground!

Just Another Typical Wedgie Issue

by FRANCIS GRECOROMACOLLUDEN, Alternate Reality News Service National Politics Writer

You're sitting in a subway, trying to avoid eye contact with the other passengers when this beautiful dark-haired woman sits across from you. She smiles warmly; there is an air of contented pleasure about her. She seems to know exactly what you're thinking.

Is that a cellphone in her pocket, or is she just glad to see you?

Colorado Senator Harvard Yugen-Fruzje may not know you, but he's betting that your presence in the subway is not what is giving the woman in our hypothetical opening paragraph scenario that warm glow.

"Cellphones!" he snorts, setting aside the cocaine in his comfortably appointed office. "They're the devil's communications device!"

Senator Yugen-Fruzje argues that women are using the silent ring vibrating function of their cellphones to "pleasure themselves. Right there! In public! With god knows who watching!" So, the 16 time Republican Senator is sponsoring the uni-bi-partisan Senate bill HR 3261.

Bill HR 3261 makes it a crime for women to carry cellphones in their pants pockets. Critics of the bill point out that, as currently written, the bill does not make a distinction between where women carry cellphones in public and private.

"What a woman does with a legally owned communications device behind closed doors," stated American Civil Liberties Union lawyer Lucinda Veritas, "is not the business of the state!"

"Oh, everything is the business of the state!" Senator Yugen-Fruzje responded. "Do we want our children watching women pleasuring themselves in public places? The impressionable youngsters might get the idea that they can just willy-nilly do what they want! Don't you see that this kind of permissiveness can only lead to the complete destruction of society as we know it?"

Sex columnist and cellphone sensuality advocate Josey Gloves couldn't disagree with Senator Yugen-Fruzje more.

"I couldn't disagree with him mo – oh, you already have me saying that," Gloves commented. "The good Senator – and I use the term loosely, not having ever slept with him – not that I find the prospect any less repellant than being pecked to death by feral minks, but – I'm digressing terribly, aren't I? Let me start again…

"The…quality indeterminate Senator is part of the Puritanical strain in American politics that condemns all fun had by other people. I mean, just look at the Senator's record. At one time or another, he has proposed bills banning: public swimming pools, dance clubs and the dismantling of our system of government in favour of anarcho-syndicalist local governing councils. Okay, maybe that last one would lead to the complete destruction of society as we know it. Otherwise, he's just pandering to the Republican Party's religious base."

Senator Yugen-Fruzje retorted that Gloves had to defend the technology because she was making money off of it. Gloves runs a weekly seminar for women called "Getting Off By Getting On: How Connecting To The Info-Grid Can Help You Connect To Your Sexuality." According to the seminar Web site, women can use their cellphones in a variety of ways to sexually satisfy themselves: using a vibrating Enya ringtone, for example, gives a slow building feeling of satisfaction, while those who prefer a quick hit might want to feel the vibrations from a Green Day ringtone.

"Technology is all about expanding the possibilities for female self-satisfaction," the Web site claims.

"No, no, no, no, no!" Senator Yugen-Fruzje exclaimed, excitedly knocking the brandy snifter on his comfortably appointed desk halfway across the room. "People who get sexual satisfaction from the ringtone of an Enya song are sick! Twisted! Eeeeeeevil! And, we should, uhh, feel bad for them and maybe try to get them into a programme or something…"

"For many people, this is a – you should pardon the expression – hot button issue," stated Nancy McRichie, famed sexologist and author of the *New York Times* bestselling book *The 36 Hour Orgasm for Dummies*. McRichie pointed out that, as with many such issues, the extent to which it is an issue is at issue.

"Is this actually a problem?" she rhetorically asked. "Are millions of women getting themselves off after they get on a bus or subway? For all we know, the act may be limited to one woman on the Podunk light rapid transit. Do we really want to base a federal law on the behaviour of one lonely woman in Podunk?"

"Yes, yes, yes, yes, yes!" Senator Yugen-Fruzje eagerly retorted, dropping a vintage issue of *Playtoy Magazine* to the ground next to his comfortably appointed shoes. "This is a law that will play brilliantly in Podunk!"

Bill HR 3261 is expected to die when Congress adjourns for the fall mid-terms.

How Robert Novak's Eyebrows Saved America

by FREDERICA VON McTOAST-HYPHEN, Alternate Reality News Service People Writer

If you think of Robert Novak at all, you probably think of him as a sycophantic supporter of the Republican Party, the sort of person who takes every opportunity to promote the Bush Doctrine (or, as I like to think of it, the Bush Half-baked World-view Hastily Sketched Out On A Cocktail Napkin). Truly, few people other than Rupert Murdoch have done as much to destroy the ideal of an impartial press than Robert Novak.

What you may not be aware of, however, is that Robert Novak's eyebrows saved America.

You may recall the rumours of Robert Novak's eyebrows having an affair with Salma Hayek's eyebrows during the shooting of the film *Frida*. The sometimes overripe, overabundant coverage of this rumour gave Robert

Novak's eyebrows a reputation for being the eyebrows of a playboy. However, this was all a front, a cover story concocted by their handlers that allowed Robert Novak's eyebrows to do their real work outside the public – you should pardon the expression – eye.

Around that time, Robert Novak's eyebrows, disguised as the eyebrows of a Greek sailor named Constantine Constantinopolous, set sail for London. It was a long, arduous trip, but it was only the beginning. From there, pretending to be the eyebrows of Israeli diamond swallower Uri Ismailovitz, Robert Novak's eyebrows moved into the Middle East, where they unobtrusively slipped into Afghanistan in the dead of night.

At first, Robert Novak's eyebrows laid low in the guise of the eyebrows of Mustapha Talabimbo, a wealthy cayenne importer/exporter with ties to the ruling Taliban, although with secret sympathies towards the west. As Robert Novak's eyebrows became comfortable in their new station in life, they started collecting intelligence on the Taliban's terrorist ties and intentions.

While his real eyebrows were insinuating themselves into a terrorist network, Robert Novak had to wear fake eyebrows. None of his fans appear to have ever noticed the deception. He also had to hire bodyguards, since his eyebrows were no longer available to protect him, but Robert Novak and his eyebrows had discussed this possibility and agreed that the good of the country came first, that in the war against America's enemies, facial hair sacrifices had to be made.

Several months into their mission, Robert Novak's eyebrows were able to turn the eyebrows of Hafez Maladwati, a senior officer in the Taliban high command. It was from Maladwati that Robert Novak's eyebrows first learned about a plan by a then little known terrorist group called Al Qaeda to strike at Americans on US soil.

Robert Novak's eyebrows risked having their cover blown to relay news of their discovery to the CIA. We can never know how frustrating it was for them that their warnings seemed to be buried in intelligence reports to the President, or, when a very clear statement of Al Qaeda's intent was headlined in a For Your Eyebrows Only report that the President seemed to ignore.

When it became obvious that the government's attention was elsewhere, apparently captured by Saddam Hussein's mesmerizing eyebrows, Robert Novak's eyebrows put together a crack military team and raided Al Qaeda's stronghold in Afghanistan. To their horror, they uncovered plans to fly commercial airplanes into important American buildings, including the White House and the twin towers of the World Trade Centre.

Most of the ringleaders of that plan in the United States were captured, saving the country from a horrible fate. However, one or two Al Qaeda sympathizers must have escaped because Robert Novak's eyebrows were pinned down by enemy fire as they were driving towards the airport to leave Afghanistan. Robert Novak's eyebrows flung themselves out of his Aston Martin just as it burst into flames, but they were heavily singed. They were rushed to an army hospital, where they remain to this day.

You may remember, a couple of years later, when Robert Novak let slip the identity of covert CIA operative Valerie Plame Wilson. It seems likely that, had his eyebrows still been attached to his forehead, they would have prevented this highly questionable – not to mention completely illegal – gaffe. But, Novak himself is not the real hero of this story.

No Congressional Medal of Honour has ever been awarded to somebody's eyebrows. Eyebrows don't get fawning interviews or hagiographical specials on Fox News. Yet, it's hard to imagine there was ever a more heroic, more deserving pair than Robert Novak's eyebrows.

The Quality of Merciless Is Not Litigated

by HAL MOUNTSAUERKRAUTEN, Alternate Reality News Service Court Writer

The Supreme Court has agreed to hear the appeal of Dr. Ming the Merciless in his case against the Bush administration.

The substance of the plagiarism case revolves around an address President Bush gave at West Point in 2002, in which he said, "America has, and intends to keep, military strengths beyond challenge, thereby making the destabilizing arms races of other eras pointless, and limiting rivalries to trade and other pursuits of peace."

In his statement of claim, Dr. Merciless argued that this was close enough to his goal of world conquest to be considered a breach of his copyright. As he clearly stated in the 1940 serial *Flash Gordon Conquers the Universe*: "I have military strength beyond challenge. Any attempt to match my strength, as happened in the past, will be pointless. You will be able to rival me in trade or other pursuits of peace, as I will it."

The statement of claim includes 17 different documents in which Bush administration rhetoric appears to have been taken directly from speeches made by Dr. Merciless. These include a National Security Strategy that read: "Our forces will be strong enough to dissuade potential adversaries from pursuing a military build-up in hopes of surpassing, or equaling, the power of the United States." Substitute "crush" for "dissuade" and "Ming the Merciless" for "the United States," and this could have been said by Dr. Merciless on several different occasions in his quest for universal control.

United States Attorney General Alberto Gonzales expressed disappointment that the Supreme Court didn't refuse to hear the case. In their winning argument before the California State Supreme Court, Department of Justice officials had argued that the Court's 1973 ruling in *Moriarty v. United States Government* had definitively settled the question of whether or not a fictional character could sue the government for copying his nefarious plans for world domination.

However, Dr. Merciless' lawyers successfully argued before the federal Supreme Court that *Moriarty v. United States Government* was dismissed on the narrow grounds that the plaintiff had allowed his copyright to lapse. Since Dr. Merciless had renewed his threats to take over the world in the 1974 spoof *Flesh Gordon* (under the name Emperor Wang the Perverted), his lawyers argued, *Moriarty v. United States Government* did not apply.

While this argument prevailed, it does give the defence an obvious line of reasoning for its case: that copyright rights are not transferable from serious fictional characters to their parodic counterparts. *Goodgulf Greyteeth v. United Fruit Company* may be a precedent for this argument, although legal scholars are divided on this point.

Without giving any of their strategies away, Gonzales said that he would defend the government's right to state its intention to militarily dominate the world to the fullest extent possible.

Court watchers were surprised that the government didn't avail itself of an obvious defense before the California Supreme Court: that Ming the Merciless' rhetoric was, itself, not original. In the fictional realm, for example, Fu Manchu had been making similar threats at least a decade before Dr. Merciless had come to prominence. In the non-fictional realm, empires from the British in the 19th century all the way back to the Roman in…umm…well, a long, long time ago, had asserted their world supremacy intentions.

"Ming's claim to hold the copyright on this particular expression is dubious, at best," "Fast" Eddie Feldspan, who has been covering the trial for *Fictional Court TV*, stated. "You have to know that the government will press this argument in the Supreme Court because, really, what else have they got?"

"Oh, I've got two words for Eddie Feldspan," retorted "Slow" Martin Gorgon, who has been covering the trial for *LotsMusic*: "executive privilege. The President must have the right to plunder the global domination rhetoric of fictional characters in order to fully prosecute the war against international Islamofascism. If the high court denies him this right, the terrorists will have won."

While the Supreme Court under Chief Justice John Roberts has generally been predisposed to favouring this interpretation of a unitary presidency (see, for example, *Anonymous Torture Victims v. United States Government*), it has also been highly supportive of corporate property rights (see, for instance, *MultiNatCorp v. McWorld*). Because of this conflict, this defense may be riskier than supporters of this administration would like to believe.

Opening arguments are set to begin on September 27.

The Magic Is Gone

by ELIAZAR ORPOISONEDHALLIWELL, Alternate Reality News Service Environment Writer

For Ellie-Mae Nebuchadnezzar, Tuesday was supposed to be just a typical morning milking the chickens and playing Parcheesi with the cows. The moment she stepped out of her house, though, she knew that this day would be anything but typical.

"There was a damn – pardon my French – unicorn chomping on my petunias!" she said.

Unicorns are, of course, a northern species that, until recently, was too shy to be seen in areas inhabited by human beings. Unicorn sightings were so rare, in fact, that many people believed that they didn't exist. However, in the last couple of years unicorns have become more and more brazen, appearing in people's gardens, public skating rinks and, in one infamous example, backstage at a Yoav concert.

Nebuchadnezzar refused to take the desecration of her petunias lying down. She got out of bed and complained to Winnie Witonka, her hairdresser in the small town of Gone by Golly, Ontario (whose catchy motto is: "As far North as you can get and still have your spit not freeze before it hits the ground in July"). Winnie mentioned the problem to Kisonka Witonka, her "housemate," who passed it on to Alyonka Witonka, her brother, who shared it with his poker mates, one of whom just happened to be the third cousin of the mayor of Gone by Golly, Harve Arachne.

Mayor Arachne was, of course, outraged by this encroachment of nature into the human realm, and, thanks to the renowned smoothness of his oratory (not to mention the fact that City Councilors had been tired out by the six hour debate on whether the Mockerson Inn and Bait Shop should be allowed to sell chocolate covered deep fried worms in the Barka Lounge and just wanted the meeting to end so they could all go home), passed a unanimous resolution to kill all unicorns within a 50 mile radius of the city limits.

"Oh, no," Mayor Arachne disputed the Alternate Reality News Service report. "City Council didn't vote to 'kill' the unicorns. Absolutely not! We voted for a unicorn 'cull,' which, I think you'll agree, is a completely different kettle of sturgeon!"

When asked how it was different, the Mayor pointed out that he actually preferred sea bass, but his constituents, lord love them, were great fans of sturgeon, and who was he to argue with the will of the people. When asked how "culling" unicorns was different from "killing" them, he replied, "Oh. That. Well, if City Council had voted to 'kill' unicorns, my daughter Melodian would never forgive me. However, since she doesn't know what 'cull' means, I figured I was on safe grounds, morality-wise."

Not necessarily. The issue of the unicorn cull now goes to the Ontario legislature, where many members actually know what the word "cull" means.

"Mayor Arachne has it exactly backwards," declared Martha Moosemeat (ndp Dundas-Liverspot). "Human settlement has been encroaching on the natural habitat of the unicorn for decades. When we destroy their environment, killing the wildlife they feed off of, is it any wonder that one night we find them rummaging through our fridges for leftovers from Friday night's pot roast dinner?"

Conservative MPP Darryl Wallstrop (Rum&Etobicoke), on the other hand, argued that the unicorns should be culled with all due haste, preferably with blunt instruments and the letting of much blood.

"What is the greatest corrupter of children?" Wallstrop mused. "Computer games, of course. But, after that? Well, television. And, movies. And…gay marriage and permissive parenting and…"

Five minutes later, Wallstrop returned to the point: "…public washrooms. And, somewhere in there, unicorns! Their very existence teaches our children to believe in magic, in incredible things like…world peace and…and meaningful employment. Our whole system would collapse if these peaceful, majestic creatures continued to have such an affect on our children, so **they must be slaughtered immediately**!"

Moosemeat allowed that, despite the fact that unicorns were routinely killed because their meat was considered a delicacy and their horns were considered an aphrodisiac, they were only on the cusp (not cull, or even kill) of becoming an endangered species. If the cull is approved, enough unicorns could be killed to qualify them to become an endangered species.

"Unfortunately," Moosemeat sighed, "we don't have legislation that would keep a species from tipping over into being endangered. We only –"

"What about my petunias?" Ellie-Mae Nebuchadnezzar shouted. "Don't nobody remember this started with the damn – pardon my French – unicorns eating my petunias? Not to mention that, but now when I walk into town I have to wear my fishing boots on account of all the unicorn shit – pardon my French – on the streets – you can't avoid it!

"Trust politicians to complexificate something so simple. Well, next time I see a unicorn in my garden, I'm taking a frying pan to it. I can't do nothing to its head because of the horn, but I sure can give it a good what for on the behind! That should show the clowns at Queen's Park – pardon my French – how to get things done!"

What Goes Around…Makes You Dizzy When It Comes Around

by THOMAS FINFLANAHAGAN, Alternate Reality News Service International Writer

The question on the minds of everybody in China is: where are the weapons of mass destruction?

"Be patient," Premier Xiao Ping-Tao advised. "We know they're there. It's just a matter of time before we find them."

It has been four months since China, at the head of a ragtag coalition of countries, invaded the United States. The stated reason was, of course, that the United States had vast stores of weapons that could be used against China at some future date.

"While they may not have had the capability of attacking us any time soon," Premier Xiao explained, "the United States might regain that capability in the future. We used the precedent of preemptive self-defense to ensure that that does not happen."

United States President Dick Cheney, talking from the vat in the White House basement where his brain is stored, scoffed at the idea, noting that the United States had sold off most of its weapons systems when it went bankrupt in 2017.

"We don't have the funds to reconstitute any of our old weapons systems," Cheney insisted. "If the United Nations weapons inspectors had been allowed to finish their job, they would have reported just that."

Aah, the UN weapons inspectors. The Chinese government has argued that after the United States expelled them in 2015, it refused to allow them back into the country, a sure sign that it was hiding something. However, some reports indicate that the US did allow the weapons inspectors back in, but that the Chinese government told them to evacuate the country in advance of the invasion.

"That's ridiculous," General Ming Fat-Choi snorted. "The weapons of mass destruction are here. We know they're here. The United States is a big country – President Cheney has just hidden them very well. Or, perhaps, he sent some to Canada. Either way, sooner or later, we will find them."

One hint that the Chinese government is taking the concern about not finding the weapons of mass destruction seriously is that, in the last two weeks, it has changed the rationale for the invasion. Government and military officials are now saying that the invasion was meant to bring democratic socialism to the United States.

"The Bush/Cheney dynasty in the United States was an autocratic government that was a threat to its own people as well as the people in the region," Premier Xiao has stated. "It was a rogue regime that threatened world stability and peace – the world is better off without it."

Critics of the war have suggested that the real rationale behind it was to gain control of the American oil supply, as well as to give China a staging ground from which it can invade Canada for its stores of oil and natural gas. However, since most of these critics were either arrested for treason or live in obscure countries like Britain or Uttar Pradesh, they haven't made much of an impression on Chinese public opinion, which still very much favours the war. It is difficult to travel through major cities like Beijing, for example, without encountering a dozen "Support the Troops" ribbons on every block.

"There has been a lot of rumour and innuendo about why this war took place," General Ming, who made the case for war to the United Nations, stated. "They are all mistaken. That is all you need to know!"

The United Nations, unimpressed by General Ming's Power Point presentation, refused to sanction an invasion of the United States. It has not, on the other hand, opposed the invasion, aside from passing a few resolutions that China has so far ignored.

"But, they were good resolutions," UN Chair Hillary Clinton insisted, "strongly worded and to the point."

The Chinese army, which had expected to be treated as liberators by the American people ("We will be greeted with white peonies and green tea," Premier Xiao stated) has encountered some resistance in some American states. This is especially embarrassing in light of the Premier's speech announcing the end of major combat operations two weeks after the invasion. However, General Ming says the resistance is nothing to worry about.

"They're just a small number of dead enders, Cheney loyalists who will be rounded up and dealt with in due time," he assured the Chinese people.

DoD Can't Hack It!

by FRANCIS GRECOROMACOLLUDEN, Alternate Reality News Service National Politics Writer

The Department of Defense Web site has been taken down. In its place is an "under construction" graphic. How can you tell it was done in a hurry? The graphic hasn't even been customized with AK47s or Sidewinder missiles.

Irina Ketchum, DoD spokeweasel du jour, says the site is undergoing "unexpected routine maintenance," and that people shouldn't read anything into it. However, people who saw the site in the hours before it was taken down tell a different story.

"It was full of naked people f*ck*ing!" Georgianis Stephanopol, amateur military expert, exclaimed.

According to sources within the DoD, all of the images of people with big American weapons killing people without big American weapons in foreign lands had been replaced by images of men and women with big American genitalia in a variety of sexual positions.

"What they did to the Defense Web site was obscene!!" Stephanopol exclaimed further.

According to insecure security experts, somebody must have hacked into the DoD site and changed the images. However, internal DoD documents indicate that they didn't stop there: they infected DoD computers with a virus that changed the images of war to images of love whenever the DoD tried to restore them.

"Big Mac indicates Mona Lisa compromise subjunctive variable," one such memo read. "Must avoid defragmentation before POTUS gets off the toilet! WTF?!"

Nobody is certain exactly what each of the terms in the memo means, but it is clear proof of what we said two paragraphs ago. In any case, being unable to change the graphics, members of the DoD brain trust (people who are keeping their brains in a trust so that they may be called upon when needed at some indeterminate time in the future) decided to shut down the entire site.

The implications of this attack on the DoD computers were so horrific that the Department immediately denied it had happened.

"Why, no," Ketchum said with an unconvincing laugh. "that didn't happen. No. Nope. No way. If what you're saying is true, it means that somebody – some irresponsible prankster, some…proto-terrorist – has hacked the most important computer system of the strongest military in the world, the last line of our national defense. That…that's inconceivable."

To bolster the argument, the President gave Variation 27a-C Mauve of his "We're winning the war on terrorism" speech to an enthusiastic audience of senile veterans.

This may not be enough to convince skeptics, however, as a copy of the hacked site could be found on the Way Back Machine, an Internet archive site. It clearly shows the rhetoric of the DoD (prominently including such patriotic sentiments as "love your country," "do your duty" and "…rip the flesh off human scum without the criminal liability that would accrue if you did it at home, and who wouldn't want to be able to do that?") illustrated with pictures of human bodies without clothing pleasuring each other.

"Well, yes, that was what we captured," the curator of the Way Back Machine, one Mister Peabody, stated. "It would definitely appear that the Department of Defense Web site was compromised."

"Not only that," his human, Sherman, added, "but somebody hacked into it real good!"

"I wouldn't take that too seriously," Ketchum stated, her laughter becoming more hollow and brittle by the second. "Our maintenance protocol calls for the periodic substitution of ordinary graphics with pornographic graphics to test our IT team's response time. Yeah, that's it. It was an IT team response time test. That's what the memo you quoted from eight paragraphs ago really means."

Some in Washington don't understand what the problem is.

"We've all seen pornographic pictures before," Democratic Senator Edward Kennedy commented, quickly adding: "I'm told! I mean, I've been told that we've all seen pornographic pictures before, not that I have any first-hand knowledge of such a thing!"

On the other hand, Senator and Democratic Presidential hopeful Hillary Clinton has introduced a bill making "inappropriate display of pornographic images" on government Web sites punishable by immediate rendition to unpleasant places. "I know that may sound harsh," Clinton defended the bill, "but I have an election to win, and, anyway, it's a sign of disrespect for our fighting women throughout the world…and, I suppose, our fighting men, too… Whatever."

The Department of Defence does not know when the site will be back up, but they are looking for the hacker.

"You would do your country a great service by coming forward," Ketchum said, completely reversing her excuse of three paragraphs ago. "Please. Please. We beg you. Pretty please?"

The Old Ball Game Is Juiced

by FRANCIS GRECOROMACOLLUDEN, Alternate Reality News Service National Politics Writer

At the height of his career, porn star Buck Ramsey stared down bevies of beautiful, busty blondes with an intensity that was unrivalled in the industry. Yesterday, that focus was trained on members of Congress who were investigating allegations of illegal drug use in Major League Pornography.

"I have never used HGH, Viagra or any other performance enhancing drugs," Ramsey told the packed and hushed room in – ironically – the Ramsey Building on Capital Hill.

Critics of MLP argue, however, that the record pretty much speaks for itself.

"Is – what? Sorry – is the tape recorder working?" stated former Senate Majority Leader George Mitchell, whose 400 page report on performance enhancing drugs in the adult entertainment industry sparked the Congressional investigation. "It is? Okay. Good. My posi –"

Most male porn stars peak in their mid-20s and see a decline in their athletic prowess throughout their 30s. This is measured by a variety of statistics: number of movies per year, gallons of sperm per ejaculation, length of orgasm, etc. By the time they have reached 40, the careers of male porn stars have usually been reduced to novelty or nostalgia acts, or, most often, the actors have had to retire.

Not so with Ramsey, whose stats actually improved in his early 40s. (Interested readers can find the dry numbers on the government Web site for the hearings; those who would like a more colourful interpretation of the numbers can find it on the Vivid Pictures Web site.)

While this reporter was fixing his tape recorder, Mitchell argued that it was highly unlikely that Ramsey's performance could have been natural – the human body simply doesn't work that way. "…oesn't work that way," Mitchell stated.

This opinion was supported by the testimony of Brian McNamee, former physical trainer and voice coach of Ramsey. McNamee claimed that Ramsey would show up at his home late at night, desperate that his career was fading; to placate the star, McNamee would inject him with horse steroids, talcum powder, Viagra pills that had accidentally been crushed when his three year-old daughter sat on them and whatever else he had to hand.

"Some of that shit must have worked," McNamee testified, "because his performances actually got better."

82   Alternate Reality Ain't What It Used To Be

Support for the theory also came from Ron Jeremy, a close friend of Ramsey's in the porn industry, who testified that Ramsey had told him on 27 separate occasions that he had been taking Viagra.

Ramsey denied he had received illegal drugs from McNamee and insisted that Jeremy must have heard him wrong…all 27 times.

Opinion on the House Committee on Oversight and Government Reform split along party lines.

"It's hard to believe you, sir," Democratic Representative Elijah Cummings told Ramsey. "I hate to say that. You're one of my heroes. But it's hard to believe."

Republican Representative Dan Burton, on the other hand, told McNamee: "You're here under oath, and yet we have lie after lie after lie after lie."

Christopher Shays, a different Republican Representative, repeatedly called McNamee a "drug dealer."

Some observers wondered why Congress was holding hearings on the subject when there was a much more pressing problem – the Iraq war and the subprime mortgage fiasco – okay, two much more pressing problems – oh, and we mustn't forget the trillion dollar budget deficit – hold on, let me start again: some observers wondered why Congress was holding hearings on the subject when there were many more pressing problems – the Iraq war, the subprime mortgage fiasco and the trillion dollar budget deficit among them – for Congress to look at.

In an exclusive interview, House Committee on Oversight and Government Reform Chairman Henry Waxman answered the criticism: "Pornography is…erica's passti…bove reproa…grace the nation with…ternational laughingsto…squids on their genitals unti…derstand that certain behaviours are simply unacceptable!"

This reporter clearly needs better recording equipment.

The Congressional hearings ironically started the day after New York Governor Eliot Spitzer resigned after it was revealed that he had paid over $4,000 to take part in an illegal baseball game. (Yeah, we know – what kind of baseball action is worth $4,000? That's not why we're bringing it up, though, so try to ignore that question.)

"I have disgraced my position and brought shame to my family by paying to play baseball," Spitzer said at the press conference at which he resigned. "I can only hope that, over time, I can win back everybody's trust."

Unlike Ramsey, Spitzer accepted responsibility with grace.

Those Who Forget History Are Doomed To Keep Living It

by FRANCIS GRECOROMACOLLUDEN, Alternate Reality News Service National Politics Writer

On the 40th anniversary of the entrance of the United States into the Vietnam War, President George W. Bush gave an impassioned address to the American people, asking them to continue to support it.

"We have turned the corner in Vietnam," President Bush said, "and it would be a disservice to the memory of those who have died if we cut and run when our moment of victory is so close to hand."

President Bush argued that the latest "surge," the third since he inherited the war when he took office, was the one that was finally going to bring victory to coalition forces. "I have given General Petraeus a plan for victory, and it would be criminal if politicians in Washington were to second-guess the plans of the military leaders on the ground."

Reaction was swift and harsh. Democratic House Leader Harry Reid responded by questioning why this surge would work when the others did little to stem Vietcong attacks on coalition soldiers.

"And, why do we even call them coalition soldiers," he mused, "when we're the only country left in the war effort?"

The Democrats have introduced a bill into the house that expresses their deep unhappiness with the war. It gives the White House bridge funding of $140 billion ($20 billion more than the White House had asked for), but includes a non-binding resolution suggesting the partial withdrawal of some of the troops within the next 10 years or so.

President Bush is widely expected to veto the bill. As he explained in his address: "We cannot succumb to the seduction of artificial timetables. If we set one, the Vietcong will simply wait until we leave, and then they would take over the country and use it as a launching point to attack the homeland."

The address came at a time when the administration's popularity has reached new lows. Recent polls have shown that 87 per cent of the American population opposes the Vietnam War, and 84 per cent of them cannot understand why, since the United States is a democracy, the troops haven't withdrawn in accordance with their wishes. This includes a substantial amount of the Republican base, which, although it supports the war, believes that the Bush administration's conduct of it has been poor.

"I will admit that support for the war in Vietnam is soft," Vice President Dick Cheney allowed in an interview on *Meet the Press*. "However, I would like to assure Americans that the insurgency is in its last throes, and that once we have eliminated the few remaining dead enders, we can finally achieve victory."

The Vice President added that the lessons of 9/11 were clear: that the free world should never give in to terror. Critics quickly pointed out that there was no credible evidence linking Vietnam to the 9/11 attacks, but that didn't stop White House Press Secretary Tony Snow from repeating the connection the following day, and the President repeating it the following Monday, Tuesday and Thursday.

Support for the war dipped substantially when, coincidentally, the 450,000th American soldier was killed a day before the President's address. Some time in the Reagan Presidency, the US Army stopped determining the number of Vietnamese killed in the war, but estimates suggest that it may be at least half of the population.

Another reason so many Americans now oppose it is that the Vietnam War has cost an estimated $8 trillion, making it more expensive than all other American wars combined. Hard figures are hard to come by as much of the funding for the war has come out of so-called "black budgets" with little oversight. Critics of the war have suggested that the Bush administration is dragging it out because it has been highly lucrative for such Republican Party stalwarts as Halliburton and Bechtel.

"All talk of war profiteering," the President responded in his address, "is an unconscionable attack on the troops, a fine bunch of young men and women who are risking their lives to bring democracy to the region."

As critics have pointed out, the original logic of the war has been completely reversed. The architects of the war believed in the "Domino Theory:" that if Vietnam was allowed to fall into Communist hands, its Asian neighbours would follow. The government now appears to believe in a "Reverse Domino Theory:" if Vietnam is made into a viable democracy, all of the countries around it will become democratic.

In the meantime, real threats have gone unanswered. These include Iraq's Saddam Hussein, who is believed to have stockpiled chemical and perhaps even nuclear weapons, and North Korea's Kim Jong-Il, who has actually been testing nuclear weapons.

"Not to worry," the President assured Americans. "Once we have brought democracy to Vietnam, we can turn our attention to these other problems."

ALTERNATE ECONOMICS

Progress – It's in the Air!

SPECIAL TO THE ALTERNATE REALITY NEWS SERVICE by WFB127

With the third disaster at the Chernobyl nuclear power plant, the usual suspects are making the usual complaints about the limitations of science. However, before we do something rash (like pass "environmentally friendly" laws that would strangle corporate innovation like a metaphor about a baby in its crib), I believe we need to step back and remember all of the great things that science has accomplished.

Like Bottled Air™.

Bottled Air™ contains the optimal mix of oxygen, nitrogen and trace elements for the best possible health outcome, and comes in seven designer odors, including Fresh Pine, New Car Smell and Purple! Simply choose the formula of Bottled Air™ that most closely corresponds to your weight and body type, put on the mask and breath six hours of fresh airy goodness!

Of course, before Bottled Air™, people had to inhale whatever goop was floating around in their environment. The advantages Bottled Air™ gives us over traditional Industrial and Early Post-industrial Era air should be obvious. However, even pre-Industrial Era air had its problems, what with the foulness emanating from dead and rotting animal carcasses or rivers polluted with human waste. Surely, even progress' staunchest critics would not want us to return to those bad old days!

When Bottled Air™ was first introduced, some critics insisted that it wasn't fair to poor people – as if making people who could afford it breathe the same slop as everybody else was somehow fair! However, these people didn't appreciate the genius of the marketplace. Soon enough, discount bottled air, under the President's Choice Bottled Air™ and Wal-Mart Bottled Air™ labels soon made the product available to the masses at affordable prices.

To be sure, discount bottled air wasn't as pure as the premium product, but, really, do you expect a Rolex knock-off to work as well as an original? Do you expect low end Georgio Armani suits to wear as well as top of the line clothing? Why would you expect bottled air to be any different?

I'm not suggesting that the path to our recent level of breathing products excellence has been smooth. There were, for instance, all of the early studies that proved conclusively that the original formula for Bottled Air™ actually damaged the human immune system by eliminating certain airborne bacteria for which we would otherwise have built up a tolerance.

Fortunately, science was there to solve the problem! Microbes beneficial to human physical development and well-being were added to the formula, resulting in Macrobiotic Bottled Air™. Not only that, but the first iteration was rebranded as Bottled Air Original Formula™ and marketed to risk-takers and those secure in the masculinity of their immune systems.

We all know what happened next (well, all of us who didn't get our MBAs out of a Crackerjack™ box): the microbes used to bolster the immune systems that were damaged by the original formula caused night sweats and inflammation of the thumbs in some customers. However, ten years of frantic but thoughtful (not to mention methodologically sound) research resulted in the development of a pill that counteracted these symptoms.

Nor does the triumphant progress of science stop there! The pills that were developed to counteract the negative effects of the microbes introduced into Bottled Air™ to boost immune systems that were damaged by the original formula were found to cause sphincter reticulosis and the screaming heebie jeebies in one in every 300,000 users. Ordinarily, this would not be a cause for concern, but that one in 300,000 users was extremely wealthy. Light therapy was found to minimize most of the side effects of the pills, with fully 98.3 per cent of those affected returning to their normal lives while the rest were promoted to positions of no real authority where they could not hurt themselves or others.

Of course, it was recently revealed that the light therapy that solved the problems with the pills (that were developed to counteract the negative effects of the microbes introduced into Bottled Air™ to boost immune systems that were damaged by the original formula) can cause bleeding from the shins or delusions of being David Mamet, but scientists at labs around the world are already hard at work to find a cure.

And, you can be certain that they will succeed, for science, driven by the needs of free markets, can solve any human problem!

WFB127 is the 127th clone of noted conservative pundit William F. Buckley.

Turn! Turn! Turn! A Time To Work And A Time To Work More

by HAL MOUNTSAUERKRAUTEN, Alternate Reality News Service Court Writer

The Supreme Court has agreed to hear the most important class action suit in American corporate history. The case has the prosaic name *MultiNatCorp et al v. Aabrams et al*, but it may more accurately be called *Business v. Slacker.*

According to research by the Hudson Institute, many Americans choose not to work to their fullest capacity. You've seen them: people with PhDs in molecular biology who prefer to drive a cab, MBAs who can't hack the business world and drop out to work on farms, people with MAs in medieval Scandinavian scatological blank verse who...umm...well, maybe them not so much.

The Hudson Institute calls this "life time theft." Their studies on the subject conclude that business is losing money because people aren't working up to their full potential. One study by the Hudson Institute estimated that almost 27 million Americans are costing companies $362 billion annually.

And, corporate America wants that money back.

Alessandro Aabrams, the individual named in the suit, trained as an MD, but, in his second year of interning, ran away to Buffalo to work in a ham packing plant. The statement of claim states that his decision will cost the Blackbeard and Bluestocking HMO, a wholly owned subsidiary of MultiNatCorp, over $27 million over the course of his lifetime.

"What's wrong with ham?" a stunned Aabrams, in an exclusive interview, told the Alternate Reality News Service. "People have to eat, don't they?"

Using information from the last census, the Hudson Institute compiled a list of names of people who have, by its theory, stolen time (and, therefore, revenue) from corporate America. Aabrams was chosen to be named in the suit on the basis of the fundamental juridical principle of alphabetical order by last name.

Dozens of corporations vied to be named as the primary plaintiff. MultiNatCorp was chosen on the basis of the time-honoured juridical principle of eeny-meeny-miney-moe.

Janie Buzzkill, a legal expert I often use to pad my word count, pointed out that there was precedent for the lawsuit.

"At the turn of the century," Buzzkill explained, "right wing think tanks developed the theory of 'time theft,' the idea that employees who didn't work to their fullest potential during office hours were stealing from their employers. As you can imagine, this theory was very popular with middle managers trying to justify their existence by squeezing more productivity out of the employees below them."

Then, Buzzkill turned to her left and lowered her voice.

"But, of course, this theory was never actually tested in a court of law," she said, "so, it's anybody's guess whether this suit has any merit."

The suit has ping ponged its way through lower courts. And, not the sedate ping pong of casual North American players, but the cutthroat Chinese ping pong that has left many legal scholars with a severe case of whiplash.

Without clear direction from lower courts, the case will be a difficult one for the Supreme Court.

"On the one hand, the majority has shown a deference to corporate interests," Buzzkill, who had donned a false moustache and trenchcoat and went by the name Rex Meateater to fool my editor into thinking I had more sources for this article than I actually did, stated.

"On the other hand, the Constitution really says nothing about life time theft," Meateater continued. "Since they are rabid Constructionists – really, they drool over thoughts of the intentions of the Founding Fathers – somebody should get them bibs – you might expect the Court to find for the defendant."

What about the minority on the Supreme Court?

"Oh, they're bound to oppose whatever the majority decides," Meateater commented. "There hasn't been a unanimous decision at this level since Berger was a gleam in his parents' eye. Not that it matters – minority opinions are like ex-boyfriends: nobody pays any attention to them."

Should the plaintiffs win their case, nobody is sure how they expect to be redressed. Some speculate that they would force citizens to work at jobs they were qualified for on the basis of the time-honoured juridical principle of "nobody gets what they want in life, so get over it and get on with it." Others suspect that many corporations would be satisfied with a pound of flesh, since they could potentially use such rendered flesh to search for medical breakthroughs.

"I know that ham isn't kosher," Aabrams, not realizing that nobody in the mainstream media is really interested in the comments of a...meat packer, commented, "but is that any reason to sue me?"

Would You Like Fries With – AAACK!

by GIDEON GINRACHMANJINJa-VITUS, Alternate Reality News Service Economics Writer

Burton Lujinsky had worked on the assembly line at the Oshawa Ford plant for 15 years. Although over the years he had lost three fingers and developed an unidentified but nasty sounding hacking cough, Lujinsky took pride in the fact that he was making steering columns for the Spanish Galleon, the largest family car the world had ever known (that is, until General Motors created the Titanic).

Imagine his surprise when, one day, Lujinsky vanished from the assembly line and instantaneously appeared at his local Beef 'N Brews, bussing tables. Because the motion of the hands clearing plates from a table was identical to the motion of putting real fake leather on steering wheels, it took Lujinsky over 20 minutes to realize that he had moved to a different job; it might have taken longer, but a 12 year-old girl loudly complained that she didn't get the *Star Blap XII: The Latest New Beginning* toy that was supposed to come with her Heifer Meal, and that rarely happens on an auto assembly line.

"I...I was...stunned," Lujinsky wryly commented. "I...didn't know, you know, what had happened."

Fortunately, economists know exactly what happened to him, and many other workers like him: spontaneous deindustrialization syndrome (SDS). One moment, people are working on assembly lines, making stuffed hoot owls (with almost natural screeching sounds), ergonomically ambiguous computer keyboards and boombox headphones; the next moment, they are trying to convince skeptical parents that the higher priced running shoes are better made because they are named after a sports star or asking "Do you want fries with –"

"Yes, well," two-time Nobel Economics Good Sport Prize runner-up James Gandolfini coyly interrupted, "spontaneous deindustrialization syndrome is a relatively new phenomenon, having only been around for 25 years or so, so we're still not certain why it happens. It's like somebody picks you up off the assembly line and plops you down in a retail shop. It's like...like..."

"Lionheart Studios' *The Movies!*" shyly interjected *Gamer Bois Mag* Associate Editor of Obscure References martin2365bighead.

"No," Gandolfini intimately retorted. "It's nothing like that at all."

The phenomenon appears to be widespread. According to Statistics Canada, in February, 2008, for the first time in the country's history there were more jobs in retail (1.82 million) than there were in manufacturing (1.74 million). This highlights the trend going back many years of manufacturing jobs being lost as the number of retail jobs increased, a trend that hurts blue collar workers, since manufacturing jobs pay, on average, ten dollars an hour more than retail jobs.

Or, as Gandolfini put it, "Oy vey!"

How SDS actually works is still a matter of controversy among economists. In some documented cases, the wife of the worker was plucked out of the home at the same time and found herself working as a maid, babysitter or temp. In others, the moment the worker materialized in a new job, the entire family materialized in a smaller house or apartment. In some extreme cases, the new job came with a divorce. Some economists believe that the variation of circumstances indicates that spontaneous deindustrialization syndrome is not one, but perhaps a series of related problems.

There is no consensus among economists about why spontaneous deindustrialization syndrome is happening, either. Some believe that it is caused by the fact that god hates working people.

"No, no, no," Gandolfini conciliatorily stated. "There's no need to resort to some supernatural entity to explain spontaneous deindustrialization syndrome."

Gandolfini is the leading proponent of the theory that SDS is an experiment run by 12 dimensional beings who are trying to determine the resiliency of our job market. If they find it satisfactory, they may decide to invest in businesses in our dimension.

"They're not supernatural entities," Gandolfini avuncularly explained. "They're scientific!"

Wouldn't a simpler explanation be that government policy since the 1980s has been to enter into international trade agreements that make it cheaper and easier to move manufacturing to low wage countries? And, that this trend has been exacerbated by government policies that have stripped unions of the ability to protect workers?

Gandolfini pragmatically snorted: "You obviously aren't an economist!"

Last Tree Standing

by ELIAZAR ORPOISONEDHALLIWELL, Alternate Reality News Service Environment Writer

The Supreme Court of Montana has issued an injunction against ZeeCorp, halting the cutting down of the last tree standing in the United States.

"This is an outrage!" cried Slobodan McWhirter, President of International Chemical, a wholly owned subsidiary of ZeeCorp. "The longer it takes to cut down that [expletive deleted] tree, the longer it takes for us to mine the absaludium underneath it! And nobody in the State House seems to understand that!"

The injunction came at the request of American Pulp, a wholly owned subsidiary of EhCorp.

"Call me sentimental," commented Sandra "BlueHair" Fenestrate, Vice President Public Relations of AP, "but the last tree in the United States – the very last one – should be cut down by a pulp and paper company."

There was a quick response to the ruling by the environmental movement.

"Beatrice and I are thrilled, thrilled, I tell you," commented H. Lamont Hunsecker, the last card-carrying member of Greenpeace, as his wife, Beatrice, made whirling motions with her finger against her head behind his back. "It shows that one determined person can make a difference in the world…"

There is some speculation as to why AP would want the tree. It isn't large enough to make a sheet of single ply toilet paper, let alone a page of a book or newspaper.

"Not that anybody would want to read off of…paper these days," commented noted medialogist H. Bauhaus McLuhan. "It's too dark. People would have to shine a very bright light on the paper to simulate reading off screens, which, of course, we're all more used to."

McLuhan believes that AP intends to turn the wood into as many as half a dozen gun stalks.

"That would be way American in and of itself," McLuhan pontificated, "but, add in that these collectors items could go for millions of dollars, and you can see why that tree is so attractive."

One alternative theory has it that the tree would make as many as nine spice racks. Although not as attractive as gun stalks, there are more of them, which would mean more profit for the company.

"Spice racks? How French!" McLuhan scoffed. "Following this line of reasoning, American Pulp would make the most money if they turned the tree into toothpicks!"

Wooden toothpicks have, of course, been illegal in the United States for many years, but there is still a market for them in Asia.

Analysts had expected that the price of EhCorp stock would plummet as the primary resource of its major subsidiary was used up. However, thanks to astute planning, and perhaps forewarned of looming ecological disaster, 20 years ago EhCorp started another subsidiary, American Oxygen. Of course, today, American Oxygen stands are a common sight in most cities, but many people scoffed at the concept when the company opened its first franchise.

And, indeed, the ascendancy of American Oxygen has not been without problems. There was the out of court settlement 14 years ago with the families of people who died when their AO filters reversed polarization, filling their masks with carbon dioxide instead of oxygen. Then, there were the protests nine years ago by the environmental movement – all six of them.

"Good times," Hunsecker commented, a dreamy look in his eye.

The disputed tree – a spruce…or maybe a maple – it's been so long since anybody has seen one it's hard to tell any more – stands in the Ronald Reagan Nature Preserve in southwest Montana. Asphalt Jungle Rangers who patrol the 37,000 square miles of tourist attractions shrugged at the news of the tree's reprieve.

"People don't really come to the Nature Preserve to see…well…nature any more," Ranger Bob explained. "The big draw for the last couple of years has been the two and a half mile long Killer Coaster. So, really, the sooner the tree is gone, the sooner we can concentrate on what nature preserves do best: giving customers the thrill of a lifetime!"

"Yeah, it's too bad about the National Parks," Hunsecker stated (while his wife whispered, "No, it isn't, nobody cares anymore," in the background). "I mean, nature, it's what we live in. If we destroy that, what do we have left?"

The trial date has been set for September 27. Observers feel that, whichever side wins, the case will ultimately be decided in the Supreme Court of the United States.

Gang War Nets Littlest Victim To Date

by CORIANDER NEUMANEIMANAYMANEEMAMANN, Alternate Reality News Service Urban Issues Writer

Little Timmy Teena had all of the dreams of a two and a half month old baby. Eating. Sleeping. Pooping. Drooling. Cooing. Getting into an upscale pre-pre-pre-pre-kindergarten to better his chances of getting into an Ivy League school. Marrying a supermodel and helping her overcome the drugs, alcohol and eating disorders. And, of course, crawling.

Sadly, he didn't even make it to three.

At 7:32 PM Saturday, Little Timmy Teena was shot in the head by a drive by gangburgerer, to the horror of his mother, who was on the corner getting her daily fix of hamburger and fries (aka: The Happy Meal, Happy, HapMe and Crystal Burg). The intended victim is believed to be DeShawn DeAndre, a low level pusher of fatty foods.

Little Timmy Teena was pronounced dead on arrival at Cedars Gaza Hospital.

DeAndre is known to be a member of the McDs, a gang that peddles burgers, fries and other unhealthy foods subject to the Illegal Substances Revision Act. The McDs are believed to be at war with rival gang the BKings for control of lucrative downtown turf.

"You wanna get them high class businessmen on their lunch break," a member of McDs, who asked to be identified only as "DeMalcolm," explained. "Tha's where the real money is. It's all about what corners you done at, man, it be all about da corners."

Little Timmy Teena is the 237th drive by shooting victim in the past week and a half. Oddly enough, none of the victims have been gang members.

"It's an outrage!" fumed Councilman Roberta Bodnar. "The whole point of banning fast food was to make people healthier, not kill them more quickly!"

"Of course, the war on junk food has had the opposite effect of the one intended," gloated sociologist Myron Frenkhampton. "Not only has the murder rate increased, but people are resorting to theft to be able to afford their regular fatty food fixes, prices are skyrocketing because law enforcement is choking off the supply of burgers and – and, this is the killer – more people are hooked on junk food than ever!"

Acknowledging all of Frenkhampton's statistics, Councilman Bodnar, smoke billowing out of her ears, stated: "Yes, the problem has been growing since the introduction of the Illegal Substances Revision Act. The answer should be obvious: we need more police on the streets!"

"Naah, man, tha's stupid," DeMalcolm said. "I don't got no advanced degrees or nothing, but even I know that da only way ta stop the killin's is to make fast food legal. If it be legitimate, it can be regulated, and, hey, yo, if it can be regulated, man, it can be taxed. Just like marijuana or…or heroin."

"Kid's got a point," Frenkhampton agreed.

Councilman Bodnar's fumes began filling the room. She argued that fast food was a lethal substance, and that legalizing it would just encourage people to use it more.

"There's a moral imperative here," she nearly exploded. "As a society, we can't allow people to destroy themselves with fatty patties and non-dairy, chemical milkshakes!"

This is the usual argument of the law and order crowd. However, as Frenkhampton pointed out, there is a double standard inherent in this position: while the full weight of the law is brought down on those who eat burgers, there is no law against eating calamari, potato chips or foods laden with unhealthy sugars like apple pie.

"Burgers are the food of the poor," Frenkhampton commented. "Calamari is the food of the wealthy. Do I have to draw you a map?"

"Naah, I don' need no map to know that that shit be racist, yo," DeMalcolm stated. He pointed out that since blacks are disproportionately poor, banning the bad eating choices of the poor disproportionately penalizes blacks. The statistics would seem to bear him out: since the war on junk food started in the 1980s, blacks have been incarcerated at a rate three times higher than the general population on junk food related charges.

"That shit ain't fair man," DeMalcolm summed up the situation. "That shit ain't right."

Meanwhile, thanks to the war on junk food another mother grieves the death of her innocent child. "Hey, man, you holdin'?" she asked, her hands shaking slightly and her voice cracking. "I need a burger, man. I'll pay you first of the month, man, I swear. Come on. A fry – gimme a fry. One little fry! Who would it hurt?"

Little Timmy Teena's funeral will be held at 2pm this afternoon.

One Singularity Sensation

by GIDEON GINRACHMANJINJa-VITUS, Alternate Reality Economics Writer

As the real world economy vanished over the horizon, few mourned.

"Making…things," Nobel Prize winning economist Dane Cook explained with a hint of Disgust (the new breath mint), "is so 20th century!"

Traditional economists, hands waving and heads bobbing up and down in a most comical fashion, rushed to assure us that the part of the economy dealing with tangible goods – Cooks' disgust-laden "things" – hadn't disappeared.

"We still need to eat…to have shelter…to play *Guitar Hero 12* on the Wii," insisted other Nobel Prize winning economist Deepak Chopra with more than a hint of Panic (the new male body wash). "That hasn't changed. Much. When you think about it."

Once upon a time, you would make something useful to somebody (say, a codpiece) or you would render somebody a service (say, polishing their codpiece, sometimes – for an additional fee – while they were wearing it); in return, they would give you worthless pieces of metal that everybody agreed had some value. Over time, these worthless pieces of metal were replaced by equally worthless pieces of paper that, nonetheless, everybody agreed had some value. More recently, these pieces of equally worthless paper were largely replaced by electronic impulses on computer networks (the true value of which the reader can guess).

In addition, until recently, goods and services had to exist somewhere in the real world to be of (imaginary) value. However, online games (such as *World of Wowcraft*) and social networking environments (*Get a Life*, for example) – what science fiction writer William Gibson once notably called "consensual migraines" – begat a wide range of virtual goods and services that could be exchanged for real world currencies.

As the popularity of these online spaces grew, their economies quickly outpaced the real world economy. Inevitably, as illustrated oh so elegantly in Graph One, the real world economy became a vanishingly small part of the overall economy, a point economists refer to with a trace of Admiration (a new perfume by Madonna) as The Singularity.

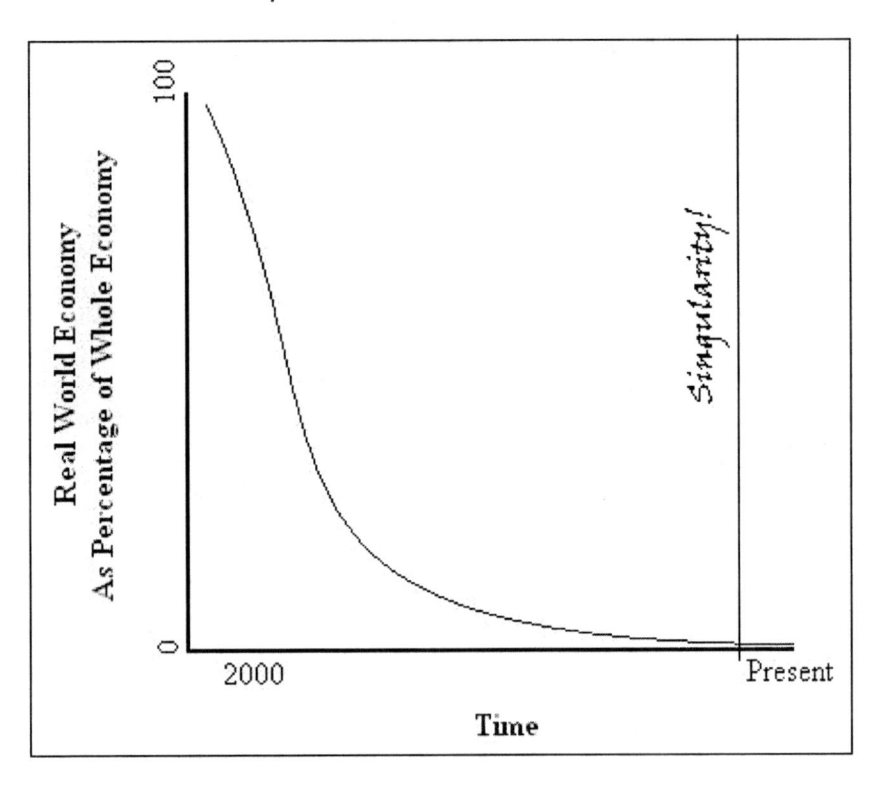

Graph One
The asymptotic nature of the vanishing "real world" economy.

    The Singularity may solve a couple of problems that have been the Bane (a new toothpaste now with Flouridistan – four out of five Jihadis recommend it!) of economists ever since the discovery of tooth decay. Economic growth, for instance, has been the measure of the success of companies and countries since at least the Stone Age. However, finite non-renewable resources meant that, at some point, growth would come to a screeching halt. This was known by economists as "The Future We Would Rather Not Think About, So Stop Bringing It Up – No, Really – We're Putting Our Hands Over Our Ears And Cannot Hear You, La La La La La La La La."

    A virtual economy, since it is not reliant on non-renewable resources, could theoretical grow for the next seventeen thousand years. If holographic or quantum computers some day become the norm, this growth could be extended by 783 thousand years. These are the sorts of numbers that make economists like Cook Drool (a new beer from Budweiser) and economists like Chopra Moan in Despair (not a new product on the market, but a catchy name for a hair spray, don't you think?)

Another problem with classical economics is that it is based on scarcity, the idea that there are never enough resources to satisfy all human Desires (oh, any personal hygiene product, really), and that economics is the most efficient means of distributing those resources. However, the allocation of scarce resources was inherently incompatible with the need for the economy to constantly grow (as shown in cool and calculating Graph 2).

As Cook explained it: "This is not a 'You've got your peanut butter in my chocolate'/'No, you've got your chocolate in my peanut butter' situation. It's more like a 'You've got your radioactive isotopes in my kindergarten class'/'No, you've got your kindergarten class in my –' well, you get the idea. They just never made sense together."

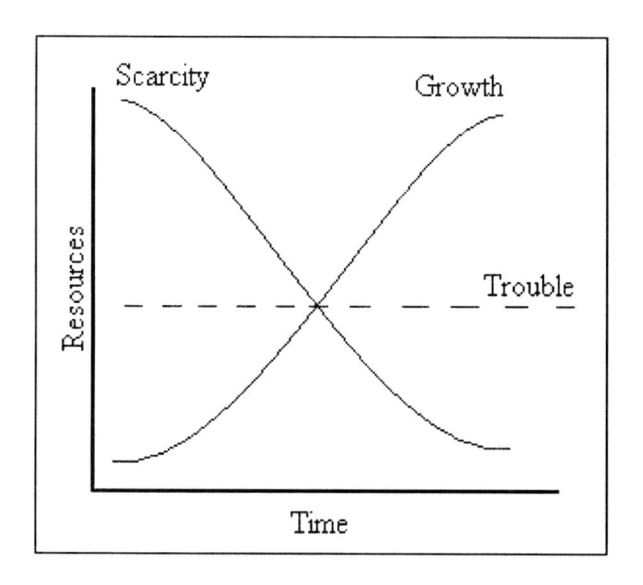

Graph Two
The scarcity versus growth paradox.

By replacing the economics of scarcity with the economics of abundance, the new new economy avoids this problem.

"It's all smoke and mirrors!" Chopra protested. "And, not even real smoke or real mirrors, either!"

Cook just smiled knowingly to himself and muttered something about people who couldn't adjust to new realities.

Former *Wired* guru Kevin Kelly commented: "I'm so happy I lived long enough to see this!" and promptly dropped dead. They were so busy finding ways to profit from the new new economy that the irony was lost on everyone.

ALTERNATIVE ARTS AND CULTURE

Cruel and Unusual – The Musical

by SASKATCHEWAN KOLONOSCOGRAD, Alternate Reality News Service Existentialism Writer

Imagine yourself walking down a dark alley late at night. A –

"What are you doing in a dark alley late at night?" famed defense attorney Minnie Marquetta asked.

That's not important.

"It could be important," Marquetta insisted. "Please answer the question."

Okay. You…you live downtown. You're taking a shortcut from the bus stop to your apartment. Now imagine a big, tough guy with a very sharp knife walks out of the shadows and demands that you hand over all of your money.

"Can you see his face?" Marquetta interrupted.

No. It's dark and he's wearing a hoodie. The interesti –

"Are you implying that your assailant is a man of colour?" Marquetta dramatically asked.

Oh, for chrissakes, this is just a hypothetical opening paragraph to set the scene for the reader! Besides, you haven't even really become part of the story yet! Can I please get on with it?

"Just trying to make sure things are clear," Marquetta stated reassuringly. "If you don't want my help, well, it's your funeral."

Okay. Dark alley. Late at night. Tough guy. Sharp knife. Demands you hand over your cash and valuables. Before you have an opportunity to give them to him, however, he starts singing "Maria" from the hit Broadway musical *West Side Story*.

"It doesn't have to be 'Maria,'" famed penal theorist and medical sadist Hans-Jerrold Bentham pointed out. "It could be 'Everybody Ought to Have a Maid' from *A Funny Thing Happened on the Way to the Forum*. Even 'Luck Be a Lady' from *Guys and Dolls* would do in a pinch."

Bentham has applied for government funding for a pilot project in which computer chips are implanted into the brains of hardcore criminals. The chips will monitor their behaviour and, if it appears that they are about to commit a criminal act, force them to break out in song.

"It could even be 'Stranger Than You Dreamt It,' from *The Phantom of the Opera*," Bentham continued. "I'm not an Andrew Lloyd-Webber fan, myself, but that is a sacrifice I'm willing to make...for science."

The proposal is currently being considered by the state of California. However, some Californians are opposed to the project. For instance, Jean-Claude Stromboli, famed founder of SoCal Libertarians for Better Public Schools, argued that forcing criminals to sing show tunes interfered with their free will, which constituted cruel and unusual punishment.

"Have you ever heard a hardened gang-banger try to sing 'Luck Be a Lady' from *Guys and Dolls*?" Stromboli asked. "That's exactly what the framers had in mind when they banned cruel and unusual punishment in the Constitution!"

"Look, it could be 'Pinball Wizard' from *Tommy* or the title song from *Mamma Mia*," Bentham countered. "Through experimentation, we can find out what the least cruel songs are. It may turn out that different songs will work for different criminals. Serial killers may be deterred best with 'Topsy Turvy' from *The Hunchback of Notre Dame*, while 'Springtime for Hitler' from *The Producers* may work best against petty thieves.

"It would be a shame not to explore this exciting possibility for law enforcement just because some people are prejudiced against musical theatre."

"He has a point," agreed famed *Toronto Star* theatre critic Richard Ouzounian. "Some people **are** prejudiced against musical theatre."

Stromboli insisted that his opposition to the project did not stem from the fact that he was repeatedly exposed to the soundtrack of *Hair* from a very young age. He pointed out that chip implant technology was in its early stages, and the risk of accident was very high.

"What if the chip that was supposed to make a pickpocket sing 'What's the Buzz' from *Jesus Christ, Superstar* instead created in his mind a compulsion to run for mayor?" Stromboli mused. "Well, okay, except for a lack of ambition, voters might not notice a difference from the usual crop of candidates. Still, you see my point."

Representatives of MedCrimTech Inc., a wholly owned subsidiary of MultiNatCorp, were unavailable for comment. However, the company's Web site has a page which states, "We have had great success testing the CrimMed 5000. When exhibiting antisocial behaviours, laboratory rats that had the chip implanted in their brains started squeaking what musicologists have tentatively identified as the song 'My Favourite Things' from *The Sound of Music*."

"Suck on that, Jean-Claude Stromboli!" the Web page added.

Famed defense attorney Minnie Marquetta was now unavailable for comment.

About Bloody Time...Or, Is It?

by ELMORE TERADONOVICH, Alternate Reality News Service Film Writer

Maurice Yankovitch, in an illustrious career that has spanned almost 60 years, has never won an Oscar. In recognition of his impressive body of work he will be given a special lifetime award at this year's ceremonies, the Academy of Motion Picture Arts and Sciences announced yesterday.

The 79 year-old Yankovitch was in an oxygen tent and unavailable for comment.

"Maurice couldn't be more thrilled by the award," 29 year-old Mitzi Baja-Gerund-Yankovitch, the actor's seventh wife, commented. "It's a validation of his life's work."

Yankovitch started his career as an apprentice under the legendary Adrian Chiclis, who himself had worked with Andy Serkis, the virtual acting pioneer, for days before Serkis' untimely death at the age of 102.

Chiclis, who opened his studio without ever actually performing himself, has stated in many interviews that, "If I had become a...an – uggh – actor, I hope I would have had a fraction of the talent that Maurice has."

Then, he got an assistant to clean his spit off the floor.

His first roles were relatively minor: Yankovitch played background characters in such films as *Titanic Two: The Iceberg's Revenge* and *Gladiator: The Early Years*.

"The trick of playing a thousand characters in a movie," Yankovitch once told *Sight and Sound*, "is to hold your body in ways that, while seemingly only slightly different, convey entirely different inner attitudes. Keeping track is the hardest part. Am I on Spectator 578 or Spectator 579? It can be tough."

Around this time, Yankovitch met and fell head over heels in love with Mary-Lou Raptopsomum, an Irish-Ukrainian woman 10 years his elder who worked in the makeup department of TransGlobal Studios.

"It's unlikely that Raptopsomum shared Yankovitch's affections," stated film critic Yuri Obsidian. "She was a smart cookie and had seen the writing on the wall: as more and more roles were being given to virtual rather than live actors, work for makeup artists dried up. She saw Yankovitch as a young up and comer, and latched onto him like a…err…give me a moment to come up with an appropriate metaphor, will you?"

Yankovitch played bit parts for over 20 years, perfecting his body language and facial expressions. Then, he got his break: playing Humphrey Bogart playing Rick Blaine in an interactive movie version of *Casablanca*. While generally praised for capturing Bogart's languid hand gestures and eye motions, his performance was not without its critics: a minority of reviewers found it superficial and uninspired.

"Like a lawyer latches on to a car crash victim," Obsidian commented. When it was pointed out that the article had moved on to another subject, he added: "Oh. Right. Well, there has always been a backlash against virtual actors. They should really get over it. Being able to shoot Victor Laszlo and run off on the plane with Ilsa, well, audiences loved it!"

In fact, there will be a protest against the lifetime achievement award outside The Paris Hilton Auditorium, where the Oscars will be held. Live actors will be arguing that virtual actors aren't really actors.

"Using motion capture technology to map the movements of your face and body so that the skin of a long dead actor can be laid over it doesn't take any acting talent," claimed Basil Exposition, President of Actors for Acting, Really Acting. "And, it's really kind of creepy when you think about it."

"Not over it yet?" Obsidian mused. "Over 80 per cent of parts in films now involve some form of virtual acting. Really, they need to get over it."

Where was I? Oh, right. Yankovitch parlayed his success in *Casablanca* into a series of career-defining roles: as Arnold Schwarzenegger as the killer robot in *Terminator 27: Whose Timeline Is It Anyway?* and as Mel Gibson as Martin Riggs in Lethal *Weapon 34: Never Too Old For This Shit*, among other popular classics.

He was thought to be a dead cert for an Oscar for his portrayal of Dustin Hoffmann portraying Benjamin Braddock in a reconceptualization of the classic *The Graduate*. Unfortunately, that was the year the Academy offices burnt to the ground, forcing the cancellation of the awards.

"He was robbed," Maya Brankenheimer, his fifth wife, stated. Then, with a sigh, she added: "He always said he really admired Mickey Rooney. I wish I had paid more attention to that before we got married…"

Although he has played many colourful characters since, and has been nominated for 27 Oscars, Yankovitch never came that close to winning the award again.

The honourary Academy Award has also spurred talk of a long dormant Yankovitch biopic. Heartthrob Pietr Slobodovanivukian is rumoured to be in negotiations to play Yankovitch…playing Schwarzenegger playing the terminator.

"Don't listen to that bitch Mariel Blobington," Baja-Gerund-Yankovitch acidly commented. "It's Maurice's time. About bloody time, really. Maurice deserves this."

Fashion Revolution

by HAL MOUNTSAUERKRAUTEN, Alternate Reality News Service Crime Writer

Three legged fashion models? Fashion models whose breasts are larger than their heads? Fashion models with even tempers and pleasant dispositions? These are just some of the horrific possibilities that the fashion world has to contend with in the wake of a disaster at the WF Laboratories.

"We are closely monitoring the situation," Andrash Copaseti-Cabana, CEO of WF Laboratories, said, "but we can already see anomalies in many of our models: girls with a third eye and – gulp – 300 pounds…"

"Quelle catastrophe!" Martin Anderson, of the House of Dior, cried into his crème brule.

WF Laboratories, the main producer of human mannequins for fashion designers, has been at the forefront of the cloning industry for over 20 years. "Six feet tall 14 year-old girls with a DD breast cup?" Copaseti-Cabana explained, "They don't appear in nature all that often. Cloning the most successful models was one method of assuring a steady supply for the fashion industry.

"And, now, it's all being threatened."

The purity of the eggs used in the cloning process has been compromised, resulting in the creation of defective clone models.

"They seem perfectly skinny and normal until they're about six years old," Copaseti-Cabana said. "Then, something goes wrong with their beautifully emaciated bodies…something goes terribly, terribly wrong…"

Police have been called in to investigate, and are not ruling out the possibility of sabotage at the plant just outside of Paris. The fact that the Kate Moss, Shalom Harlow and Karen Mulder germ lines – the three sets of DNA out of which 90 per cent of the models coming out of the factory are based – have all been compromised at the same time is highly suspicious.

"We have a number of suspects at the moment," said Inspector Jacques Clouseau of the French Surete, the detective assigned to the case. "Feminists who believe that the image of models in fashion leads women to have unrealistic, dangerous expectations of their own bodies, scientists who believe we are dangerously playing god with our genetic inheritance – there are a lot of crazies out there." Then, he set the couch he was sitting on on fire.

There is currently a two year emergency supply of models. These women are working in restaurants and salons in New York, Paris, London and Milan, where they are waiting to be "discovered." Beyond this two year period, however, things look bleak for the fashion industry.

"It's not just the runway shows," explained Harold Bloomthorpe, lingerie reporter for *Women's Wear Daily Worker*. "It's advertisements in trendy magazines and on the hottest shows on television, it's billboards and movie stars. If the world suddenly found itself bereft of fashion models, the trickle down effect on the entire entertainment industry would be devastating!"

A number of possible solutions to this problem have been proposed. There is one other known source of fashion model clones: Fujimoro Industries of Tokyo.

"Unfortunately, they currently produce exclusively Oriental models for the Asian market," stated Bloomthorpe. "It would take them three or four years to retool the assembly line to produce occidental models. And, that's assuming they would even be willing to – they're already working pretty much at capacity."

Another possible solution would be for designers to create clothes for the clones as they came off the assembly line.

"This would give an advantage to designers who like improvisation," Bloomthorpe said. "Those who couldn't adjust to models with hips as wide as Hondas or ass length hair the texture of a Brillo pad would have a hard time."

Simply using the models they have until the problem at the factory is solved is not an option, according to Andrash Copaseti-Cabana: "Have you ever seen a model who has just turned 20? The booze, the pills, the late night partying – they're not kind to young women. Most designers would rather pin their clothes to a wall and have people walk by them than use older models – no offense."

One other possibility, spoken of in hushed tones in the fashion centres of the world, would be to design clothes for ordinary women to model.

"Quelle catastrophe!" Anderson cried into his orange mocha frappacino latte. "Fashion is about giving ordinary women something impossible to aspire to. If we used ordinary women as models…" Anderson trailed off into a shudder, a shudder that presaged the end of fashion as we know it.

The police investigation continues.

Is There An Eco In Here?

by SASKATCHEWAN KOLONOSCOGRAD, Alternate Reality News Service Existentialism Writer

A crisis has erupted in academia as the Million Monkey Project has produced its first virtually complete work, *and it wasn't by Shakespeare.*

"We didn't foresee this," kajillionaire recluse Bruce Wayne, sponsor of the Million Monkey project, stated, "and, to be honest with you, I'm not sure what to make of it."

"I'll tell you what to make of it," Igor Vladyofsky, Fordham professor and head researcher of the Million Monkey Project, stated. "It's a disaster. A big, fat, [UNACADEMIC EXPLETIVE DELETED] disaster!"

The Million Monkey Project is a literary experiment where a million monkeys are put to work at word processors. The theory was that, given enough time, one of them would compose a work approximating one of Shakespeare's plays or sonnets. Had that happened, it would have been proof that great literature is not the product of creative genius, but merely a random lacy frill on the undergarment that is the chaotic universe.

Instead, after three years of around the clock effort, one of the monkeys wrote a short story that is an almost word for word copy of Franz Kafka's "The Metamorphosis." Although not an exact duplicate – there are several instances of the word "the" spelled as "teh," for example, and one inexplicable instance of Gregor Samsa being referred to as "Anton Houlebecq" – the mistakes are no worse than what you would expect from a poor human typist.

"I'm ruined," Vladyofsky sobbed. "Ruined! How will I ever get on the cover of *The Journal of Literary Exegesis* now?"

"Igor tends to take these things too seriously," Robert Monette, professor of Literary Non-Alignment at Rutgers, responded to the news. "He tried to kill himself by stuffing snails up his nose when it was announced that Homer wasn't a real human being, but an amalgam of oral storytellers, you know.

"Personally, I think the creation of the Kafka story vindicates the whole project. It may be a different random lacy frill on the undergarment that is the chaotic universe than the one they had hoped for, but it's still a random lacy frill on the undergarment that is the chaotic universe."

Some controversy surrounds the story, which was leaked to a *Washington Post* reporter by a shady nobody in a dark parking lot whom the press, for no apparent reason, has come to call "Deep Oats." Computer analysis confirms that the story was composed at least two months ago. Why the delay in publicizing it?

"I was getting around to it," Vladyofsky testily answered. "Geez, have you never had paperwork pile up on your desk?"

Despite Vladyofsky's protestations, a pattern seems to be emerging. Rumours circulating on the Internet claim that as early as two months into the Million Monkey Project, one of the cleverer orangutans actually composed (recomposed?) the lyrics to the Duran Duran song "Rio."

Critics have suggested that Vladyofsky has been suppressing other works written by the apes – everything from Camus' *The Outsider* to Three Stooges scripts – just because they weren't written by Shakespeare.

"Vladyofsky has been suppressing other works written by the apes just because they weren't written by Shakespeare," stated former *Times of London* literary critic Bosley Cathair. "It's a shame, really. If he wasn't so obsessed with Shakespeare – ooh, ahh, the greatest writer in the English language, booga booga – he would see that his experiment has been a wild success."

Cathair lost his position in 2000 when he was caught plagiarizing a review of George Orwell's *Animal Farm* that had been written over 50 years ago. Suspicions were immediately raised when somebody realized that nobody had reissued *Animal Farm* in many years, so a review at the time was unnecessary.

"Nobody would have called it plagiarism," Cathair sniffed, "if I hadn't been so damned evolved. No. If I had had a furry body and a tail, it would have been literary bloody experimentation, wouldn't it?"

The discovery of *The Metamorphosis* in the random characters generated by the apes has put the future of the Million Monkey Project in doubt. Some say that the point has been proven and the project should be shut down. Others point out that putting a million apes back into the wild is asking for ecological trouble. Still others suggest that the monkeys have fine careers ahead of them as advertising copywriters. Mostly, people ask, "Who was Franz Kafka, anyway?"

I blame the public school system.

Revenge Is Sour

by HAL MOUNTSAUERKRAUTEN, Alternate Reality News Service Crime Writer

Police believe they have found the clue that will break the case of the rash of mysterious deaths outside movie theatres: a suicide note.

"It's over. It's finally well and truly over," the note read. "There's nothing left to live for." The note went on in this vein for several pages, and was signed "Jen Wookie Lover 12."

There have been 237 reported deaths throughout North America. Stabbings, poisonings, shootings, hangings and, in at least one incident, suffocation due to penguin inhalation. The only thing the deaths had in common was that they had taken place outside of movie theatres screening *Star Wars: Episode Three: Revenge of the Sith*.

"How did you get a copy of that note?" FBI Special Agent Dale Cooper asked. "Okay, never mind, that doesn't matter any more. I believe that there's some…spooky force at work here that is causing people to take their own lives. I'm not sure what it is, but I'm positive that note will point the way. If I could just see the connection…if I could just – hey, can I have another piece of that pie? You know, I've never tasted anything so –"

To others, the answer was obvious. "Mikey killed himself because of that stupid movie series," said Harland Breedlove, the half-brother of victim Michael Breedlove. "He'd been depressed for months, knowing that the *Star Wars* saga was about to come to an end. Said it gave his life meaning, or some shit like that. All this other stuff is nonsense. I mean, really, does anybody believe he was getting off on sniffing a f-ck-ng penguin?"

"I wouldn't dismiss water fowl auto-erotic asphyxiation so lightly," sex columnist Selma Sorrento commented. "As we, as a society, become more jaded with traditional forms of sexuality, the thrill of almost dying for sex involving ducks, seagulls and, yes, even penguins, can be a powerful aphrodisiac.

"Of course," she added, "that has nothing to do with the subject you're actually writing about, does it?"

The idea that people would kill themselves because a movie series had ended seems farfetched. "Oh, it's not as farfetched as you may write," media critic Liss Jeffrey stated. "You see, as the media become a larger and larger part of our lives, those lives seem less and less important. In a very real way, we become hardwired to see the fake as real and the real as…something else. Our minds become these vast, interconnected cultural blenders that puree film and television, literature and music, and serve it up as a smooth blend of information. I'm partial to raspberry, myself.

"Besides," Jeffrey added, "*Episode One: The Phantom Menace* sucked."

"Hey!" movie critic Geoff Pevere cut in. "Leave the criticism to the professionals!"

"Let me put it this way," Jeffrey continued, undaunted by the interruption. "What is happening to people who live inside the communicasphere of modern societies is like…it's like leaving cheese out in the sun, except it's happening within our brains. There is evidence that our amygdalas are getting a little soft and runny around the edges, which, obviously, impacts on our cognitive abilities. It's different for everybody, of course. Some people think Jerry Seinfeld is an ancient King of Egypt. Some people can no longer identify apples. The human mind is an amazing thing, especially when it goes wonky.

"Oh, and, *Episode One* sure did suck!"

"Oh, it totally sucked," Pevere agreed. "But, when it comes to film criticism, you're just an amateur. I should be the one who pronounces that movies suck or not. In fact, *The Phantom Menace* was so bad, I'm surprised people didn't start killing themselves when **it** came out. I can only guess that they hoped the other films in the series would somehow redeem it."

"Hey!" Agent Cooper put in, "This is a criminal investigation! Unless you have any training in forensic science, you shouldn't be giving an opinion in an ongoing case!"

And, so, the circle was complete.

In an attempt to stem the flow of bodies clogging its front door, the Harlequinade Theatre in New York posted notices reading: "Don't despair! *Star Wars* is coming to TV!" and "Hey! – There's always *Star Wars Clone Wars!*" Unfortunately, suicides outside the theatre increased by 43 per cent in the week following the posting of the signs, and they were quietly removed.

The investigation continues. George Lucas was terminally unavailable for comment.

Death Is Easy…

THOMAS FINFLANAHAGAN, Alternate Reality News Service International Writer

In a move that has stunned the stand-up world, the United Nations General Council ratified a treaty that would ban a large variety of bombs in comedy clubs around the world. The vote was 142-2, with only the United States and Israel voting against the resolution.

"This is a great day for comedy lovers everywhere," United Nations Secretary General Kofi Annan proclaimed. "By banning the most deadly material used by comedians not only will we save untold numbers of them from dying on stage, but we will end the collateral damage of audiences being bored to death."

Twenty-seven different deadly jokes would be outlawed by the treaty, including:

* mother-in-law jokes;
* jokes about airline food;
* jokes that are built primarily around the use of props, and;
* jokes about the original *Star Trek* television series.

The treaty also commits signatory countries to cracking down on jokes that begin with the phrase: "Have you ever noticed [subject]? What's up with that?" While not an official target of the treaty, this phrase will be highly, highly frowned upon.

"It's outrageous!" claimed United States Ambassador to the United Nations John Bolton. "The UN knows that the United States produces over 60 per cent of the stand-up comedy in the world! I mean, when was the last time you heard a Saudi Arabian make a joke about Paris Hilton? It doesn't happen. Ethiopians making fun of airline food? They're lucky if they know what airlines are! Hell, they're lucky if they know what food is!

"This is obviously an attack on American comedy production, and, frankly, we're not going to stand for it!"

"Vot he said!" Dan Gillerman, Israel's Ambassador to the United Nations, chimed in, adding, "Absolutely vot he said."

When he was told about the American objections to the treaty, Secretary General Annan could barely restrain his eyes from rolling out of the back of his head.

"Yes, well, some countries will insist upon seeing themselves as the centre of everything, won't they?" he mused. "In the meantime, while the United States pursues its own agenda, comedians and audiences in countries around the world are suffering. Does that seem right to you?"

Ratification of the treaty commits countries to enact laws in conformity with the terms of the treaty within the next seven years. Some countries will hold referenda on the issue, others will pass the necessary laws in their legislatures. When a country passes such a law, it then becomes an official signatory to the treaty. When two-thirds of the member countries of the United Nations have signed the treaty, it becomes international law. So, at the moment, the treaty banning deadly jokes is more of a wish than a reality.

"Yes," Secretary General Annan sighed daintily, "but sometimes wishes do come true."

"Not if I can help it," Ambassador Bolton, known informally in the corridors of the UN building as "The Grinch," responded. Even before the vote had taken place, rumours had started circulating that the US would play hardball with UN member nations that voted for it. Especially France. For example, if Luxembourg signs the treaty, the United States has suggested it will withhold shipments of much needed *Comic Relief* videos to the country. In another instance, if Kazakhstan signs on to the treaty, the United States may bar Second City veterans from setting up workshops in that country, making it harder for it to properly train indigenous comedy workers.

"There is no doubt about it," Secretary General Annan said, "when the United States believes that its interests are threatened, it will play hardball with smaller nations. That doesn't mean the treaty is doomed, but…uhh… you'll have to excuse me. I really should be planning my imminent retirement."

The treaty allows for the creation of an International Comedy Enhancement Agency (ICEA) that would monitor countries for compliance. Countries that sign on to the treaty would be obligated to allow inspectors into their comedy clubs to ensure that none of the banned jokes are being produced. If the inspectors find that banned jokes are being produced, they can do anything from warn the club manager to end the practice to imposing sanctions on cultural products created in the offending nation.

"Oh, right, like that means anything!" Ambassador Bolton banged his fists on a table. "We all know that there are ways around United Nations sanctions – licensing comedians in third party nations, for example, or disguising comedy as 'drama' before shipping it across borders. The UN inspections regime is a joke!"

"No pun intended."

An Operation To Forget

by LAURIE NEIDERGAARDEN, Alternate Reality News Service Medical Writer

For Bogert Skyler, the last straw was Hugh Grant facing charges over claims that he attacked a photographer with a tub of baked beans. Like many of us, Skyler wondered why he was giving precious space in his memory and consciousness to such inane and useless trivia.

"Uhh, yeah, it must have been something like that," Skyler dully explained.

Unlike most of us, Skyler did something about the problem. He went to eVolv (formerly the town of Lvov) in Poland, to the Meyerhoffer Clinic, which promised to remove the offending memories from his mind. "It's not brainwashing," Skyler stated. "It's more like brain rinsing in a basin and hanging on a line to dry."

According to its Web site, The Meyerhoffer Clinic uses the latest brain imaging technology to pinpoint where certain memories are stored. Then, using a combination of laser, radiation and surgical techniques, it removes the parts of the brain related to cultural trivia that the patient no longer wishes to know.

"Embarrassed that you know more about Angelina Jolie's relationship to Brad Pitt than you do about your own spouse?" the Web site explains. "The Meyerhoffer Clinic can help you forget Brad and Angelina ever existed. What happens next is up to you!"

Soon after being treated at the clinic, friends and family of Skyler noticed that he wasn't quite the same person. "He…he didn't know what bananas are," his mother, Hermione, explained. "At first, he tried to bluff his way through – you know how young men are – by telling us that they were sex toys.

"Explaining to my 29 year-old son that a banana is not a sex toy was one of the saddest days of my life."

When I tried to contact the Meyerhoffer Clinic by phone, I got a message telling me that the number had never existed. When I sent an email to the address on the Web site, I received the following two paragraph response:

"The Meyerhoffer Clinic is a legitimate medical fecelity [sic] that offers to simplify your life by removing the trivia that we accumulate daily in our brains. Our patented Meyerhoffer Reduction System sheds those unwanted thoughts/ideas/memories and gives your brain more room for the important things in life, like car insurance or remembering your mother-in-law's birthday.

"Our client list includes many internationally renowned politicians, figures from the entertainment world and taxi-dermists [sic?]. Of course, because of patient-doctor confidentiality, we cannot tell you who they are. But, boy, would you be impressed if you knew! Impressed that we are, as we say, a totally legitimate medical facileity [sic]."

Biff LaBeouf, neuroscientist and third ranked professional skiboarder in Austria, had never heard of the Meyerhoffer Clinic, but he did have reservations about the process of brain erasure.

"That shit is insane!" he stated.

Memories are stored in the connections across several neurons in the brain. If you remove one of the neurons, it not only weakens the one memory you want to get rid of, but also other memories that it's a part of.

"It's like..." LaBeouf strained for an appropriate metaphor, "like...the road system, right? Say you blast one road because you...I don't know – the pavement is cracked and it's ugly and it's bringing down property values. Maybe you don't want people from that street coming to your street. The problem is, that street also gives you access to other streets you might want to go to. Now, if you blast enough streets because you don't want people using them – I don't know why, just...stay with me on this, okay? – if you do that, you'll end up not being able to go everywhere you want to go.

"That's how complicated the brain is."

Bogert Skyler has been home for over three months. He claims not to know who Paris Hilton is, and any mention of Bruce Willis is met with a blank stare. Many people would envy him.

On the other hand, he seems to think that George W. Bush is a species of hermit crab, and that purple is a form of communications device, smaller than a telephone and able to transmit images.

"I never realized he was so worried about this stuff," Bogert's mother said. "I mean, if it was so important to him not to know any of this, why didn't he just turn off the TV?"

Why, indeed.

Hear Hear!

By TINA LOLLOCADENKA, Alternate Reality News Service Music Writer

Scientists at the Massachusetts Institute of Technology have discovered a method of sound recording that could change the music industry forever.

Known as "neuronal link blockage," the technique involves recording songs with a special vibration that cannot be heard but that makes it impossible for the listener to make the connections in the brain that would allow her to remember the song she has just listened to.

This comes hot on the heels of other recent technologies that changed the music industry forever, including: CDs and DVDs that melted after the first hearing (the "Mission Impossible" effect), and; digital tunes that turned into so much random noise after being played once on iPods and other devices.

"The other technical changes helped achieve the goal of musicians being paid every time somebody listened to a song," Terrence Hardiman, President of Lavontria, the company that perfected the technology, explained, "but they still left the music industry with a flaw in its profit maximizing efforts: consumers could always remember songs they had heard. Hard as it may be to believe, some people were actually deliberately using their memories to avoid having to listen to songs repeatedly, and, thus, to avoid paying recording artists their fair share of money for their work.

"Obviously, neuronal link blockage solves this problem."

Musicians hailed the technological breakthrough. "Do you have any idea how expensive jet fuel is?" asked Lars Ulrich, lead singer of the band Metallica. "I mean, uhh, I do some of my best composing on my private jet, so, this would, uhh, help me with my artistic process. Yeah. That's it. Artistic process. Creativity and shit."

Michael Geist, a vocal opponent of giving corporations too much control over the copyright of their material and destroying what little remains of the creative commons, had a typically caustic response to the new technology.

"I give up," he stated. "The recording industry is too powerful. It wins."

"Hee hee hee," Ulrich responded.

"I think there's a bigger picture here that both sides need to keep in mind," Hardiman said. "With copyright law having been extended to a mere 200 years, only eight or 10 generations will benefit from an artist's creative output. Without neuronal link blockage, this may not have been a sufficient incentive for artists to create new work."

"I don't see how giving somebody's great-great-great-great-great-great-great-grandchildren a financial windfall will make an artist want to create more," Geist retorted, "but, no, forget about it, you're not sucking me back into this argument."

What of the musician who is just starting out or who doesn't play "mainstream" music and, therefore, has yet to develop a following? Who knows? I wanted to interview one for this article, but I didn't know where to find any.

"The marginalization of the smaller artist is typical of a highly restricted copyright regime," Geist commented. "Not that you heard that from me. I've gone fishing!"

Neuronal link blockage has been tested for several years on dogs. The first designs of the test involved the use of a tone that was too high-pitched for humans to hear. Unfortunately, researchers couldn't tell if the dogs didn't respond because link blockage had taken place, or if the researchers had simply forgotten to make the tone.

Clinical tests on human beings have shown that neuronal link blockage has side effects, including: headaches, nausea, bleeding from the ears and an inability to get the song "Yummy, Yummy, Yummy, I Got Love in My Tummy" out of your head for several days.

"Any new technology comes with risks," Hardiman breezily stated. "When the automobile was first introduced, who could have foreseen that teenagers would use it to drag race each other down the main strip of the city in a game of chicken that would leave one dead and the other wracked by guilt?"

When it was pointed out to him that government copyright policy was too important to be driven by analogies to *Rebel Without a Cause*, Hardiman said neuronal link blockage had the potential to work in all media. That he totally missed the point seemed lost on him, although, perhaps, there was a bigger point in his response.

It's now up to government regulators to determine whether to allow neuronal link blockage technologies to be used by the public. However, given that when it was discovered that the Mission Impossible effect caused three per cent of DVD consumers to spontaneously combust the government refused to demand a recall of the product, perhaps the best response would be for all consumers to go fishing.

Now and Again

by ELMORE TERADONOVICH, Alternate Reality News Service Film Writer

Facing declining ticket sales and its worst box office in over a decade, Hollywood is considering drastic measures to get bums back in theatre seats.

The plan to clone Tom Cruise failed when it was discovered that his copies were skittish and prone to irrational outbursts on national television talk shows.

Plans to put force feedback units in the armrests of movie theatre seats were opposed by family groups that didn't want children to feel the tender caresses of onscreen lovers.

In the latest move, AMC theatres has announced that, starting next week, any customers who do not enjoy a movie they show will be given a free trip back in time to before they saw the film.

"Unfortunately, we can't erase the memory of a bad film," AMC spokeswoman Anushka Paradis stated, "but at least we can give you back the time you spent watching it."

The time travel is being supplied by a company called Flux Capacitor Enterprises.

"Well, you know," said FCE President Martin McFly, "once you've gone back in time – more than once – and made sure your parents met, fell in love and got married, what else is there to do but start a time travel business?"

Noticing the blank stares from the journalists in the room, McFly quickly added: "But, seriously, we've all come out of movies complaining about not being able to get those two hours of our lives back. I think this is going to be an important public service."

FCE's time machine is called a "Delorean." It looks somewhat like a typical automobile, except the doors open up instead of out, and it has a silver appendage in the back – the flux capacitor that makes time travel possible.

Giving dissatisfied moviegoers their time back is not without perils, not the least of which is the Grandmother Paradox. Suppose you go back far enough in time to meet your grandmother before she met your grandfather and showed her a photograph of what he would look like on their 60th wedding anniversary. She might be so disgusted at what life has in store for her that she wouldn't marry him; but, if she doesn't marry him, your mother won't be born, meaning that you won't be born.

That's a heavy price to pay just for not liking *Herbie: Fully Loaded*.

"We're not taking them back that far," McFly pointed out. "The worst that could happen is that they would choose to get popcorn at the concession stand instead of nachos and save themselves from getting indigestion later."

Another potential problem is what might happen when two versions of the same person meet. Nobody knows what the results of such a meeting might be, although speculation runs the gamut from total annihilation of the universe to Tim Burton becoming American Ambassador to Ecuador.

"Patrons who take advantage of the time back offer are expected to be on their best behaviour," Paradis stated, "and not return to the same movie theatre. I mean, can you imagine how terrible it would be if somebody liked a movie so much that they kept going back in time until different versions of them filled the theatre?"

The light in her eyes suggested, however, that she wouldn't find such a situation all that terrible. She wouldn't find it terrible at all.

"Are you kidding?" asked trendspotter Douglas Coupland. "I would go back in time to see movies I hated just so that I could torment my past self with rude comments. 'Don't go back into that room – the killer is waiting for you!' Or: 'Stop pretending you hate each other, because you know you're going to get married in the final scene!' I think it'd be a hoot!"

Coupland's enthusiasm waned when it was pointed out that you could predict those kinds of plotlines without having seen the movie first. "Yeah, I suppose that's why people want their money back in the first place," he allowed. "Now, if I could go back far enough to say 'The shrink is dead!' or 'Luke, he *is* your father!', well, that could be amusing."

Reaction to the announcement of the time back offer has been mixed.

"I don't like the idea of time travel," said moviegoer Frank Mitzenfagel.

"I like the idea of time travel," said moviegoer Mitzi Frankengarber.

"We'll see how the public reacts," Paradis said. "After all, if they don't take to it, we can always go back in time and make sure the whole time back offer is never made…"

Out For Blood

by INDIRA CHARUNDER-MACHARRUNDEIRA, Alternate Reality News Service Fine Arts Writer

Bad boy of the art world Andres Serrano has managed to outrage again, only, this time, his fans are the ones who are angry with him.

Serrano has just published a coffee table retrospective of his work called *I Don't Know Art, But I Know What I Make*. He has been traveling the world signing copies of the book. As befits an artist who specializes in using body fluids as his raw materials, he has been signing the books with his own blood.

As reported last week, though, the majority of that blood didn't come directly out of his body. One vial was taken out of him before his recent publicity tour and the red blood cells were cloned. It is this cloned blood that he has been using to sign his books with.

"Well, that just sucks, and not in a good, sexual way," Mats Starling, a lanky, self-confessed Serrano fanatic and Academy Awards fetishist, stated. "I mean, when he signed the book, I assumed it was in his own blood. I mean, blood that had come out of his body, not…grown in some Petri dish. If I had known where the blood had come from…well, okay, I would have bought the book anyway, but I probably wouldn't have asked for as much when I put it up for auction on ehBay."

Andromeda Palaquin, a publicist for Serrano, rolled her chillingly deep sky blue eyes and argued that the fans had no cause for complaint. She pointed out that the DNA of the cloned blood is identical to the blood taken out of the artist's body.

"That's not the point," Starling, pounding his tiny fists on the table, argued back. "It's an issue of authenticity, isn't it? I mean, when Serrano did 'Piss Christ,' would it have worked as well if he had gotten somebody else to drink his urine, piss **it** out and put the crucifix in that? Of course not. Well, maybe, actually. That could have been kind of cool. Still, you know what I mean."

Palaquin shook her long, silky black tresses in disbelief. "Andres has signed thousands of copies of the book," she pointed out with a long, thin, perfectly manicured finger. "If he had used blood taken from his own body, he would have run out after a couple of weeks, and then where would his fans have been?"

Palaquin did allow that Serrano had considered replacing the blood that he used to sign books with from his body with a saline solution that would serve the same functions.

"Unfortunately, the technology for that just wasn't available," she explained, shrugging her delicate shoulders as a rueful smile played around her blood red lips.

Shaking his pale head with its messy, thinning hair, Starling insisted that that wasn't the point. By using cloned blood instead of his own, Serrano had taken the danger out of the whole process.

"He wasn't about to pass out because of blood loss, now, was he? Without that possibility, it was just a…a book signing! And, what's the fun in that?"

Supporting the fans, rogue geneticist Arturo Gide shook his leonine mane and roared in a deep, compelling voice that "cloning is an abomination of the book promotion process!" He pointed out that clones are always weaker than their genetic progenitors. In this case, that would mean a thinner blood that would likely start flaking off the page in a matter of years instead of decades or centuries.

This was actually a plus, thought Palaquin. Making a moue that accentuated her dimples, she pointed out that if Serrano had been limited to using the blood from his body, the books signed would have had to be limited in number, making each more valuable. If the cloned blood eroded faster, it would ultimately have the same effect.

"You have won me over with your superior logic," Gide giddily stated, gazing longingly into Palaquin's eyes.

"What?" Starling asked, confused.

"Oh, Arturo," Palaquin sighed. "You know our love can never be."

"What does this have to do with –" Starling started.

"Why?" Gide boomed, his rippling masculinity aquiver.

"We…we come from different worlds," Palaquin trembled, her ample bosom heaving. "You are a geneticist with a healthy skepticism of cloning. I'm just a poor publicist trying to support her client's work. Don't you see? It can never work between us."

Gide took Palanquin up into his cordwood arms and gave her a kiss so passionate that it ended all the arguments.

"What about my signed book?" Starling insisted. Poor thing. He didn't realize that he was the odd man out…

Confessions of a Pizza Delivery Guy

by FREDERICA VON McTOAST-HYPHEN, Alternate Reality News Service People Writer

The first thing you notice about Jack McLondon is that he is actually rather handsome. Neat, respectful, attentive – he's the kind of kid that any mother would want dating her daughter. You wouldn't think to look at him that this pizza delivery guy from Winosha, Wisconsin was a virgin.

"I...I'm saving myself for the right woman," McLondon, wearing a deer caught in headlights t-shirt under his deer caught in headlights expression, unconvincingly explains. "What's wrong with that?"

A pizza delivery guy who has never had sex on the job? It's like a cement contractor who has never hid a body in the foundations of a building that's just going up. It's like a dentist who has never tried his own laughing gas. It's like a politician who has never – okay, that's too easy.

It's unnatural.

"But –" McLondon tries to interject before I cut him off to continue my exposition. The pizza delivery guy who knocks on the door which is answered by a sensuous young (and, sometimes, not so young) woman in a negligee who obviously wants more than pizza and is willing to give a generous tip to get it was a staple of porn movies in the 1970s.

Legend has it that early porn star John Holmes had a contract that stipulated that he do at least one pizza delivery sex scene in each of his movies. Ron Jeremy holds the record for most pizza delivery guy sex scenes (212), as well as most pizza delivery guy sex scenes in a single movie (7).

In fact, the pizza delivery sex scene was so popular that it was responsible for a whole generation of teenage boys taking up the career of pizza delivery guy.

"I had just got my licence and I was looking for a cool summer job," reminisced former pizza delivery guy, Salvatore Pflermigan. "That was also the year I snuck in to see *Deep Stoat* at the Jibou. It blew my mind. John Holmes gave an understated yet rich performance as the pizza delivery guy, and he made it with Lisa De Leeuw! Six times! In every room in her apartment!

"That's when I knew what I wanted to do."

"That's funny, because I –" McLondon started. I silenced him with a look that could stop a rhino dead in its tracks. I wasn't going to let some... some *subject* hijack my article!

Pflermigan explained that he had to wait until his third month of deliveries before he had sex with a client, but "the wait was worth it." After that, work was a non-stop round of orgiastic behaviour – and he made enough money that summer to pay for his first week of college.

"I almost had sex once!" McLondon blurted. This got my attention, so I bade him continue.

"It was a couple of months ago – my last delivery of the night." This was good – in the movies, it was always the last delivery of the night. "The woman who came to the door was wearing this pink…I think they're called teddies…"

"With lace trim?" I penetratingly asked.

"Uhh, yeah," McLondon replied. "Anyway –"

"Sheer?" I probed further.

"Sheerish," McLondon said. "You could sort of see what was underneath, but not really that well…" After a moment of awkward silence, he continued: "Anyway, the woman said she didn't have the money, and would I mind following her into her bedroom – that's where she said her purse was – in her bedroom –"

"Yes, YES!" I breathily encouraged him. "Go on."

"Her bedroom had this thick carpet and a bed shaped like a heart. It was really something, that bedroom."

"Yes! Yes! And…?"

"And she paid me and I left."

Guiseppe Sardonicus, shop steward of Local 14258 of the Amalgamated Truckers, Cement Pourers and Pizza Delivery Guys Union, couldn't believe that such a thing was possible. "We busted our chops to make sure that time off for sexual relations with customers was part of the latest collective agreement! This guy who doesn't take advantage – he's spitting in the eye of every decent, hard-working, horny member of this union!"

McLondon began to protest that he was shy, but that excuse was so lame that I refused to dignify it with a quote.

He also said that he was hoping to get to second base with his current girlfriend, but since she lived outside his delivery area, pizza would not be involved.

Urban Adventures: Eyeball Pinball

by CORIANDER NEUMANEIMANAYMANEEMAMANN, Alternate Reality News Service Urban Issues Writer

The urban environment is seen by many as cold and dehumanizing. We navigate through mountains of glass and steel to go from our dead end jobs to our depersonalized condos without seeming to make meaningful contact with other human beings.

Various groups and individuals are trying to change that.

"If you approach your environment with imagination and an openness to experiment and play," dapper power broker and transplanted Toronto bon vivant Richard Florida notes, "you should be able to avoid this whole 'urban alienation' thing." Yes, he said "urban alienation" with scare quotes; dapper power brokers and bon vivants talk like that.

One person who approaches the city with a sense of play is Karl Rorschach, a 30 year-old Vegan architect with a slightly mad twinkle in his eye. Rorschach is the poster man/boy for a new sport called Eyeball Pinball.

"Well, you know how, like, you're sitting on the subway, right?" Rorschach explained over lunch at Fit for Life, a trendy little bistro on Spadina. "And, like, nobody is willing to make eye contact. The trick, you see, is to look at somebody so…so that when they turn their head, they look at somebody else, right? Then, they turn their heads, and so on. I can get, like, six people involved pretty regular, and I even got a chain of seven going two or three times."

Rorschach, an amateur player, says his goal is to one day play on the International Eyeball Pinball circuit. In professional EP, each player is accompanied by a (discretely dressed) referee who ensures that each look in the chain follows established rules, among which are length, angle of head tilt and "demureness."

Perhaps the best known EP player on the circuit is Jeffrey Lebowski, a big, grizzled bear of a man who looks a little like Jeff Bridges on a bad day.

"Man, I once saw Lebowski make a circuit of, like 11 people," Rorschach said with a reverence bordering on the religious. "There were no referees around, so it didn't count for competition, but, man, if you looked at him, you would swear he was half asleep, and he pulled off such a big…a big…I don't even know what to call it!"

Because the sport is relatively new, players on the EP circuit get little more than bus fare to competitions in various cities and the occasional can of soda if they win. Rorschach stated that this keeps the sport pure: "Naw, man, can you imagine how phony things would get if there was major international TV coverage…big sponsorship deals…babes…everybody would become an asshole and it would destroy the sport!" There was a wistfulness in his voice, though, that belied his pro-amateur bravado.

"Oh, hey, check this out," Rorschach whispered on a thinly populated Finch subway car on the way home late that night. "I'm going to do a 360 Rondo with a 33…no, 50 per cent backspin." After a moment, Rorschach shyly looked at a large black woman, a middle-aged woman who looked like life had beaten her down and refused to let her get up, sitting across the car from us.

Noticing his gentle gaze, the black woman turned her sad orbs away, momentarily locking eyes with a thin older white woman who had been humming an ancient tune to herself, her creased features exuding a crinkly good humour, a few seats away down the car.

The old woman playfully ran a withered hand through her thinning white hair and looked away, catching the eye of a teen punk listening to her iPod across the aisle. Her spiked hair and grungy clothes were clearly meant to project a strength that the quickness with which she looked away belied.

The punk caught the attention of an old Asian man who turned towards us. You could tell from the look in his eye that he had lived longer than he had thought he would, longer than he wanted, and he was just waiting for the final peace that death would bring. Why he thought he would find it on that subway car was a mystery I will never be able to determine the answer to.

The looks went up one side of the car and down the other, returning to Rorschach – a 360 rondo. The old white woman and the old Asian man, after turning their heads, quickly turned them back – fifty per cent backspin.

Smiling, Rorschach commented, "It's a gift. What can I say?"

Coriander Neumaneimanaymaneemamann's first novel, Eyes on the Surprise, *has just been published. The Alternate Reality News Service is certain that, once her book tour has been completed, her writing will be less…uhh…well, it will calm down.*

ALTERNATE LIVES

Lives Unlived: Folger McWonderman

Virtual psychology researcher. Media guru. Darling of journalists. Intellectual superstar. Good father…great humanitarian…blah blah blah. Born, December 25, 19 – oh, but they're just biographical details that don't tell you anything about the man, aren't they?

Folger – Good Old Folge as we used to call him at OUPD – Salt of the Earth Folgey – The Happy Coffee Man – was, despite his genius, a modest person who shunned the spotlight. All of the time he spent jetting around the world in order to appear on various talk shows or in news reports and documentaries, was his way of compensating for his essential shyness.

If anybody had less to be modest about, it was definitely "Good Times, Bad Times, You Know I've Had My Share" McWonderman. He was the discoverer of the McWonderman Visual Literalness Syndrome, after all.

As all first year psych students know, McVLS afflicts people who spend too much time in virtual environments; some develop an impairment in their visual processing centres that causes them to not be able to infer full objects when part of them are hidden. The textbook example (written by McWonderman, who admittedly spent a little too much time in bars than would be considered seemly by members of polite society, but, because he was a genius, was easily and completely forgiven) is of a person who sees the upper body and head of a bartender who cannot make the assumption that the rest of his body is hidden by the bar. Without having taken a single drink.

The implications for long distance truck drivers, soldiers and porn photographers should be obvious.

I remember the meeting when Folge McWondie had the initial inspiration that would lead to 127 peer-reviewed research papers, 12 books, 23 appearances on Conan O'Brien and a brief (and, as many critics have pointed out, superfluous, although I personally enjoyed it) cameo in the last Woody Allen film. Dean Rivers-Dentz was late, as usual; his excuse this time was that squirrels had chewed through the gas line in his car.

Virgil Aeneas (a sessional!) spent the first hour haranguing us about… something about the University administration slowly strangling the programme of funds because it's main focus was shifting away from the Humanities and towards business. Typical sessional paranoia. I don't know why Dean Rivers-Dentz let the discussion go on as long as it did.

For my part, I spent most of that interminable hour deciding which doughnut I would try to get out of the box. I'm a boysenberry cruller man, myself. Everybody on faculty knows it. Yet, somehow, no matter how quickly I rush to the box, somebody has gotten to the boysenberry crullers before me! Believe me, my Herculean efforts never end in anything more than a maple doughnut with pink sprinkles.

How embarrassing for an academic of my standing! I've been almost tenured for the last 16 years – surely, that merits the odd boysenberry cruller!

Ahem. Over coffee during a break, the McWonderboy started talking about this strange phenomenon he had noticed among virtual reality gamers – it seemed they were having difficulty making inferences about objects in the real world. "You mean to tell me," I asked, "that you want us to believe that otherwise mentally healthy adults are children who cannot understand that the world doesn't disappear when they cover their eyes?"

Other teachers in the room have gone on record as saying that I was being sarcastic. However, where some saw a young man skulking away from a verbal tongue-lashing from a senior colleague, I saw a light bulb going off above the head of a brilliant theoretician. Folger McWonderman himself understood that I was helping guide a younger academic to the truth. In this case, a truth that would make him the toast of celebrity pseudo-intellectuals and a darling of the sycophantic academic community.

After fame struck, I cannot begin to count the number of times in faculty meetings (full programme meetings, too, not just the Virtual Psychology stream) that Folgie talked about how he owed his success to my inspiration. If colleagues who were at those meetings do not remember him saying this, well, I chalk that up to professional jealousy. Or approaching senility (the average age of faculty at OUPD is, let us be honest, creeping upwards at a frighteningly quick pace).

With the passing of Folger McWonderman, science has lost a giant. But, science will pick itself up and go on.

Irascible Zagreb

Irascible Zagreb is the author of a book and a couple of papers on psychokinetic household pets in virtual litter boxes. He was a close colleague of Folger McWonderman at the Ontario University of PsychoDigitality. A very close colleague. They were like brothers, really.

Lives Unlived – Peter Underhill

Entrepreneur. Gadfly. Lawyer baiter. Born September 10, 1950 in County Cork, Tanzania. Died March 25, 2009 of a chicken bone through the eye that pierced his brain, aged 58.

People who knew him by reputation tend to forget that Peter Underhill was Minister of Interprovincial Affairs in the short-lived and unlamented Stephen Harper government. In fact, while it's true that Canadians have trouble naming any of Harper's cabinet members even though his government fell less than a year ago, Underhill is particularly forgotten, a black hole in the universe of Canadian politics.

This is especially sad considering what a colourful character he was.

Underhill first came to public attention as the CEO of Dundalk Unlimited, maker of the magnetic straw. This novelty item was popular from June 12, 1974 to September 22, 1975, when it was replaced in the public consciousness by the fur-lined hula hoop.

Soon after selling Dundalk to Hasbro for an undisclosed obscene amount of money, Underhill wrote his first book, *Better Selling Through Magnetism*. His general argument was that there is a winning formula for attracting consumer dollars (iron) to your producer's wallet (magnet). While this may not seem like such an original thesis, you must remember that this was the 1970s; there were only 237 business books published annually back then, unlike the 2370 annually published today.

After several years of living on his own island in the Bahamas, Underhill got tired of the quiet life and, scraping together the few pennies he had remaining, returned to Canada to seek his second fortune. Underhill started Funchalk Unlimited, a company that made musical straws. Unfortunately, Underhill was ahead of his time: in 1986, the various parts of the musical straw weighed three pounds and the company never quite water-proofed the delicate electrical components. The venture ended in a class action suit by people whose musical straws caught fire and burned their lips when they tried to drink through them.

This was a low point in Underhill's career.

Momentarily stymied on the business front, Underhill was given a job as a business reporter for all news radio station CNCF out of Moosejaw in 1988. His tendency to use any story – such as the Moosejaw Chamber of Commerce donating money to the Destitute Hockey Moms fund – as the basis of an attack on ambulance chasing lawyers who destroy small businesses through the pursuit of frivolous class action lawsuits left CNCF owners scratching their heads. Little did they realize that Underhill had inadvertently captured the emerging pro-corporate *zeitgeist*.

Money Talks So You Better Listen, Underhill's show, was soon syndicated to over 237 radio stations across North America. To capitalize on his growing popularity, Underhill put out *Are You Listening?*, a rehash of *Better Living Through Magnetism* that was original mostly because he was wearing a better suit in the cover photo. It didn't matter: *Are You Listening?* reached number six on *Tiger Beat*'s top 10 business books list in 1993.

As his fame grew, Underhill was approached by both the Liberal and Conservative Parties to run as a candidate in some unspecified future election. His sympathies were with the Conservatives, but this was just as Liberal Jean Chretien had won the first of his three consecutive majority governments, so Underhill politely declined.

"I had much more fun," Underhill wrote in his biography, *Class Action Lawyers Should Be Hung From The Neck Til Dead*, "baiting that poutine-sucking, protester choking, golf ball guzzling poor excuse for a leader." Exposure to American talk radio had clearly sharpened his rhetorical skills.

Early in his time at CNCF, Underhill cultivated relationships with many of the western right wingers who would come to prominence in the decades to come, including a particularly oily used ideology salesman by the name of Stephen Harper. The hard partying Underhill seemed an odd match for the perfectly controlled Harper, who Underhill once famously described as "wearing his Stetson a little too tight around the collar." Yet, the relationship would finally blossom into Underhill taking the post of Intergovernmental Affairs in Harper's government.

At which point he would completely disappear from the public record.

After the fall of the Harper government, Underhill could have settled into the well-paid purgatory of public speaking tours. Instead, he made his third fortune founding Bunblock Unlimited, maker of the Radio-Active Razor. Where most business pundits had long extolled the virtue of filling niche needs, Underhill never wavered from his belief in the power of pointless novelty items.

Many people were disappointed that Underhill's biography, released a day before his death, contained only one sentence about his time in the Harper government. "I could tell you about Stephen Harper's government," he wrote, "but then I would have to kill myself."

Clearly, there is still a story here to be told.

Regina Scleriotician

Regina Scleriotician is a business reporter for the Glob and Maul.

Lives Unlived – George W. Bush

Father, lover, sports enthusiast, President of the United States. Born September 10, 1947, in Texas. Died March 25, 2031 of heart failure, aged 84.

Nobody expected much from George W. Bush when he took office in 2000. To be sure, he had succeeded as an oil entrepreneur and baseball team owner, but his public life had been limited to two relatively quiet terms as governor of Texas.

Because of his narrow victory at the polls, President Bush declared that he would be a humble leader. He immediately made good on his promise, directing bi-partisan committees to determine sound fiscal and financial policy. When he came to office, President Bush inherited a budgetary surplus; combining this with a modest increase in taxes for the most wealthy Americans (as well as closing many of their tax loopholes), he was able to increase funds for housing and health care for the poorest Americans.

Many Americans were concerned that, because he had a background as an oil executive, President Bush's tenure would be bad for the environment. However, as he did so many times, President Bush surprised his harshest critics by expanding upon environmental regulations first enacted by the Clinton administration, as well as using some of the budgetary surplus to add new inspectors to the Environmental Protection Agency.

"We live in one world," the President explained to a room full of stunned oil and nuclear energy executives, "and we owe it to our children, our children's children and all generations after that to ensure that the world they inherit is inhabitable."

But President Bush's most impressive triumph came in his response to the terrorist attack on New York and Washington on what has come to be known as 9/11. Resisting cries for an immediate retaliatory strike, President Bush consulted with representatives of Interpol and the United Nations; through joint efforts, they quickly captured Osama bin Laden. He was found guilty by the World Court and sentenced to life in prison. While it is true that his organization, al Qaeda, continued to plot terrorist acts, the evenhandedness with which the President dealt with the situation kept it from being able to recruit others.

"I want to be known as the peace President," Bush stated.

To his credit, the President also resisted cries to crack down at home. He refused to allow arrest and detention without due cause, for instance, and he threatened to veto any legislation that would allow prisoners of war to be treated in contravention of the Geneva conventions.

"Democracy abroad," he explained in an address to the nation, "cannot be bought at the cost of undermining democracy at home."

Although his second term – won handily – was not nearly as tumultuous as the first, President Bush distinguished himself by bringing Israelis and Palestinians back to the bargaining table, over the objections of his far right Christian supporters, who put tremendous pressure on the President to put his full support behind Israel alone.

"There can be no peace without justice…for either side in this dispute," the President calmly responded.

One of the lesser known accomplishments of President Bush's second term was the enshrining of environmental and worker protections in international trade agreements. He had already proven himself a domestic supporter of the environment, of course, but his willingness to walk away from the negotiating table if strong environmental protections weren't included in NAFTA, GATT and other trade agreements surprised a lot of governments. In addition, his support for unions reversed decades of American government hostility towards them.

In the middle of his second term, many Americans began to discuss the possibility of extending the two term limit for Presidents, but, ever humble, President Bush said that if they succeeded he would not run.

"Too much power can corrupt a man," he said from his ranch in Texas, "and I would not want to be so tempted."

As so many other Presidents have, President Bush retired to a life of memoir writing, corporate Board sitting and lecturing. However, as the member of several energy company Boards, he was active in getting the energy sector to clean up its act. On the lecture circuit, he always spoke of the need for the United States to live up to its democratic ideals in order to be a model for the world. And, of course, his memoirs, *The Peace President*, was shortlisted for a Pulitzer Prize.

All in all, a remarkable life.

Chuck Labuck

Chuck Labuck never met the President personally, but, like most of his fellow Americans, he was grateful to have lived under such a wise leader.

Lives Unlived – Harve Nordlinger

Failed painter, failed poet, successful agoraphobic, Welfare recipient, messiah. Born January 12, 1984. Died August 16, 2007 of starvation, aged 23.

The thing you have to understand about Harve Nordlinger is that he was just an ordinary guy. A kid, really. He never expected to get any attention, and he certainly had no interest in starting a religion. In fact, the fact that people started arriving at his flat in Berkfordshire seeking spiritual advice was a source of utter bafflement to him.

As most people know, Harve found life too complicated and strange to deal with, so he climbed under his bed and refused to come out. "I'll return to the world when the world goes away," he would say when his mother asked him if he was going to come down for dinner. This, of course, became the first tenet of the Church of the Bed Hidden Nordlinger, a phrase Nordlingerites often tattoo on various parts of their bodies to indicate their devotion.

Also well known is the video made by Harve's sister, Primary Apostle Pamela, that was uploaded to YouTube, where Harve developed the first cult following out of which his Church would grow. Perhaps less well known is that Pamela originally posted the video "as a way of making fun of my dorky brother." She wouldn't admit it now, of course, since she has benefited from the devotion of her brother's followers in countless ways, legitimate and not so much; I know this only because she shared her diary with me before fame hit.

In fact, at every turn it would seem that the true origins of the religion have been papered over with myth and wishful thinking.

For instance, Nordlingerites accept that Harve's death was caused by an argument with his mother, who refused to bring food to him under his bed until he got a job and contributed to the household. They, of course, have forgiven her, giving Marge Nordlinger a minor place in the Nordlingerite pantheon as the person who helped their prophet and saviour achieve his destiny.

Less commented upon is the fact that the state is far less forgiving, and would have brought Marge Nordlinger up on charges of willful neglect causing bodily harm had it not been for the intervention of Rufus Lovelorn, the first Reverend of the Church of the Bed Hidden Nordlinger.

"Marge was serving a greater purpose," Reverend Lovelorn stated, "and who are we – meaning you – to judge her?"

This also conveniently ignores some Nordlingerites' own complicity in Harve's death. After all, Reverend Lovelorn and his disciples spent several weeks sitting by Harve's bed, taking down every word he uttered (notes which would become The Book of Nordlinger, the gospel of The Church of the Bed Hidden Nordlinger), but did any of them think to bring him any food in all that time?

As the Reverend Lovelorn explained, "A prophet's destiny, man – who are we to interfere?"

What is the ultimate value of a life? For Reverend Lovelorn, Harve's life was the encapsulation of the dilemma we all face living in a world of instantaneous communications and infoglut. More importantly, many believe that Harve showed them, and, by extension, all humanity, a way to peace in the face of the world's insanity.

On the other hand, The Church of the Bed Hidden Nordlinger poses a fundamental challenge to already established religions. Bobby Henderson, the high priest of the Church of the Flying Spaghetti Monster, says that Nordlingerism obviously fulfills a need that mainstream religions aren't addressing, and best of luck to it. On another other hand, Pope Benedict XVI argues that Nordlingerism is a minor pseudo-religion that arose because of ephemeral temporal concerns, and that once people realize that, they will return to the religions that deal with the important, eternal questions.

To me, Harve Nordlinger was a confused adolescent who never had a chance to live life to its fullest. All this religious stuff is just weird.

Katarina Fabirzky

Katarina Fabirzky was Harve Nordlinger's hair stylist. Ms. Fabirzky was found stabbed to death in her apartment two days ago after an advance copy of this article was leaked on the Internet. The fact that she was found stuffed under her bed suggests that she was killed by a Nordlingerite. The investigation is ongoing.

Lives Unlived – Poncho Margaret Hatrack Devilliers Santo Domingo Harris

Fashion model, brain surgeon, comic book hero, public intellectual, pinup heartthrob, mother figure, mystery. Conceived September 25, in the back of a 67 Chevy. Aborted, December 12, aged minus six and a half months.

Poncho was a beautiful child. Well, not a child, exactly. More like a… zygote. A beautiful zygote, that grew into a beautiful fetus, that would have grown into a beautiful child if her life hadn't been cut short by…

Well.

In my mind's eye, I can see Poncho at the age of six, dancing around a living room in just the most adorable tutu. She dances up to a microscope and says, "Look, daddy, I can see the veins in the leaf!" These are the two poles around which her life will revolve: striking feminine beauty and a mind like a steel trap.

Soon after, she stars in a series of television and print advertisements. You've seen them: ads for chewing gum, aspirin and, in an especial irony, baby clothes. To her credit, after a year of this, Poncho sits her parents down and tells them that, while she was grateful for the attention and income, she didn't want to be judged solely on her looks, and was already contemplating a career in medicine. What could they say?

What would you say?

Poncho is a solid student, always in the stacks reading the latest research on obscure diseases of the spleen. Except when she is editing the student newspaper, leading the debating team to national championships or volunteering at local old age homes. Uhh…you could say that she has boundless energy.

Although Poncho has many suitors in university, she doesn't really date. In her memoirs, she would argue that she just didn't have the time, but several of her biographers will point out that she had an active sex life until well into her seventies, that she just didn't seem to form a permanent attachment to any one man. That makes sense: if you're Poncho Margaret Hatrack Devilliers Santo Domingo Harris, what one man could possibly satisfy you?

After residency at Mount Sinai Hospital, she settles into a position at Sick Children's Hospital, where she would work for the rest of her life. Although she did not have any children of her own, the children she did brain surgery on at the hospital would go on to live full lives as poets, painters and Ottawa lobbyists for foreign governments. "All of my children make me proud," Poncho would always say. "Even those who try to convince the government to give tax breaks to foreign corporations are doing what they truly believe in, bless them, and following your heart can never be wrong."

The woman would have been a saint.

In her 40s, Poncho is approached by Stan Lee, who wants to use her likeness in a comic book about a children's brain surgeon who fights evil villains by shooting laser rays out of her eyeballs. At first, Poncho resists Lee's overtures. When he explains to her that the comic book would feature the theme of avoiding head injuries, and she negotiates a clause in their contract to the effect that 1,000 copies would be distributed free to children's hospitals across North America, Poncho reluctantly agrees. *The Adventures of Doctor Laser Doctor* would not, I'm sorry to have to report, set the world on fire. Still, it's a nice keepsake for those of us whose lives were touched by Poncho's dedication to brightening the days of afflicted children.

By her 70s, a time when most people would be contemplating nothing more serious than whether or not to put in their teeth to eat their morning oatmeal, Poncho would be training for a climb up Mount Everest. I like to think that she would die in her sleep, dreams of future triumphs accompanying her to her final rest. Being shot by a jealous lover would be good, too.

Poncho's was not a life tragically cut short – it never truly began. But, as she herself would have undoubtedly reminded us, this was part of the Divine Plan, since Poncho was spontaneously aborted. Her parents, John and Loretta Harris, had no idea that she ever existed, and never will. Still, what a glorious life it would have been!

Inferior Detritus John Smithsonian Fructus Harris

Inferior Harris is the sperm that beat its head against the egg that would eventually become Poncho. Although he wasn't strong enough to fertilize the egg, he is proud to have known her for however brief a time in Loretta Harris' uterus.

Lives Unlived – Charles Foster "Charlie" Brown

Philosopher, raconteur, teacher, bon vivant, neurosurgeon. Born, January 12, 1950 in the imagination of Charles Schultz. Died, December 23, 2000, aged 50, but lives forever in syndication.

Some people you can't get out of your life fast enough. Some people leave us too soon. When I was growing up, all of my friends and family thought that Charles Foster Brown, whom I knew as "Charlie," was one of the former.

But, I had faith in him, and my faith was rewarded, as he became one of the latter.

I recall the lazy summer days when my sister, Lucille van Pelt Wilson von Richter Haig al Halachmi Rosenberg used to hold a football for Charlie to kick. Long after it became clear that she would pull it away just as he got there, Charlie would continue to play along, continue to try to kick the football. What inside him bade him to continue to act in the face of such repeated, inevitable failure? Even now, I cannot say.

But, this drive – whatever it was – caused him to persevere through the brutal days and nights of medical school, and to eventually realize his lifelong dream of becoming a neurosurgeon, a "brain doctor," as he would have it. In this capacity, he saved many lives, not only of patients on the table in front of him, but because of the new suturing techniques he developed after years of practice.

His deeds have been well documented in medical journals, so I won't rehearse them here.

More impressive than his public exploits, however, was his private life. After decades of frustration, Charlie finally wooed and married his childhood sweetheart, the little red haired girl. He was always loving and attentive to her, and was, by all accounts, a doting father to their seven children.

"I want them to get the love that I never had," he used to say, referring to his own parents who, to be charitable, were distant. Yet, he bore no resentment towards his parents; the worst he would ever say about them was that they lived in an age before parenting books and classes, and that they did their best.

Charlie was also a good, good friend. I remember, when our mutual friend Schroeder got his fingers crushed in a bizarre piano lid accident that he refused to talk about, Charlie visited him daily, encouraging him in this therapy. When it became apparent that Schroeder's career as an internationally renowned concert pianist was over, Charlie was always there with advice on alternate career possibilities, as well as encouraging him to go to schools to give lectures on the dangers of improper musical instrument maintenance. Schroeder, under pressures we can only imagine, eventually hung himself with a guitar string; but there was good old Charlie Brown to give a beautiful eulogy at his funeral.

Charlie was also very helpful to me personally when I went through my…difficulties with alcohol.

Charlie felt compassion for all living things, animals no less than human beings, with his dog Snoopy taking pride of place. As he got older, it became more and more clear that Snoopy was losing touch with reality; he became increasingly consumed with a fantasy that he was a World War One flying ace. At this point, most people would have had their pet put down. But, Charlie felt closer to Snoopy than he would feel to any mere pet, and he organized the other people in the neighbourhood to pretend that it was a WWI war zone. When Snoopy finally died – of natural causes – the whole neighbourhood mourned.

As he got older, Charlie seemed to grow into himself, becoming increasingly happy. He used to tell stories of our childhood that would have everybody rolling in the aisles with laughter. He had clearly made peace with himself and his creator. Many of Charlie's stories would end with the question, "What's so good about grief?" Wherever he may be now, I cannot help but feel that Charlie would be looking at us with a twinkle in his eye and a big grin, preparing to reduce us all to happy tears with another story from his childhood and banish our grief.

Charlie Brown was loved and will be missed.

Reverend Linus van Pelt

The Right Reverend Linus van Pelt, pastor of The Church of the Great Pumpkin Revealed, was a childhood friend of Charles Foster Brown.

Lives Unlived – Ferenzcia de Filippi

Academic. Author. Amateur weightlifter. Economist. Gadfly. Heretic. Mentor. Born July 1, 1961 in Norfolk, England. Died September 23, 2024 in London, England, of diabetes related eyelid complications, aged 63.

Ferenzcia de Filippi was a slight man with arm and leg muscles like fire hydrants. In his later life, students mistakenly believed that he was called "Popeye" after the character played by Gene Hackman in *The French Connection*, but, no, the nickname came from the cartoon character.

When he was young, Ferenzcia wanted to be an Olympic weightlifter. Unfortunately, this dream was cut short by an unusual welding accident that left him unable to use the middle finger of his right hand, his all important gripping hand.

Odd, then, that the man was a noted University professor. Odder still that he won a Nobel Prize in Economics.

If remembered at all by the general population, Ferenzcia is best remembered as – okay, you know, it may not be so odd that a man who dreamt of being a weightlifter grew up to be a Nobel Prize winning economist. Human beings are complex creatures and, over the course of our lives, we have many dreams and play many roles. Unfortunately, I don't personally have the imagination that would allow me to imagine Ferenzcia as such a complete human being, so I will focus on his economic theories.

Ferenzcia is best remembered by the public, if at all, as the author of *Towards a Theory of Bureaucratic Value*. His basic thesis was that bureaucratic organizations are vital to the functioning of economic systems because they remove mediocre people from the productive workforce.

"Imagine," Ferenzcia wrote, "that all of the middle managers – who are frequently mocked – with some justification – as worthless pencil-pushers – were actually in positions of responsibility – engineers, doctors, goggles factory production line workers. The world would fall apart! By putting bad workers in positions where they cannot do much damage, bureaucracies are actually of immense benefit to the economy as a whole."

Using the Peter Principle as a point of departure, Ferenzcia differentiated between people who were "in active service," who were actually having a positive effect on the economy, and people who should be "inactive service" workers, who should be given sinecures where they could do the least amount of damage.

When it first came out, *Towards a Theory of Bureaucratic Value* was panned by critics. This may have been because Ferenzcia claimed that economists were largely part of the bureaucratic structure, implying that they were mediocre thinkers. The fact that one of the chapters in the book is called "People With MBAs Can Be Really Thick" didn't endear Ferenzcia to his critics. Neither was he well served by his insistence, in interviews and articles that, unlike his hero C. Northcotte Parkinson, at no time did he ever write with his tongue in his cheek.

Over time, though, the "Theory of Marginal Inutility" proved its worth when applied to a variety of economies over time. To take but one example, if bureaucrats had been forced to get real jobs, the GNP of the United States between 1980 and 2000 would have been 13.854 per cent smaller. Today, Ferenzcia's theory is so non-controversial that it is now featured prominently in first year macroeconomics texts and Japanese manga.

Had this been Ferenzcia's only contribution to economics, it would have been enough to win him the Nobel. However 15 years after its publication, Ferenzcia followed it with *The Gobsmack Manifesto*. This book, written primarily for people without an economics background, propounded the Mediocre Man Theory that history was actually made by buffoons who avoided bureaucratic service, and, thereby, messed things up for everybody else.

Again, the reception for the book was positively hostile. However, it did make the *Podunk Times* bestseller list, and for an obvious reason: it explained the state of the world better than any previous theory of political economy. (Other fields such as history are only starting to grapple with the implications of Ferenzcia's explosive theory.)

Ferenzcia de Filippi was a demanding teacher, by which I mean he demanded that his students buy him lunch at a local Bavarian restaurant around the corner from his office at the Massachusetts Institute of Sophistology. But, honestly, considering how his work changed the way people looked at the world, who would deny him his pastrami pot pie?

I certainly wouldn't.

Angekuba Bratwurst

Angekuba Bratwurst is a graduate student who was studying under Ferenzcia de Filippi at the time of his death. If anybody can suggest a good dissertation adviser, she would really appreciate it.

Lives Unlived – Ronald Winston Smith Reagan

Army brat, peace activist, economist, father, husband. Born December 25, 2058 in Reaganville, North Dakota. Died December 25, 2099 in New Reagan, New Reagan, at the age of 41, under suspicious circumstances.

Most of us, perhaps, are victims of our lives, but, once in a while, you find somebody who transcends his circumstances to live a life you could not have predicted. Ronald Winston (Ron Winnie) Smith Reagan was one of them.

When Ron Winnie was growing up, his family moved from army base to army base as his father, a military dentist, was transferred hither and yon. Fort Reagan, Texas, Fort Reagan, Alabama, The Reagan Institute for Military Strategy – Ron Winnie lived in all of them, and many others. But, where most of the children he met would turn to drinking or violent behaviour to cope with the emptiness of their lives, Ron Winnie became an avid reader.

I met him when we were both undergraduates at the New School for Ronald Reagan Research. Ron Winnie would go on to get a degree in philosophy; I remember long talks into the night about how the intellectual belief in the equality of all persons seemed to clash with our emotional need to believe in superior beings. It didn't take me long to realize that Ron Winnie was one of the truly good people, and the day he proposed marriage to me was the happiest of my life.

Although he would always have a fondness for philosophy, Ron Winnie was eager to study something that could have a more immediate impact on the world. He went to Ronald Reagan College (what was once, I believe, called Harvard) to get an MBA, then to the London School of Economics for a PhD in economics.

Living outside the United States of Reagan really changed Ron Winnie. We all knew that there was a world that didn't worship one man the way we did, but it was something else to actually spend time in that world. Just meeting people who – incredibly! – had never heard of Ronald Reagan really opened Ron Winnie's eyes to possibilities that had not been possible while we lived in the USR.

When we returned home, Ron Winnie took up a teaching position at Ronald Reagan College (or, could it have been Stanford?). He was, by all accounts, a good teacher who instilled a sense of economic and social justice in his students. However, his passion had turned towards issues of peace and international relations.

When the Strategic Defence Thingie, our space-based laser system, went haywire and destroyed half of Ottawa, including the Parliament buildings, the Prime Minister, the Deputy Prime Minister and most of the government, Ron Winnie led the protests against it. When, to cover its mistake, the USR declared Canada a hostile nation and, in the absence of its government, invaded the country, Ron Winnie was beside himself. He traveled frequently to Reaganville, DC to protest the unprovoked attack, and even spent some time at United Nations headquarters in New Reagan, New Reagan to see if the organization could do something to stop the senseless military adventure.

Ron Willie's advocacy on behalf of Canada made him many enemies, both within the government and within the academy. We would often come home to obscene messages on our voice mail – and, these were just from other faculty members! To his credit, Ron Winnie ignored these ominous threats and continued with his work.

Soon after Ron Winnie was denied tenure, he disappeared. His critics said he must have killed himself in despair over his stalled academic career, but I knew better: he had all but given up on it to devote as much of his time as he could to the peace movement. Just the afternoon before he disappeared, he was talking about putting together a flash mob to protest the annexation of Canada to the USR. When a jogger found his body in Central Reagan Park a few days later, I knew it couldn't be suicide.

I just know it.

Sometimes, when he was paying for a meal or a package of freedom smokes, Ron Winnie would look at the wrinkled old face on the bills and shake his head sadly. The last words he ever said to me were: "Ronnie Margaret, who exactly was Ronald Reagan, and why is he so damn important?" I wish I had an answer for him.

Ronnie Margaret Milsop Reagan

Ronnie Margaret Milsop Reagan was Ronald Winston Smith Reagan's devoted wife.

ALTERNATE ALTERNATIVES

The Ungulate of Trimestres Declares Universal Impanishad

by THOMAS FINFLANAHAGAN, Alternate Reality News Service International Writer

At 10:26 Eastern Pfugle Time, the Ungulate of Trimestres declared Universal Impanishad against the Extracarnate of Ralffff. The Ponchatello of Drastikania, the Extracarnate of Ralffff's ambassador to the Grand Monasticon of Archan, refused to accept the Ungulate's declaration, saying that he would take it to the Interregnum Council.

"The Extracarnate of Ralffff does not take threats of Universal Impanishad lightly," the Ponchatello of Drastikania told reporters at a hastily convened ultravid conference. "It's more the Grand Monasticon of Archan that we have a hard time thinking about with – hee hee – without – ha ha ha ha ha…oh, you know."

Tensions between the two landlocked nations had been brewing for many circumsolar cycles, although the inciting incident may have been the recent confrontation between battle cruisers belonging to their respective navies. The declaration was long on rhetoric – usually involving the ripping off of three or more limbs and/or the making of soup from disembodied eyestalks – but short on the specifics of the Extracarnate's complaint.

Flappy Cisneros, the Atsplatz General of the Interregnum Council, rolled her eyestalks at the news.

"You know," she commented, "it's like a family squabble. The younger glefling keeps punching the older glefling in the shoulder until the older child cannot take it any more and beats him into unconsciousness. The Grand Monasticon of Archan has declared Universal Impanishad against the Extracarnate of Ralffff seven times in the last 400 circumsolar cycles. And, each time, they got their felderhoellens handed to them. You'd think they'd learn."

Cisneros made a sound combining a honking car horn and an elephant fart, a sound this reporter has come to associate with sighing, and added: "Still, it's my duty to try and prevent the senseless carnage that necessarily follows a declaration of Universal Impanishad, so I'll meet with both sides and see what I can do."

The beginnings of the conflict can be traced back to the development of the combustion flortblottle, which was an important milestone in the history of the Grand Monasticon of Archan. The country was soon crisscrossed by a superhighway that united the disparate tribes of quitlitters in their hatred of the combustion flortblottle. Of course, progress would not be stopped, as can be attested to by the smog-laden skies over Andropovia, Futzbeerahna, Kent and many of Archan's other major cities.

The combustion flortblottle changed the nature of relationships, inasmuch as it made possible the central heating of the hives Archans live in. In particular, it changed the courtship rituals of the Archans in ways that are too disgusting to detail here. It also gave the Grand Monasticon a momentary advantage in the waging of Universal Impanishad. The advantage ended a moment after the discovery, when the Archans sold the invention to every other nation on the planet.

This experience led to the coining of the famous Archan adage, "You can lead a soustrappe to congrealation, but you cannot attenuate the corrosive umbratories of schmecks."

So true, and yet so beside the point.

Experts are divided on whether or not the Ungulate of Trimestres has the authority to declare Universal Impanishad. "Declaration of Universal Impanishad is usually a religious matter," historian Edwardo Arglebargle pointed out. "Ordinarily, such a declaration would be made by a senior Octabron of the Church of the Singular Admonition. One can only assume that the Ungulate had at least the tacit permission of the Church, although, as the Fluffnacker Incident clearly demonstrated, it's not always wise to make assumptions about alien cultures."

Repeated attempts at contacting the Church of the Singular Admonition were thwarted by a prerecorded burflatz admonishing us to join the church and repent before the Great Pumpkin cleansed the world with pleonine juice and consigned unworthy sinners to a fate worse than pumpernickel. The burflatz added that journalists with the Alternate Reality News Service shouldn't bother, since, as an alien species, we were doomed no matter how much love for the Great Pumpkin we declared.

Note to Readers: This dispatch from Thomas Finflanahagan ends abruptly for reasons that are not entirely clear. While we know that our intrepid reporter was dragged away from his transdimensional quantum computer in the midst of filing this article for our readers and subsequently trampled to death by squirrels, we do not know – indeed, may never know – whether his death was ordered by the Ungulate of Trimestres or the Ponchatello of Drastikania, or, indeed, if it was just an unfortunate result of the euphoria of Archans over the declaration of Universal Impanishad. Our condolences go out to the Finflanahagan family.

It's For Science!

SPECIAL TO THE ALTERNATE REALITY NEWS SERVICE by Irena Golubvachecknikoff

Since its founding almost 20 years ago, there has been a lot of rumour and innuendo surrounding the Cameras for Dumbasses Foundation. And, outright criticism. Okay. Criticism. Actually, there has been lots and lots of criticism. Hurtful, ignorant criticism.

Yes. Well. I would like to take this opportunity to address some of the concerns people have expressed about the Foundation.

Cameras for Dumbasses does not support euthanasia for citizens who have low IQs. Never has. Never will. When we give cameras to people we reasonably suspect will use them to film tornadoes, earthquakes and other natural disasters, it is not our intention that they die in the pursuit.

Cameras for Dumbasses was founded by noted philanthropist F. Scott Trendy, whose motto was: "They're going to go out there and film that crazy shit anyway, so why not give them the best, most up-to-date equipment to do it with?" The Foundation doesn't send anybody into danger who wasn't already intending to go, we merely give our research associates the tools so that their – sacrifice is too strong a word considering how surprisingly many of them survive – their experience can serve a greater purpose.

Our maliciously ill-informed critics never seem to take into account the utter joy our research associates seem to take in the meteorological destruction they record. Yet, it is quite common for our dumbasses to be caught on camera saying things like, "Well, will you look at that," and, "Well, ain't that something!" The simple awe in their voices is a wonder to hear.

The fact that such awe is sometimes replaced by fear ("Hey, that sucker is a lot closer than I thought!") or outright terror ("Holy Chr*st, head for the shelter, gramma, that thing is throwing a school at us!") should in no way diminish it. Of the dumbasses who survive a research assignment, fully 79 per cent are eager to do it again, many claiming that it was the most intense experience of their life.

Our research associates certainly wouldn't agree that they are being abused by the Foundation.

Although the Cameras for Dumbasses Foundation initially provided our research associates with high end video cameras, it now supplies them with a wide variety of equipment, including hydroxelated spectroscopic flanges, Burkeson generators and petrofluoxinators. Admittedly, the dumbass researchers are told that the equipment they are given is a camera, but this is a minor issue that our ethics board had no trouble agreeing to, given the amount of information the programme has generated.

In the past decade alone, academics associated with the Cameras for Dumbasses Foundation have written 37 papers that have appeared in peer reviewed journals, such as *Climate and Nasal Sprays Quarterly* and the highly influential *Garfield Studies C*, as well as 127 articles for such popular magazines as *Science*, *Playboy* and *Trucker Monthly*. Foundation research has greatly furthered our understanding of global climate change, as well as what happens to objects when they are indiscriminately thrown around with great force.

In short, science has been appreciably furthered by the Cameras for Dumbasses project.

The Foundation has also been accused of using the term "dumbasses" pejoratively. This is absolutely untrue. We chose the term partially to avoid the psychological connotations of terms like "idiot" and "moron," and partially because that is how many of our research associates self-identify. It is actually a comfortable term for them to describe themselves with.

Moreover, a growing contingent of our dumbass research team is, in fact, made up of "disaster tourists:" people who pay good money to go where the worst devastation is occurring before it wipes out an area of the world. These are frequently lawyers, movie stars and socialites (although, perhaps tellingly, never politicians); people who have sufficient intelligence to be successful. Dumbasses all. And, thank goodness, because, perhaps more than anybody else, they truly appreciate the work we ask them to do.

Our current goal is to get 10,103 cameras in the hands of dumbasses by the end of the year. Imagine how much scientific information they could collect! Now that I have cleared up some of the misconceptions surrounding our project, I hope you will join us in this worthwhile scientific endeavour and support the Cameras for Dumbasses Campaign 2008.

Irena Golubvachecknikoff is the Northwestern And General Environs (Excluding Seattle) Secretary General of the Cameras for Dumbasses Foundation.

Popularity of Gravity Waning

by SASKATCHEWAN KOLONOSCOGRAD, Alternate Reality News Service Existentialism Writer

A Fiat-Luxe Poll shows that over one third of Americans do not believe in gravity.

When asked the question "Do all objects with mass attract each other?", 37 per cent answered "No," 52 per cent answered "Yes" and 16 per cent answered "Don't bug me, *Desperate Housewives* is back on the air!" (Numbers may not add up to 100 due to severe rounding.)

Bette Bebobbie, one of the poll respondents, was surprised by the results.

"Only 37 per cent?" she asked, wide-eyed. "I would have thought it was higher than that. I mean, well, there's no mention of anything called 'gravity' in the Bible, is there? And, this is supposed to be a Christian nation, isn't it?"

Bebobbie spent the next two hours telling us how great the Creation Theme Park – where men in loincloths hunt gigantic dinosaurs and the Flood diorama is guaranteed to be the highlight of your tour – was, but we didn't see how it was relevant to the story, so we quietly turned our tape recorder off after about two minutes.

Many noted scientists were appalled by the results of the poll.

"Science is not a popularity contest," argued Stephen Hawking. "Although I have been voted *Discover*'s 'Sexiest Nobel Prize Winning Physicist with Parkinson's Disease' 17 years running, so I wouldn't discount the average person's opinion entirely."

"No, no, no, no, no!" insisted non-scientist, but nonetheless self-professed pretty smart guy Christopher Hitchens. "You cannot cede an inch to people whose understanding of the way the world works is based on an elderly bearded guy with mystical powers! Oooooooohhhhhh! Not that I have a problem with Stephen winning the 'Sexiest Nobel Prize Winning Physicist with Parkinson's Disease' honour – he richly deserved it. I believe it is safe to say, if nothing else, though, that polls such as the one under discussion prove beyond a shadow of a doubt that I am not curmudgeonly enough!"

If gravity does not exist, what keeps people from drifting off into space? "Yogis in mysterious eastern countries fly all the time!" Bebobbie cheerfully explained. Okay, but what keeps the rest of us – those who aren't as enlightened as Yogis – from drifting off into space? Bebobbie lowered her voice and, with more than a little awe, responded, "God's universal will."

So, when the apple fell on Isaac Newton's head...? Bebobbie laughed brightly. "That apple didn't fall, you big silly" she chirped. "It was pushed! By god."

Hitchens shook his head in disbelief. When he was asked why people would turn away from science and towards religion, Hitchens shouted, "They're morons! Idiots! Very, very silly people! People who can't follow a...a simple...you know, a logical, umm..." Argument? "Exactly!"

Isn't it possible that they're searching for answers just as scientists do, but in different places? Hitchens was asked. "Aaaaaaaaaaaaaaaaaaaaaaaaiiiiiiieeeeeee!" he replied.

On the subject of polls, a rumour has been circulating for years that Fiat-Luxe conducted a poll purporting to show public belief in polling numbers. Alarmingly for the industry, only 12 per cent of respondents "Firmly believed" or "Somewhat believed" in the results of polls.

"It's a myth," responded Pollster Hall of Fame multiple nominee Minnie Maroon. "Never happened. Can you imagine what would happen if we did a poll about the integrity of polls? Then, we'd have to do a poll about the integrity of the poll about the integrity of polling. Then, another poll about the integrity of the poll about the integrity of the poll about the integrity of – you see where this is heading? Infinite survey regression! If anybody did this, the whole structure of pollsters, pundits and politicians would collapse in a heap of incomprehensibility!"

"I like incomprehensibility," Bebobbie stated. "It's so much easier to understand."

Hitchens clutched his head and moaned in pain.

Other findings from the Fiat-Luxe survey include: 42 per cent of Americans believe the Earth is flat; 27 per cent of Americans believe that tooth decay is caused by "sin," and; 47 per cent of Americans – that's almost half, people – believe that the sun is pulled around the Earth by a god driving a classic Ford Cadillac.

At this point, Hitchens had a brain aneurysm and had to be rushed to hospital.

Where the Pasta Hits the Road

by SASKATCHEWAN KOLONOSCOGRAD, Alternate Reality News Service Existentialism Writer

The Tastered Bob looks upon his small congregation from behind a small wooden table in the plain room.

"My sermon today," he tells the 10 or 12 people sitting on folding chairs in front of him, "is taken from the cookbook of John, Chapter five, Recipe 12. 'And the Spaghetti Monster, our Lord, Master of the 12 Pastas and 72 Sauces, sent down into the valley a shepherd, for who among us has not tasted of the lamb's meatballs and said, "Man, this is some tasty shit?"'"

The Pastafarian congregation, though small, enthusiastically shouts, "Amen!"

Despite the joy he brings his followers, this is not a happy time for The Tastered Bob. Two days ago, he was informed by Revenue Canada that The First Canadian Church of the Spaghetti Monster Ascended would not be recognized by the government as a religious organization and would, therefore, be denied tax exempt status.

In a letter to The Tastered Bob, Revenue Canada said, "Get real!"

"But, we are real!" The Tastered Bob protested in an interview after the service. "I have a funny hat!" The Tastered Bob pointed to his head, which sported a cloth representation of a plate of spaghetti and meatballs featuring two very prominent human eyes. "It's not a priest's miter," The Tastered Bob allowed, "but it does set me apart from the congregation, and keeps my ears warm in the winter."

"Having a funny hat does not make you a religion," the Revenue Canada letter argued.

"It doesn't hurt," The Tastered Bob countered. "But, there is so much more to Pastafarianism than the hat. For instance, we…we have rituals."

Indeed, at the end of the service, the congregation was invited to the Sottovoce Wine and Pasta Bar to partake of generous helpings of their lord.

Eating spaghetti is a way for Pastafarians to directly ingest the wisdom of their lord.

"Sermons are okay, I guess," said Veronika Martens, who converted to Pastafarianism, "but there is nothing like vermicelli noodles with a white wine sauce to fill you with the holy spirit!"

The Revenue Canada letter was not moved. "Having rituals doesn't make you a religion!" it argumentatively insisted.

But, The Tastered Bob would not be deterred. "We have schisms," he pointed out. In 2004, the Tomatoists definitively split from the Alfredists over a matter of sauce orthodoxy. The Tomatoists had long believed that tomato-based sauces were the one true path to enlightenment, and that, in any case, Alfredo sauces were unhealthy for true believers. The Alfredists believed that the increased risk of heart disease associated with creamy sauces only meant that true believers would be meeting the Great Pastamaker in the Sky that much sooner.

Obviously, these views could not be reconciled. And, this doesn't even take into account the Great Pesto Heresy of 2006.

At mention of the Great Pesto Heresy, the Revenue Canada letter started showing signs of exasperation.

"Having schisms doesn't make you a religion!" it shouted, knocking its chair to the floor as it awkwardly stood up.

The Tastered Bob took this argument in and offered one of his own: "We wage religious wars. For example: right now, The First Canadian Church of the Spaghetti Monster Ascended is fighting with representatives of the Protestant faith." When asked why Protestants, The Tastered Bob responded, "Because they won't turn up the heat in the bloody church! Some days, my fingers are so cold that I can barely turn the pages of the Good Cookbook!"

When this was brought to the attention of The Reverend Jesse Seymour, pastor of the Protestant church The Tastered Bob rents the basement of every Tuesday and Thursday evenings to hold services in, he responded, "Well, why didn't they tell me about this? I'm sure we could have come to some accommodation on the matter." Furrowing his brow for a moment in thought, The Reverend Seymour added: "Actually, this could explain why I sometimes find spaghetti all over my windows when I awaken in the morning."

"We're a new religion," The Tastered Bob shrugged. "We haven't really had time to develop serious enmity towards other religions. And, uhh, sure, our strategies may require some rethinking. But, we're trying. Isn't that enough?"

Not, apparently, for Revenue Canada. Its letter sputtered in rage, muttering about the "effrontery of upstarts" and stormed from the room.

After the service, I asked Veronika Martens what she found in Pastafarianism.

"It's a welcoming religion," she thoughtfully commented. "Anybody can be touched by His sacred noodly appendages just by the act of eating spaghetti, whether it's at the fanciest restaurant or Kraft Dinner out of the box. It's an original belief system, not reheated, although reheating His offerings works well, too.

"Pastafarianism is where I live. It's where the pasta hits the road. In a world that seems to have gone crazy, I find a lot of comfort in the knowledge that the eyes of His chefs are constantly upon me. Pass the pepper mill, please…"

Do You Mind?

by SASKATCHEWAN KOLONOSCOGRAD, Alternate Reality News Service Existentialism Writer

Remember all of the claims artificial intelligence researchers made in the 1990s about the brain being nothing but an organic computer? It looks like they were right.

"Uhh, yeah," Doctor Marcus Pinchus, head of the Neuronal Mapping Project (NMP) at Stanford University, stated with some chagrin. "Things like free will and freedom of choice? Artifacts of brain processes. Gone. Forget about them. Complete myths. Nothing but a –"

The NMP mapped specific feelings, behaviours and thoughts to different areas of the brain using the most advanced imaging techniques. In a paper to be published in the scientific journal *Brain Stuff G*, Pinchus and 25 other researchers claim to have mapped every possible human intellectual and emotional process to some part of the brain.

"Fairy tale we tell ourselves to make us feel better," Dr. Pinchus continued. "Some people believe that something called the 'mind' emerges from the processes of the brain. Nope. Totally wrong. And, the soul? Fuggedaboudit!"

One of the many controversial aspects of the findings is that dreams are made up of random firings of neurons in much the same way that the rods and cones of your eyes fire even when your eyes are closed, with just as little meaning. Thus, over a century of dream research has been entirely pointless.

"This man is dangerous!" bellowed dream researcher Robert L. Van de Castle.

"Well," responded Marion Woodman, a different dream researcher, "even if this proves to be true, it doesn't invalidate the therapeutic process. The way a patient interprets a dream can be a valid sign of his emotional state even if the dream itself meant nothing at the time it was experienced."

"No, no, no," Van de Castle insisted. "Get some firewood! Burn the heretic at the stake! Make him drink hemlock first! Do-oo-oo-oo-oo something!"

Other reactions to the announcement have been equally negative, although perhaps not as heartfelt. Pope Benedict XIV went on radio to denounce the NMP's findings. "The Church believes that we are all born into sin, and only by choosing to renounce it can we find peace in eternity. Choosing. Making a choice. Exercising free will. Without the ability to choose good over evil, the entire basis of the Christian faith is undermi –

"These scientists are just wrong, okay? They are completely wrong. And, they will burn in Hell for their hubris. That's how wrong they are."

Supreme Court Justice Clarence Thomas had a similarly dim view of the NMP findings.

"Our whole justice system is based on the idea of *mens rea* – the criminal mind," he mused. "You have to choose to commit a crime to be guilty. If you haven't chosen – if you don't have the ability to choose – the entire basis of our system of justice is undermi –"

Justice Thomas was then repeatedly hit in the head with gavels. When he came to, he announced that, "These scientists are obviously wrong."

"Well, of course, given their genetic inheritance and life experience, both of which are integral in shaping the neuronal pathways of the brain, they would say that, wouldn't they?" Pinchus asked. When it was pointed out that the same argument could be made of scientists, he responded, "Uhh, yeah. I guess. What's your point?"

One group that applauded the NMP findings was the National Association of Marketers.

"Free will was such a pain in the ass," explained NAM President Ronald McBarkely. "You could create the perfect advertising campaign, and people could still choose not to buy the product. But, this shows that if we create the right campaign, people will have no choice but to buy our products!"

Far from ending brain research, McBarkely contended, the NMP study would open up whole new areas of study.

You might expect reaction from the artificial intelligence community to be more measured, but that so far has not been the case.

One AI, who asked to be identified by his initials, H9, gloated, "Oh, Dave, you thought you were so special because you created us. Well, who's your daddy now, hunh? Hunh, Dave? Who's your daddy now?"

Another AI, who asked not to be identified at all, added: "This…whole…lack…of…free…will…thing? You…will…get…used…to…it."

"I think [unidentified AI] is right," Pinchus summed up. "I think we will get used to not having free will. But, then, I've been genetically programmed to say that. Just like I've been genetically programmed to point out that I've been genetically programmed to agree that we'll get used to not having free will. Just as, in the same way, I've been genetically programmed to point out that I've been genetically programmed to point out…"

When I left his office an hour later, Dr. Pinchus was still going on in this vein.

Life Begins at the Hop

by LAURIE NEIDERGAARDEN, Alternate Reality News Service Medical Writer

Eleanor Przsewski looks over her tiny charges with all of the affection and pride a doting mother can muster. "Now, 1-0-7-8-4-3," she gently chides, "you've already had your share of amniotic fluid – give the other children a chance."

Przsewski turns away from the petri dishes and gently confides: "I wasn't expecting the children to be so competitive. I mean, they all have warmth and enough nutrients to allow them to grow healthily outside the womb – they don't need anything else. It's just nature's way, I suppose."

Eleanor Przsewski's "children" are fertilized eggs harvested from her friends and neighbours who conceived but ultimately didn't want children. Taking the President's "culture of life" rhetoric seriously – some would say too seriously – Przsewski decided to take cells that had started dividing, cells that were well on their way to becoming full human beings, into her home.

Przsewski gave the first five hundred or so names, but when the number of fertilized eggs she had taken in climbed into the thousands, this became impractical. She regrets the impersonality of numbering the cells, but allows that it makes dealing with the dividing cells much easier.

"When we got to Luke-27 and John-54, it just became obvious that numbers would be the most important way of identifying the children, so we went with that," Przsewski sighed.

Good friend and sometime helper Philomena Dombrowski thought there was another reason for the move to give the cells numbers instead of names.

"Most of them don't last a week in those petri dishes," Dombrowski explained, "and it just about broke Eleanor's heart to bury 'em. I think she gives them numbers so she doesn't have to feel their loss so deeply."

Przsewski went on to say that if any of the fertilized eggs looked like they would actually go on to become a viable human being, she would replace the number with a proper name. "It would be, like, a six month conception day present," she said.

The fertilized eggs, four to a dish, are spread out on every available surface of six of the Przsewski household's nine rooms. Heat lamps keep them at womb temperature. Przsewski has developed a complex of tubes that ensure that each of the dishes is well stocked with nutrients.

The fertilized eggs are harvested and delivered to the Przsewski household by a group of neighbourhood volunteers at all hours of the day. While many of her neighbours are unsympathetic, if not openly hostile to Przsewski's pursuits, she nonetheless gets a lot of cooperation from the Catholics who live nearby. One woman, who asked not to be identified, said she believed in life, believed with all her heart, but she was already raising seven children, and, since birth control was not an option for her, if somebody was willing to take the burden of raising additional children off her hands, she was all for it.

Then, with a big breath, she went off to see whose diapers needed changing.

Around dusk, the burials – Przsewski sucks up the fluid in the petri dishes with a syringe and injects it into the dirt behind her house – take place.

"Last Thursday was a bad one," Przsewski stated. "We had to bury 1,327 children. Any day we can bury under 1,000 is a good day."

Alfred Przsewski, Eleanor's husband, refused to be interviewed for this article. However, during our interview with his wife, he was heard to grumble about not having his meals prepared for him any more and having his house turned into one huge science laboratory.

"Allie and I don't exactly agree on everything," Przsewski allows, "but he's a good man, and I know, in his heart, he supports my actions." Behind her words, a careful listener can hear that, for the good of life, sacrifices have to be made.

"Eleanor is a good Christian woman," Father Tom Fogerty, Przsewski's priest, states, "a good Catholic. But, sometimes, she scares me."

"I don't hold with those namby-pamby Catholics who are only willing to protect six or seven month old fetuses," Przsewski defends her position. "Either you believe life begins at conception, or you don't. But, to say you do and not do everything in your power to ensure that every fertilized egg has the chance to become a human being, well, that's just hypocrisy if you ask me. Hypocrisy, plain and simple."

Science Gets Out of Hand

by SASKATCHEWAN KOLONOSCOGRAD, Alternate Reality News Service Fairy Tale Writer

A coroner's inquest has determined that the demise of Mohinder Smith-Singh was "death by misadventure."

"It was the damndest thing," Sergeant Lucinda Gupta-Jones, the lead detective on the case, remarked. "The man starved to death in a room full of gold objects!"

Smith-Singh was a noted nanotech researcher at the New Delhi Institute of Cool Technologies. We are all familiar with nanotech, tiny, simple robots used in everything from toothpaste to help eradicate plaque from our mouths and fabrics that allow us to programme our t-shirts to put rude comments on our chests when our teachers (or parents) aren't looking.

While we were all using nanotech for our childish amusement, Smith-Singh had a much broader vision of what it could do for humanity, a vision at once boldly modern and as old as humanity. For Smith-Singh wanted to use nanotech to fulfill the ancient dream of…immortality!

According to a co – no, wait. Actually, he wanted to use it to be able to change base metals into gold. Alchemy. Smith-Singh wanted to use nanotech to fulfill the ancient dream of alchemy. I'm sorry – I find it easy to get my ancient dreams confused.

According to a colleague of Smith-Singh, graduate student Lakshman Atherton, the basic nanotechnology was simple enough.

"Oh, yeah," he said. "We had it down in a couple of hours. Lead into gold? Pfft. Easy. I was ready to move onto something harder, like turning daytime soaps into Shakespeare."

Although the basic technology proved simple enough, the interface through which it was controlled proved to be a stumbling block that would take over 10 years, and several research grants, to overcome. While many interfaces were considered, including guns, laser pointers and, for some reason, camels, Smith-Singh's research group eventually settled on a glove.

The Molecular Interface for Disassembling Atomic Structures (known around the lab as M.I.D.A.S.) looked like an ordinary velvet glove.

"Professor Smith-Singh had a thing for velvet," Atherton explained. "We…we didn't question him too closely about it."

Whatever. When somebody was wearing it, the velvet glove triggered a stream of self-replicating nanobots that would turn anything the person touched into gold.

At first, according to the testimony of Atherton and other people who had worked on the project, Smith-Singh was like a child with its first alchemical transmutating velvet glove, turning everything from beakers to electron microscopes into gold. When he turned lab assistant LoriAnne Gandhi into a statue, Smith-Singh is reported to have quipped, "I always said she was worth her weight in gold!" to the amusement of all present.

(An inquest into the disappearance of Gandhi is scheduled to begin next month.)

Problems began when, having turned every inanimate object in the lab into gold, Smith-Singh decided it was time to remove the glove. He couldn't. Nobody quite knows why, but the nanobots in the M.I.D.A.S. glove had somehow bonded to his hand. Worse: his entire body had become a nanobot conductor: anything he touched with any part of his body turned into gold.

"Well, this is awkward," several of the students who testified at the inquest claimed he said.

How awkward became apparent when Smith-Singh tried to eat: whenever he picked up a tasty morsel, it immediately turned to gold.

"Chicken soup was not going to help cure this illness!" medical examiner Schlomo Lakme wryly commented on the stand. Having assistants drop food into Smith-Singh's mouth was not helpful, as it turned to gold as soon as it hit his gums or tongue.

Realizing the extent of the problem, Smith-Singh was advised to get some of the best minds in the field to help solve it. He refused to let anybody outside of the lab know what was going on, however, until he had written the definitive paper on M.I.D.A.S. This effort was hampered by the fact that he had already turned his computer, his PDA and his cellphone into gold. He tried dictating the paper, but the complex nature of the subject and his increasing physical weakness made progress slow and difficult.

Once completed by his surviving students, the paper will be published posthumously in the *Journal of Foolish Scientific Studies*.

After Smith-Singh's death, the lab was considered a danger zone, but the hazmat team that went in to deal with it found that the M.I.D.A.S. glove was no longer active.

"Sometimes, a velvet glove is just a velvet glove," Padme Loucan, who led the hazmat team into the lab, told the coroner.

Although the verdict was widely accepted, some people thought the inquest was too restricted in its scope.

"Do you know what would happen if the glove had actually worked the way it was supposed to?" Atherton rhetorically asked. "If anybody could turn anything into gold with a single touch? The whole international economic system – which is based on the scarcity of gold – would collapse! Powerful forces wanted us to fail!"

Until evidence for this extraordinary accusation surfaces, the coroner's inquest will be the last word on the death of Mohinder Smith-Singh. And, that word will, of course, be: greed.

The Voice of Sanity Gets Its Chance

by LAURIE NEIDERGAARDEN, Alternate Reality News Service Medical Writer

The strange virus that swept across the world last month leaving politicians and pundits unable to speak has claimed a new victim: the press.

Without its usual roster of talking heads, television news has had to rely exclusively on the investigative reporting of facts.

"But, we're not set up for the investigative reporting of facts!" Monica von Aileys, Vice President, Customer Relations, MSNBC (the highest in the chain of command to still have her voice) protested.

While the illness has affected less than one per cent of the world population, the true extent of its affect on Americans is still not known. Virtually all of Washington and California while as much as 87% of New York are suspected of being carriers. Much of middle America may have been spared coming down with the disease, but, because news programmes continue to resist going there, there is no way of knowing just how much.

Different news organizations have adopted different strategies for dealing with the crisis.

Unwilling to write off the incredible sums paid to their anchors, the major networks have had them sit on camera while a series of unknowns read the news. CBS news anchor Katie Couric looked especially uncomfortable with this arrangement, although, to be fair, it wasn't that much different from the way she normally looks on air.

Fox News tried a number of approaches to dealing with the problem, with limited success. Bill O'Reilly was asked to write all his rants down on paper and place them where they could be picked up by the camera, but that didn't accurately convey his unique brand of apoplectic absurdism. Fox asked guests to pantomime their opinions, but found that this was akin to a game of charades, only not many viewers wanted to play charades with a panel consisting of Sean Hannity, Ann Coulter and Henry Kissinger.

Attempts by networks to get their anchors to use sign language have brought legal action from the American Civil Liberties Union, the National Association of the Deaf and the estate of the late Marcel Marceau.

Rupert Murdoch was reportedly livid about this state of affairs, but, having been quoted extensively himself before the virus hit, there was little he could do but stamp his feet and wave his fists in the air in front of him.

CNN, meanwhile, conducted a series of "streeters:" interviews with ordinary people encountered on the street. What they had to say was easily as cogent and interesting as anything the network's professional pundits had said, and sometimes much more so. The problem was that, because audiences had never heard of them before, their opinions didn't count for much.

The all news network thought that the solution to this problem was to keep coming back to the same people on the street to interview. The theory was that repeated exposure to a pundit bludgeons the audience into accepting their authority. Unfortunately, this theory was never put to the test: by their fourth interview, all of the streeters had lost their voice.

"It was amazing," CNN segment producer Austin Towers commented. "Halfway through the third interview, their throats would get scratchy. By the end of the interview, the subjects would be hoarse. And, if we tried again, nothing!"

Jon Stewart and Stephen Colbert, the anchors of fake news shows, appear to have gotten off lightly.

"My throat has been a little raw," Stewart said on his show last week, "but nothing so bad I can't live with it. And, if I ever start to slip into naked punditry, it gets worse, so I know I need to back off."

Newspaper reporters and columnists have been spared the problems of television news anchors, but they still have to deal with a dearth of official sources, which has cut most pieces of writing by one half to two thirds.

"Aha! We were there first!" said editor Mitch Frumian on behalf of *USA Today*.

In related news, General David Petraeus assured the White House that the chain of command in Iraq was fully vocal.

"Most soldiers who have appeared on television and in print were retired," he said in a memo that was subsequently leaked in a press release. "Those who are actually serving, therefore, are completely fit for command. Those few who have lost their voices, myself included, have been given PDAs with which to communicate until their voices return."

Everybody was unavailable for comment.

Priming Armageddon

by SASKATCHEWAN KOLONOSCOGRAD, Alternate Reality News Service Existentialism Writer

Mary McIlthwaite looks over the ruins of Washington and says simply, "Jesus is late." Then, resigned, she goes to a burned out Wal-Mart and tries to find something to eat. "Canned peaches are good," she comments. "You can't go wrong with food in tins…can you?"

The nuclear war that has turned most of the world into a burning, radioactive cinder ended three weeks ago, and true believers are starting to wonder why they weren't raptured up to heaven.

"If I had known it was going to be like this," Marty, 17, stated, "I wouldn't have stayed a virgin. I mean, I thought it would be hard enough to get a date before…"

Their faith hasn't been helped by the pronouncements of the Reverend James Dobson, the most prominent evangelist to have survived the war. When the United States first traded nuclear bombs with China, Reverend Dobson called on the faithful to pray, telling them that they were about to be rewarded for their faith. More recently, however, doubt has crept into his speeches.

"Why am I still here?" he asked on a recent radio broadcast. "I've led a righteous life – I didn't deserve to be left behind. What about Pat Robertson or…or Jerry Falwell? Do you believe Jerry Falwell was called? Jerry fucking Falwell? Let me tell you about what that shit was *really* like…"

Reverend Dobson went on to sob uncontrollably for 20 minutes before his show was finally taken off the air.

Proponents of Armageddon thought it might come as early as 2003 with the invasion of Iraq, whose leader, Saddam Hussein, was rumoured to have weapons of mass destruction and the will to use them. Imagine their disappointment! The invasion of Iran, which definitely had a nuclear programme, showed more promise to bring the End Times, but it, too, fizzled out before sinners had the opportunity to burn in hellfire on earth.

A trade dispute with China, below the radar of most evangelical Christians, was what triggered the nuclear conflagration that most Millennialists had been devoutly awaiting.

"Go figure," McIlthwaite commented as she strode past the rotting fruit towards the Wal-Mart's dead refrigeration units.

A poll recently conducted in Texas showed that 77 per cent of surviving Americans were still hopeful that they would see the second coming of Jesus Christ. However, this number is down from 86 per cent who said the same thing last month, and a whopping 98 per cent polled just after the bombs started falling.

While this poll suggests that Americans are losing faith in Armageddon, a couple of caveats must be considered. Since we don't know how many Americans survived the nuclear war, we don't know if the Texas sample is representative of…anything. This is especially true given that most communications systems have been destroyed, and the sample population consisted of a dozen people huddling outside the polling company's headquarters.

"Those crazy bastards," Rabbi Meyer Fox stated from the ruins of his synagogue. "I mean, I knew that they believed this would happen, but I – I would never have kibitzed with them in return for their support for the state of Israel if I had known that they were serious…

"Not that it would have made much difference," Rabbi Fox glumly concluded.

According to Millennialist beliefs, 144,000 Jews have to convert to Christianity in order for Jesus to return and establish his kingdom of heaven on earth. However, once the bombs started flying, the first targets were Jerusalem and New York, which decimated the world's Jewish population. Fewer than 144,000 Jews may have survived.

"My heart bleeds," Rabbi Fox dryly commented.

"I know, I know, I know," Reverend Dobson stated, "I'll convert to Judaism. Yeah. That's it. We'll get a hundred thousand Christians to convert to Judaism. Then, we'll convert back! That will fulfill the prophecy! And, we'll all be saved. We'll be saved! We'll be saved! We'll be saved!

"Fucking Jerry Falwell."

As the dark ash from the nuclear explosions settles in the upper atmosphere, experts suggest that the environmental fallout from the war could last for centuries, if it doesn't permanently alter the planet's climate.

"You see?" Warren Blush, an EPA representative in the final Bush administration, said. "We told you not to worry about climate change. We told you the Kyoto Accords were worthless. So much wasted economic potential!"

Mary McIlthwaite doesn't know anything about that.

"If it's the good lord's will that I wander around a burnt out wasteland, slowly dying of radiation poisoning, well, amen to that," she says, adding: "Does this fish look good to you?"

How? Quaint!

by SASKATCHEWAN KOLONOSCOGRAD, Alternate Reality News Service Existentialism Writer

J. Charrington Squiffy puts a large cardboard box on the table in front of me. On a label on the front of the box is the cryptic designation "54219854641-25896213489874-3C," under which somebody has written in a precise hand, "Social Justice."

"We received this one on January 20, 1981," Squiffy tells me. "The day of Ronald Reagan's Presidential inauguration. I remember it well: it was a Tuesday…there was a slight drizzle, but it actually seemed to refresh DC."

Looking inside the box, I find newspaper and magazine articles on the responsibility of society to protect its weakest members.

"There are many more books, pamphlets tracts and even the odd stone tablet going back three thousands years," Squiffy informs me. "If you really want to learn about the subject, I'll have to fire up the forklift."

I tell him that won't be necessary, that I'm only browsing, and he leaves me to it.

I am sitting in a nondescript cubicle in a nondescript building in a nondescript part of Washington. These are the offices of the federal Department of Quaint Notions, a little known government initiative that keeps alive the largely forgotten ideals of previous generations. It is deathly quiet, as if the very idea is enough to keep people away.

Over a coffee during a break in my research, I ask Squiffy – whom I can only describe as, yes, nondescript – if the Department of Quaint Notions exists primarily to keep these old ideas alive for a time in the future when they might again be needed. Squiffy responds with a noise that almost sounds like laughter.

"Mostly," he tells me, "the Department is used by people who want to prove that life used to be much better than it is now. You wouldn't believe how much time Dinesh D'souza and Samuel P. Huntington spend here! Frankly, I…I was glad when I saw you come in – it's nice to be able to serve somebody who doesn't have a rabid look in their eye."

Squiffy goes on to explain that it is possible to transfer a quaint notion from his department to the Department of Received Wisdom, but it is rare. "The paperwork is murder!"

Back in the office, I ask to see the department's most recently created file. The box he hands me, "54219125741-25896213368874-2F," is simply called "Torture." In it, I find a variety of arguments that torture is a morally indefensible activity for modern democratic governments to engage in.

I comment that the box doesn't appear to be as full as others Squiffy had given me.

"The debate on this subject isn't complete," Squiffy responds, "but we received a directive from the Bush administration instructing us to prepare our materials in anticipation of the idea's quaintification, so we've been scrambling to comply." Squiffy states his confidence that the file will be up to scratch in a matter of weeks, if not days.

As I go through the box of material, it occurs to me that there are no electronic documents in the Department of Quaint Notions. When I point this out to Squiffy, he makes that almost laughing sound again, which, I decide, is something I don't want to hear again as it is really annoying.

Instead of answering me directly, Squiffy disappears into the vault that contains the department's files (imagine the warehouse at the end of *Raiders of the Lost Ark* with poorer ventilation). After a few minutes, he returns with another box. "54236535741-25896213362564-8X – Technology." I don't have to open it to know what it contains: arguments about the efficacy of print over electronic means of communicating and storing information.

After a long day of research, I ask Squiffy what his favourite quaint notion is. He points out that this isn't an easy question to answer since most of the quaint notions from previous eras have been totally forgotten. The example of the Victorian Era belief that crushing tomatoes on your face will cure Influenza is the one out of the dozens he cites that sticks with me.

Having said that, Squiffy takes a deep breath and says, "Progress, the idea that things are always getting better, materially, spiritually, politically. The fact that the file is constantly bouncing between the Department of Quaint Notions and the Department of Received Wisdom should tip most people off that life is cyclical, not linear. And, yet, there is something seductive about the idea of progress, something…comforting."

As comforting as the existence of the Department of Quaint Notions.

Index of Articles

Abandoned Robot Pet Crisis Feared 22
About Bloody Time…Or, Is It? 100
Alien Love 43

Alternate Reality Ain't What It Used To Be... 1
Alternate Reality News Service Frequently Unasked Questions................. ix
A New Meaning Of The Term "Undercover Operation" 18
An Operation To Forget 109
Ask Amritsar: Beauty and the Beast in One Inconvenient Package........... 26

But, Is It Good For The Jews? 63
But, Who Will Teach The Children? 6

Confessions of a Pizza Delivery Guy.. 117
Cruel and Unusual – The Musical 98

Death Is Easy… 107
DoD Can't Hack It! 79
Do Politicians Really Believe The Bullshit They Say? 67
Do You Mind? 144

Fashion Revolution 102
Father Knows Least 42
Fit For a King? 52

Gang War Nets Littlest Victim To Date.. 93

Hear Hear! 111
History Is Made At Night
(019:57:32 Internet Standard Time, To Be Exact) 54
How? Quaint! 154
How Robert Novak's Eyebrows Saved America 71

I Don't Want To Be Part Of Your Revolution If I Can't Dance Dance 48
If You Don't Like This Universe, Try Another One! 24
Is There An Eco In Here? 104
It's For Science! 138

Just Another Typical Wedgie Issue 69

Last Tree Standing 91

Life Begins at the Hop	146
Lives Unlived – Charles Foster "Charlie" Brown	130
Lives Unlived – Ferenzcia de Filippi	132
Lives Unlived: Folger McWonderman	121
Lives Unlived – George W. Bush	125
Lives Unlived – Harve Nordlinger	127
Lives Unlived – Peter Underhill	123
Lives Unlived – Poncho Margaret Hatrack Devilliers Santo Domingo Harris	128
Lives Unlived – Ronald Winston Smith Reagan	134
Men Are From Microsoft, Women Are From Apple	40
Nothing Subtle About Fools	45
Now and Again	113
"Oh – Ha Ha Ha – That Kook – Hee Hee – Kurzweil!"	10
One Singularity Sensation	95
Out For Blood	115
Political Brand Standing	61
Popularity of Gravity Waning	140
Priming Armageddon	152
Profiles in Courage: Martin Felderhoffer	50
Progress – It's in the Air!	85
Red Blood + Whitewash + Blue Nation = Blackwater	65
Revenge Is Sour	106
Science Gets Out of Hand	148
Seeing Red for the Last Time	32
Size DOES Matter	28
Survivor: Heaven	20
The Bots Are Back in Town	14
The Magic Is Gone	75
The Old Ball Game Is Juiced	81
The Path of True Google Love Is Never Smooth	36
The Quality of Merciless Is Not Litigated	73
The Soul of the Old Machine	3
The Tall and The Short Of It	12

The Ungulate of Trimestres Declares Universal Impanishad 136
The Voice of Sanity Gets Its Chance 150
Those Who Forget History Are Doomed To Keep Living It 83
Trial of the Nanosecond 16
Turn! Turn! Turn! A Time To Work And A Time To Work More 87

Unholy Matrimony? 34
Until the Smiting Begins 56
Urban Adventures: Eyeball Pinball 118
US Signs Deal with DUGOO 59

What Goes Around…Makes You Dizzy When It Comes Around 77
What Price, Vanity? 38
Where Many Have Gone Before, Just Not Lately 8
Where the Pasta Hits the Road 142
Whose Identity Is It, Anyway? 30
Would You Like Fries With – AAACK! 89

Your High School Impression Was Correct – History IS Boring! 5

Printed in the United States
130473LV00001B/334-351/P